GONE

A gripping crime thriller full of suspense

T.J. BREARTON

BARNARD LIBRARY
LA CROSSE KS 67548

D1397596

Published 2016 by Joffe Books, London.

www.joffebooks.com

© T.J. Brearton

This book is a work of fiction. Names, characters, businesses, organizations, places and events are either the product of the author's imagination or are used fictitiously. Any resemblance to actual persons, living or dead, events or locales is entirely coincidental. The spelling is American English.

All rights reserved. No part of this publication may be reproduced, stored in retrieval system, copied in any form or by any means, electronic, mechanical, photocopying, recording or otherwise transmitted without written permission from the publisher. You must not circulate this book in any format.

ISBN-13: 978-1-911021-55-1

PROLOGUE / Gone

The brown house sat back from the road on the edge of town, a single-story home with a full basement. The garage door was open, a red tricycle inside. An empty coffee mug sat on the deck. Orange leaves stirred in the breeze. As the October sun sank in the west, the house grew dark. No one turned on a light.

A teddy bear lay abandoned on the floor in one of the bedrooms. A half-drunk glass of water rested on the nightstand beside the unmade bed. Magnets held drawings and photographs on the kitchen fridge; drawings of stick figures, photos of smiling people. Water dripped from the tap onto the dishes piled in the sink.

In the basement family room, a bowl of popcorn sat on the coffee table, kernels littered about. The TV was on, light flickering over the unoccupied couch. The door to the basement office was open. On the desk, wires and cords lay disconnected.

The last log smoldered down to dying embers in the woodstove. Smoke rose up the chimney and dissipated into the air. The sun sank beneath the jagged treetops, reddish light diffused through the pines. A gust of wind twisted the tire swing hanging from an oak tree, the suspension chain creaked. The wind rustled the fallen leaves amid the maple grove, soughed through the surrounding woods, rippling the surface of a small pond.

The road in front of the house was quiet, the workday over, the people gone home to eat dinner, watch the evening news. But not in the brown house. The sunlight waned in the forest, then disappeared as the last ember in the brown house turned cold and black.

CHAPTER ONE / Shot out of the Sky

Detective Rondeau cursed under his breath. He had a wadded-up paper towel in his hand and a darkening stain on his new pants. The cup of coffee had been too full.

"Shit."

He dumped some of it in the nearby sink. He was trying to remember what his sister had once told him about how to treat coffee stains.

The office door opened. It was Eric Stokes, the new guy with the big crush on the DA. He wasn't really new; he'd been with the department for eighteen months, but he was new until someone else came along and bumped him up.

"Oh," Stokes said, and his gaze fell to the stain on Rondeau's pants. "Sorry. Personal time?"

"That's good. That's a good one."

"You want me to get you something?"

"Like what?"

"Like a K9 unit? The dogs, you know — those tongues are like sandpaper. Take the paint off walls."

"What is it, Stokes?"

Stokes came further into the room. Rondeau's office wasn't much bigger than a large closet, and it took two steps for Stokes to reach the desk. Besides the desk, there were eight — count them, eight — file cabinets, and a terrible excuse for a kitchenette with a shallow sink housed in fake-wood cabinetry. There was one window, partly obscured by a tower of manila file folders, each crammed beyond the limit. Rondeau rarely tidied up and tipped the night cleaner to stay away.

He set down his coffee and dropped the crumpled paper towel beside it. He folded his arms. "Well? What is it? Jesus, new guy, the suspense is killing me."

"You, ah, well, you're going to love this."

"Am I going to love it? Okay. Well, as long as I'm going to love it. Spit it out."

The door to Rondeau's office, left ajar by Stokes, squeaked all the way open. Two state troopers peered tentatively inside.

Rondeau straightened his back and dropped his arms, as if he were standing at attention, still that kid from Fort Bragg. He got that way whenever the staties were around, because they resembled soldiers. His heart, which was set to cruise control these days, dropped into a gear he'd forgotten was there. He stuck out his jaw at the three people crowding his small space.

"Okay. Hi guys. Now you've got my attention. Stokes? You want to let me in on something? Maize? Crowley?"

Stokes finally just blurted it out. "Someone shot down a drone."

"A what? A drone?"

"Shot it out the sky."

Rondeau tried to absorb this. He checked with the troopers to see if maybe Stokes had lost his mind. Their faces were serious.

"Okay, so, someone shot down a drone. Roger that. And you're coming to me — why?"

Stokes fidgeted. "Owner of the drone — a photographer — tracked down where it landed."

"Beginning to come a little clearer. Why don't you—"

The female trooper, Crowley, cut in. "It landed on your property."

And there it was. "Shit," said Rondeau for the second time that morning. He grabbed his coat and rushed out.

CHAPTER TWO / Them

Rondeau's home sat back from the main road between New Brighton and Hazleton. He'd taken the place over a couple years before. It was 1930s vintage, and its decay seemed to be accelerating. Roof in disrepair, sagging in the middle. Dry rot along the foundation. Lawn overgrown. The whitewashed fence was about the only thing that looked okay. He just didn't have the time to keep up with it all.

He pulled up behind the trooper vehicle in his driveway and sat for a moment, engine idling. There were rusty barrels in the yard, a junker car in the tall grass, an old refrigerator. Wooden pallets were stacked in rotting towers. Those things weren't his mess. They'd come with the place.

Rondeau got out and went to the trooper on the porch. He was a hardcase named Jaskulski, who everyone called Ski. Ski didn't look pleased.

Rondeau held the man's eye. "Where is it?"

"Gone. It's at the barracks. Photographer who owns it will probably press charges. And we could, too: first degree criminal mischief, first degree wanton endangerment. Local ordinance states—"

"Right, well, that was a revised statute . . ."

Ski looked severe. "You kidding me right now?"

Rondeau held up his hands. "Alright. I know. I'm sorry. I'll take care of it. Thank you for your help, Ski."

He waited until Trooper Ski decided for himself that it was enough, and left the porch. Ski slammed his vehicle door and tore out of the driveway. Rondeau watched him leave, took a breath, and went inside.

Millard stood in the hallway, the heaping mass of man that he was, dressed in his ragged flannel shirt and stained pants.

"Millard, what the hell happened? What did you do?"

"Hey, you don't come flying over my house with one of those things and expect me to just sit here and watch," Millard said. "*That's* what I did."

"They were taking pictures."

"They were taking pictures?" Millard's mood changed to anger. He paced around the wide hallway. Framed photos hung on the walls, family members watching them from behind patinas of dust. "I *bet* they were taking pictures," Millard yelled, "And I bet that's not all they were doing!"

Rondeau folded his arms. "What did you hit it with?"

"The Winnie." Millard was referring to his Winchester Universal, a sporting gun for bird hunting. A 12-gauge. Aside from a Bee-Bee gun he'd had since his teens, it was the only gun he owned. But Rondeau knew his brother-in-law liked to think he still had an arsenal to choose from.

Birdshot wasn't much use for home invasion, because its small light pellets wouldn't do much to halt a determined invader. But that didn't stop its use on the home defense front — in fact, if memory served, some guy in another part of the country had blown a drone out of the sky using a similar weapon. It was almost becoming "a thing."

Rondeau cocked his head. "Did you take it down with one shot?"

"Oh yah. When the guy came for it, though, I was hidden upstairs. I waited. I thought, 'You cross that fence, there's going to be another shooting. This is private property.'"

"Right," Rondeau said. And that was when the photographer had turned around and called 911, who'd sent the state troopers.

Rondeau scratched his shoulder and sighed. He started towards the kitchen, his boots clomping across the old wooden floor. "Come sit down with me," he said as he passed Millard. His brother-in-law followed and they sat at the table.

"Millard," Rondeau said after thinking for a bit, "I think you need to start seeing Connie again."

Millard look at the floor. He seemed frustrated, embarrassed. Not much had changed there; Millard hated therapy.

"Yeah, sure."

"You know you're lucky you don't have to go to County Mental Health for your therapy, right? You listening? Connie is expensive . . ."

Millard gave him a hard look. "So stop paying her. I told you I don't need any therapy."

Rondeau sat back, and ran his fingers through his greying hair. It needed a cut. "Okay," he said, "tell me why you shot down that drone."

"I told you, it was taking pictures of my goddamn *house!*" He slammed a meaty fist on the table. Rondeau briefly saw the cuts and bruises on his knuckles, they were banged up pretty bad. Like he'd been in a fight with a Chevy, and lost.

Our house, Rondeau wanted to say, but experience advised him not to. There was no point in bringing up his dead sister, Millard's wife, God rest her soul, gone three years. Rondeau was the executor of her will, and he was ultimately responsible for the property. But it wasn't worth dragging any of that out right now.

"Okay," said Rondeau, humoring Millard, "It was taking pictures of your house. Why was it taking pictures of your house?"

Millard's anger didn't entirely subside, but evolved into paranoia. Millard's voice dropped, his shoulders drew together.

"You know why," Millard said in a small voice.

"I do?"

"Yes," he whispered. "Yes, Jay, you do."

Jay, Rondeau thought. What his sister had called him. What they both called him — Jessica and Millard, when Rondeau visited in the days before she died and Millard became a paranoid conspiracy theorist. When the roof wasn't sagging as much, when the baseboard wasn't as eaten away, when the kitchen smelled like chicken casserole.

Rondeau could guess why Millard had shot the thing out of the sky. Just six months before, Millard had reluctantly submitted to an eyesight examination. When the optometrist had asked to take a picture of his retina, Millard had refused. Not only refused; he'd gone on a rant about government surveillance and demanded the eye doctor turn over all of his records. That was the level of his paranoia.

Yes Jay, you know why. You know why that drone was taking pictures of my house. Rondeau just had to ask: "You think it was them, Millard?"

Just the word — a simple pronoun, *them* — filled Millard's face with fear. Every muscle tensed. "Course it was them," he rasped. "It's always them."

Rondeau nodded. He fingered a knot in the surface of the pine table, feeling guilty. The sun streamed in through the east windows. This place had always looked beautiful in the morning light. Now the sun only revealed the dirt on the floor and the grime caking the appliances. Two men living together made lousy housekeepers.

"Okay," Rondeau said. "Okay."

"Okay?" Some life returned to his brother-in-law, but he was still drawn in. Disappearing might have been his greatest fear — just vanishing into thin air at the hands of *them*. Just turn invisible. Be gone, never to return.

What do I know? Rondeau thought. Psychotherapy wasn't his thing. That was Connie Leifson's job, Millard's therapist. "Okay," he said again, "I think I'll be able to get the criminal charges dropped . . ."

Millard finally looked okay again. *They have people everywhere,* he'd say, *especially on the inside.* That being abducted while in jail was nonsensical didn't occur to Millard — one thing Rondeau knew from experience was that delusional people didn't have delusions which were internally logical.

Of course, Millard could be afraid that *they* would kill him, even in prison, but Rondeau didn't think so. His brother-in-law wasn't afraid of death. It was that loss of freedom which made him paranoid. Being trapped. Locked away somewhere, alone. It was a phobia which had taken hold in the years before Jessica died, and had been exacerbated by her untimely departure.

"I'll be able to get the *criminal* charges dropped," Rondeau emphasized, "but you're . . . we'll likely face civil charges. That 'drone' was actually a quadcopter, not as sophisticated, but still pretty expensive. Totaled. And if this guy gets a slick lawyer, now we're talking about loss of livelihood, all that sort of thing. They could say he lost a week's worth of business. Could be a couple thousand dollars, maybe more. Who knows how much his clients pay him to take pictures . . . ?"

"Of my *house!*" Millard shouted. Not quite as enraged as before, but the anger still bubbling.

Rondeau raised his hands in a gesture of peace. Reasoning that the drone was probably just innocently passing over would be futile. "I know. I know, Mill. Of your house."

Millard slumped in his chair. Rondeau continued to poke at the knot, stealing glances of his brother-in-law while he did. Despite all the trouble, he liked Millard. Always had. The family hadn't done backflips when Jessica, their beautiful daughter from a well-to-do family married a transit cop from downstate. But all you had to do — at least back in those days — was meet Millard for about two seconds to understand why she had gone for him. Behind the outbursts of defensive anger was the man his sister had fallen in love with. The man who had been — and still was — a good man. The type of man who really would give you the shirt from his back. And he had.

Rondeau stood up. "What are you going to have for dinner tonight?"

Millard frowned. "Don't know. I'll put something on."

Rondeau eyed the pantry — just a set of shelves that had once been pretty. All he saw was a couple tins of beans and a dusty old crockpot Jessica had used for casseroles. He headed out of the room, stopped in the doorway.

"You're going to see Connie again, Mill. Alright?"

He legged it back down the hall, old boards groaning.

Millard called after him, "You wait, Jay," his voice drifting away as Rondeau went out the door. "You wait. This isn't the end. This is just the beginning."

"You keep that gun up unless you're after grouse," Rondeau called back, and stepped out into the sunlight.

CHAPTER THREE / Polarization

Rondeau stopped at the college and slipped into the lecture hall. Connie Leifson was addressing a group of students. In addition to her private practice in New Brighton, she taught sociology. He stood at the back and listened as she finished her lecture.

"Alright, so what I want from you over the weekend, is this: I want two thousand words."

The students groaned and rustled in the seats. Rondeau smiled. It had been a long time since he'd been in their shoes, but some things never changed. You came to school for an education, and then you resented the hell out of your teachers. Well, he had. Connie Leifson had probably loved it, he thought, catching himself considering her legs.

She settled the class down. "Two thousand words. Come on. Stephen King rips off two thousand words in an hour. You know what I want to hear from you: why are we so polarized as a society? Give me your take. What's going on? People arguing about politics, global warming, government. Has it always been this way? Is Facebook to blame?"

The class laughed.

"Really," she said. "Think about when you're on social media, and people are in heated dispute with one another, and the attitude polarization is there, the *tu quoques* are there, and we're calling one another, 'idiots' and 'morons.'" Connie looked up at the clock. "Okay. That's time."

The students were like horses out of the gate. They immediately took out their phones and started playing with them. No one seemed to notice Rondeau. Connie was loading papers into her briefcase and looked up as he approached.

"I don't think you want my two thousand words," he said.

She looked surprised, several emotions flashed across her intelligent face. He was used to it — Connie was friendly but very discrete, as her profession required. Surely she surmised why he was there.

"You'd write two thousand words?"

"It would take me the whole weekend." He mimed tapping at a keyboard with two clawed fingers. "And I'd only get about twenty."

She laughed and closed up her briefcase. He could sense she was busy and had somewhere else to be. He scratched self-consciously at his shoulder and said, "I'll be brief."

"No, it's okay. Here, sit down. How are you?"

They made themselves more comfortable. She turned towards him and crossed her legs, propped her elbow up on the seatback.

"I'm good," he said. "You?"

"Very good."

"Liking this?" He gestured to the lecture theater.

"I am."

There was a pause. He knew Connie had taught before, in another part of the country. He also knew she was here filling the shoes left by a teacher who had been

BARNARD LIBRARY
LA CROSSE KS 67548

13

tarnished by a series of murders the previous year, leaving a void in the department.

For a rural region, the North Country had its share of problems. There had been a prison break as well as the serial killing of the college students. And there had been the murder of a teenage boy.

Rondeau let out a breath he hadn't realized he was holding. He ran his hands through his hair and looked down. "I'm worried about Millard."

Her demeanor changed. "Oh, you know . . . I'm sorry, I can't really . . ."

"I know, I know," Rondeau began, nodding. He started picking lint from his suit jacket. Then he looked up. "We won't talk about his therapy, that's not why I'm here. He just needs to see you soon. He, ah, he shot down a drone this morning."

"A drone?"

"Yeah. A . . . quadcopter thing. Flying over our property."

"Wow," she said. "Those things are everywhere, aren't they? Don't they have to be federally registered now?"

"They are, and they do. You know . . ."

He trailed off, for a moment. He knew Connie couldn't reveal anything Millard had shared with her. But Rondeau already knew about Millard's past. The *big* story, anyway, the one which had probably caused Millard's unraveling. Millard had found a severed head by the subway tracks, duct tape over its mouth. A man. Someone Millard thought he recognized as a cop who'd turned whistleblower on corruption in the city. Someone who'd gone up against the national security state and lost. Millard had become a changed, frightened man. That was his last day as a transit cop.

Rondeau turned back to Connie. "I just think he needs you." Rondeau was self-conscious, feeling sure now that this was an imposition. He stood up, preparing an apology.

14

"I wonder if you could do me a favor, Detective Rondeau?" she surprised him.

He sat back down. "Of course. What do you need?"

"Are you going back to your office after this? I don't want to assume you . . ."

He was nodding. "Yeah, I'm headed straight back."

She pulled out a pen and paper and jotted something down. She handed the note to him. It said, Henry Leifson, with an address in New Brighton. Her parents' address. Rondeau knew them — two very nice people who lived on the outskirts of town.

"I wanted to stop and see them before I left, but I've got to be in Burlington in one hour. Will you just . . . I don't know. Drive by? Maybe even peek in, say hello? I know this is unusual, and I'm sorry . . . I . . ."

"Of course," he said. He wanted to ask her why she was going to Vermont, but it was none of his business.

"Oh, thank you. Thanks so much," she said, warmth in her eyes.

"No problem."

"You probably think I'm a worrier . . ."

"Not at all. I'd be happy to say hello to them."

"This is a quick trip. I'll be back Sunday." She touched his arm. "And we'll set something up first thing Monday morning."

"Okay." He was relieved.

She offered that soft smile, that smile that was somehow warm but completely professional. Most people's faces, when they were giving you short shrift or screwing you over, betrayed the truth. Not Connie's. It was tough to tell with her.

CHAPTER FOUR / Nobody Home

He drove south to New Brighton thinking about the last moments he'd spent in Connie's classroom. Maybe she had been in a rush, maybe she didn't want to see Millard anymore, or maybe he was just imagining things. But something had been off.

He changed lanes on the highway, wondering about the look he'd seen in her eyes. Millard was her patient so she might have considered Rondeau's visit inappropriate. "Stupid," he said to himself.

He tried not to think about it anymore. He turned up the radio, dialed it to the classic rock station, and listened to *Street Fighting Man*. Twilight was leaching the color from the day.

His phone rang. Stokes was calling. Rondeau pressed the speaker button. "Hello."

"Rondeau."

"What's going on?"

"The hospital called. A nurse there has missed two straight shifts. They've tried her at home, no answer. This would be her third shift tonight, but she's not showing up again."

"Where? She's local? New Brighton?"

"Yeah." Stokes gave him the address.

"I gotta go right by there. Tell the sheriff I'll check it out."

"Will do."

Within twenty minutes (and through *Three Dog Night* and a rocking *CCR* tune) he was outside New Brighton, passing by the few houses along the road.

One house, brown, had its garage door rolled open, vehicle in the driveway, but no lights on in the house. He read the house number and pulled in. The day was dark, it looked like people were home, yet the windows were all pitch black.

He sat in the vehicle for a moment. Nice maples in the yard, red sumac edging the property. There was a coffee mug on the deck, a fallen leaf sticking out.

The house looked brand new. Total opposite of his ramshackle place. He got out of the truck and walked towards the front door, checking everything out. He reached the door and knocked, waited. When no one came, he tried the doorbell. Still nothing.

He left the front door and walked to the garage, waiting for a light to wink on, or someone to appear in a window, wondering who the hell was out there.

No one came. He peered into the open garage at tools hung on a pegboard. There were shelves with boxes, sports gear, garden and lawn supplies, bags of blood meal and grass seed. The garage was unfinished — a doorway to the house was outlined, but not cut.

He noted two adult-sized bicycles, a child's bike seat on the back of one of them. His gaze fell on a red tricycle. So there were kids. Husband, wife, at least two little ones.

He pulled his phone out and dialed Stokes back.

The younger detective answered straight away. "Yeah, boss?"

"Got a minute?"

"For you? I got five."

Stokes was always trying to show off.

"Run a search for me on the address, see what you get."

"Yeah, okay," Stokes said. "Just a minute." Rondeau heard Stokes pecking at the keys.

He walked to the shelves and peered at the sporting gear. Basketball, lacrosse sticks, golf clubs.

"Okay," said Stokes. "Um, yeah, so, Hutchinson Kemp, and his wife Lily . . ."

"'Hutchinson?'"

"That's what it says. That's the nurse's husband. Guy's got an IMDb profile . . ."

"What's IMDb?"

"Ah, Internet Movie Database. Says he's a producer, director, writer. Known as 'Hutch.' Did a documentary a few years back, a pretty big one, about the agricultural industry. Called *Renaissance Man*. Oh wait, no, that's another one about horse racing . . . the agricultural doc was called *Citizen Farmer*. Not a very original title, sort of rip on *Citizen Kane*. Got an award, though."

"So they're living in boondocks because of her, maybe, an LPN at New Brighton Medical?"

"Yeah, sure, maybe."

"Do me a favor, call them back. Let them know we're looking into it."

"Will do." Stokes paused. "So, no one home then?"

"Don't know."

He hung up and walked out of the garage. He got a flashlight from his Chevy and circled the house. Around back, he played the beam over a long stack of firewood. There was no smoke coming from the chimney, even though the temperature was dropping. He came upon a side entrance and stopped, tried the doorknob. He hesitated, then opened it. "Hello? Anyone here?"

He froze when he heard voices. He shone the light in on a basement family room: two couches, a coffee table, TV in the corner. The TV was still on, the source of the noise. Someone was home after all. Feeling guilty, like a trespasser, he started away. But he stopped before closing the door and took another look. A coloring book lay open on the table, crayons strewn about. A bowl of half-eaten popcorn sat by one of the couches. "Hello?" No answer. Regardless of how strange it was, he shouldn't be opening anyone's door. He closed up and moved on.

Murder-suicide, he thought. It just came whistling out of the blue, the type of thing no one wanted to think about. The temptation to go back into the house was strong, but he needed to follow due process. He walked to the truck, grim ideas capering in his mind. A couple years back, a family in Alaska had disappeared. They'd left behind their vehicles, their clothing. Eventually their decomposing bodies were discovered less than a mile away. A handgun was found by the remains.

Another family had been recently found in the southwest, their vehicle located in the middle of the desert, bodies inside, everything incinerated. Police were fairly certain of murder-suicide there, too.

Sometimes it wasn't murder-suicide, but something else. One family, missing for three years, was eventually seen on video crossing the border into Mexico on foot. Investigators said it looked like there was bad business involved. But at least there was a chance they were still alive.

Rondeau stopped in the front yard. The wind picked up and sent leaves scattering from the maples. In the dark, the leaves looked like bats in flight.

He beamed the light through the front windows. The light illuminated a framed photo hanging on the wall. There they were. Hutchinson Kemp and his wife Lily. Holding two little kids, a toddler and a baby, smiling brightly. Not that you could judge a book by a cover, but they looked like a good family. A nice family.

Maybe this family had just taken a trip, left in a hurry in a second vehicle. It didn't feel like that, though.

He would give it the night. In the morning he'd have the deputies do an official welfare check. If everything looked the way it did now, they could get a warrant and search the house.

He got in the Chevy, gave the dark house one more look,   and   left.

SATURDAY

CHAPTER FIVE / Patrol Division

Deputy Peter King pulled up in the cruiser. Two men were beating the shit out of each other in the front yard. The first guy took the second guy's head and slammed it into the mailbox. The second guy stumbled back from the blow, blood running from his scalp. Peter got out of the car, Deputy Althea Bruin exited the other side. They each took their batons and slid them back through loops in their belts as they stepped onto the grass.

"Traitor," the first guy was saying. "Traitor son of a bitch." Peter knew him. Terry Rafferty. Fifty years old and a notorious drinker and brawler. Rafferty had been in a biker gang in his younger days. Tattoos covered his hairy arms and his muscles bulged from years of carpentry and heavy lifting.

Peter put his hand out in a *stop* gesture as he neared. "Mr. Rafferty. I'm going to need you to calm down."

Althea approached the second guy, John Hayes, a commercial truck driver. Peter knew him, too — he'd gone to school with Hayes. Hayes dropped to the ground and bent forward, took his head in both hands and moaned.

The bashed mailbox listed to the side, door hanging open like a tongue.

They were on Hayes's small parcel of land, where not much grew, including the grass. Hayes single-wide trailer was tucked back into the trees, swallowing it like it was some kind of bungalow in a jungle. Peter occasionally fantasized about living somewhere tropical, where you fished marlins not bass, and grown men weren't beating each other up.

"Traitor," Rafferty spat. He glowered at Hayes, ignoring the deputies.

Peter took another step. "I need you to put your hands on your head and get down on your knees, Mr. Rafferty."

Rafferty's eyes were bright blue. His big square jaw was pock-marked, his nose bent from a biker gang fight. His natural teeth had been knocked out in a motorcycle accident. Peter knew the story: after wrecking his bike, Rafferty had taken a car from a motorist who'd stopped to help, and driven himself to the hospital. They said he'd come in to the emergency room with blood spilling from his mouth, gum nerves raw.

He liked cops even less than he liked his false teeth. "Mind your business, King."

Peter glanced at Althea. *One more chance and then we pull them.* He touched the grip of his sidearm.

"Mr. Rafferty," Peter said, "we've just witnessed you assaulting this man. We are deputies of the Stock County Sheriff's Department, and we're asking you to get to the ground. Do it peacefully. I need to check you for weapons."

"I ain't got any weapons."

"Just do this nice, and everybody wins."

Rafferty stood defiant, his oil-stained shorts hanging from his waist. His face was beaded with perspiration. "Wins? No one wins." He glared at Hayes, who got to his feet.

"Woah," Althea said to Hayes. "Take it easy. Let's stay right there, okay? What happened here, gentlemen?"

Hayes had blood pouring down the side of his nose. He lowered his head and charged Rafferty like a bull. Rafferty raised his fists.

Both deputies drew their weapons. The men grunted as they collided. They fell to the ground, kicking up the dry dirt. Hayes was no match for the larger Rafferty, who rolled over and pinned him.

"Stop!" Althea gave Peter another look which meant, what the hell are we going to do, shoot them?

There was a shout from the house. Peter saw a woman bang out the screen door — Hayes's wife.

"Get her," Peter said. Althea holstered her gun and intercepted the woman.

A crackle of static emanated from the cruiser as their unit was paged from dispatch. "SCS-14, Stock County . . ."

Talk about bad timing, Peter thought.

He tried to hear the radio over Hayes's wife shouting. They wrestled in the dirt, Hayes trying to squirm out from underneath. Peter could hardly hear a damn word of the radio.

"Everybody, *quiet!*" he yelled.

He trotted to the car, listening as dispatch restated the announcement.

". . . welfare check. Repeat: Family is Hutchinson and Lily Kemp, two daughters. Lily Kemp is an LPN, and is absent without leave from New Brighton Medical . . ."

Peter leaned against the vehicle, listening as dispatch rattled off a brief physical description. He recognized the name, Kemp, and felt his chest tighten. Althea watched him while trying to stay between the woman and the men. The woman's lips pulled back in a snarl, spit flying with her words. "Get outta my way you black *bitch*," she said.

There was a lightning crack of gunfire and everybody froze. The woman shut her yap and the men in the yard halted, their limbs tangled, a fist suspended in the air. Peter stood with his gun pointed at the sky. He'd fired off one round. Bad thing to do, and he knew it.

"Thea," he said. "Let's go."

The men stared, their skirmish forgotten. Hayes' wife glared with contempt. Althea stared at Peter in disbelief. Then she took a breath, and her posture sagged. She shook her head and walked toward her partner, telling him with a look that she wasn't pleased.

"Could be a family in trouble," he explained to her.

She got in the passenger side. Peter dropped into the driver's seat. He rolled down the window and shouted at the group in the yard. "Work it out!"

Then he backed onto the main road. He dropped the transmission into drive and squawked the tires. The car shot forward, turning the fallen leaves into a cyclone in their wake.

* * *

"'Work it out'?"

Peter didn't answer as he stomped the gas and rode the edges of the turns.

"You're gunning for a career change to mental health? With earth-shattering therapies like that, you could maybe even write a book. Fire a shot, tell them to work it out, problem solved." Althea grabbed the radio and pressed the button. "Stock County, SCS-14." She waited for a response.

Peter kept his eyes on the road. He was going to pay for firing his weapon. It was something you just didn't do, even in the middle of nowhere, even when men were fighting, dispatch was paging you and someone called your partner a racial epithet.

He was coming up on an intersection — route 73 was dead ahead. Dispatch broke over the radio.

"SCS-14, Stock County."

Althea held the transmitter to her mouth. "Ah, Stock County, please be advised of a domestic disturbance at

1071 Fox Farm Road . . . we, ah, we left that call in receipt of the welfare check. Over."

"Copy that, SCS-14 . . ." The dispatcher sounded wary.

The deputies traded looks as Peter braked for the stop. Peter reached over and touched her on the leg. "I'm sorry. You okay?"

She offered an encouraging smile. "I'm fine."

We had to leave, Peter thought. *Or I would have hurt somebody.* Besides, this took priority; this could be a missing family. It sounded like the mother had no-showed a couple of hospital shifts. If he was right, and knew the family, they had two young kids.

Route 73 was quiet. Peter made a right turn and accelerated. Within moments they were passing by a dirt parking area where the state troopers often set their speed traps. A trooper sat there now.

Althea thumbed the button on the transmitter.

"Thanks, Stock County, over and out." She dropped the transmitter onto the hook.

They recognized the trooper sitting in the SUV, Trooper Ski. He was wagging his finger, admonishing them for leaving the domestic disturbance.

"Let's ask him to take it," she said as they blew past.

"No way he's gonna do that."

She raised her eyebrows at him, and Peter sighed. "Alright." He slowed and made a three-point turn in the road.

Peter quickly pulled into the lot, coming up alongside the SUV. Althea hopped out and walked over before he could protest any further.

"Morning," he heard her say. "How you doing?"

Ski mumbled a response. Some of the troopers liked to wear the proverbial white gloves, Peter thought, watching the conversation. They seemed to only respect the older deputies who worked with DEA and Border

Patrol on drug busts and tended to look down on Patrol Division.

Unlike the troopers, deputies delivered civil process papers, transported inmates to court, hospitals, doctor appointments, whatever was called for. The job could get tedious. Patrol Division sometimes felt like a taxi service. But any department could field domestic calls. It was just that a lot of the troopers didn't like to.

Althea apparently had a magic touch, though. She got back in the cruiser and flashed a smile. Ski tipped his wide-brim hat as he pulled away, churning up the dust.

Peter watched him go. "You're amazing."

Ski made the turn back towards Hayes's property.

"Anyway, maybe Rafferty and Hayes took your advice," she said. "Maybe they worked it out. Or, maybe they'll all pile on top of Ski and call him a black bitch, too."

He shook his head and tore up the dirt as they got back on the road. "If Rafferty and Hayes and his wife are still fighting, maybe Ski should just let them go at it."

"So who is this family? You act like you know them."

"I think maybe I do. I think their little girl, Maggie, goes to preschool with Benny."

Benny was his nephew. The boy attended a private preschool, and Peter knew it was pricey. He knew because his own father footed the bill, paying for his grandson to get the best early education. It pricked Peter a little bit that his father, a district judge, hadn't shown the same concern for his own kids. At least he was making up for it with his grandchildren. "This isn't the usual welfare check situation, I don't think." He figured the Kemps had some money.

She turned her head. "Oh? And what is 'the usual'?"

"Well, let's just say we're not going to find bags of poop in their bathroom because the plumbing doesn't work."

She wrinkled her nose. Sometimes the deputies found heinous things when they responded to welfare checks. It was an economically depressed county, and a lot of people went without certain amenities.

"And it probably smells like spiced coffee in their kitchen," Peter continued, "not opioids."

"Yeah." She watched the road again, the trees blurred past.

He was joking around, maybe being a little crass, but something was eating at him. He'd been bothered since he'd heard the call come over the radio. "Which means, you know, if something is wrong . . ."

"What? What do you think it is?"

He gripped the steering wheel, staring ahead. He didn't know. But a sense of dread was growing.

CHAPTER SIX / The Missing

Detective Rondeau called a meeting. His office was located in the Public Safety Complex, in a wing of the county jail. The group of law enforcement crammed into the tight space.

"Okay," Rondeau said, "we have reason to believe a family is missing. Deputies King and Bruin did the welfare check this morning. Given exigent circumstances, the deputies gained entry through a side door. They found the residence to be in the same condition as I determined last night, from the outside. No bodies, no blood; the family is just gone. New Brighton Medical confirms that Lily Kemp, the wife and mother, has missed her last three shifts."

Peter King raised a hand and spoke up. "Their daughter goes to preschool with my nephew."

Rondeau nodded. "We called the preschool. They said the child has been absent for three days as well. And the nearest neighbors are the Leifsons; I spoke with them and they told me it had been a while since they'd seen the family. So, at this stage, we're saying they have been missing for the past seventy-two hours."

He nodded to Stokes. Stokes began passing out packets, one to Sheriff Oesch, one to each of the three deputies — Peter King, Althea Bruin, and Holland Kenzie. They were a small department — Patrol Division and Jail Division, plus the newly minted detective squad of which Rondeau and Stokes were sole members, Rondeau the lead. Also present was Britney Silas, representing CSI, the forensics team. Rondeau figured it was enough to get started.

"I filed the missing persons' report myself earlier today after hearing back from Deputies King and Bruin." Rondeau took one of the packets Stokes was handing out. The heading read: MISSING PERSONS INVESTIGATIVE BEST PRACTICES PROTOCOL. The group leafed through the pages.

"First thing," Rondeau said, "we need to locate and contact any extended family members."

"On it," Stokes said.

Rondeau turned to the forensic analyst, Britney Silas. "We establish a Family Reference Sample Collection Kit as soon as we have someone from the extended family. Safe, noninvasive means for obtaining DNA references, right?"

Silas nodded.

"Okay," he said, and set the packet on his desk. "Right now this is not 'high risk.' There is no confirmed abduction, no immediate evidence of dangerous circumstances. They've only been missing three days, not thirty, no pattern of disappearances established, and we don't have any reason to believe that there is a medical issue. But just because we don't know that at the outset, doesn't mean these factors aren't, in fact, present. We need to find out everything we can about this family. Let's find their lawyer, if they have one. The family doctor. Auto mechanic. Let's look into their bank account and see if there have been any major recent withdrawals — we're not looking for the value of the account, but certain activity that might stand out, or if it has been closed or transferred."

He surveyed the group. They were still looking through their packets, but his silence drew their attention. "We are lead law enforcement agency on this," he said, glancing at Stokes.

"Stokes here is going to contact NCIC and the National Missing Persons Program . . ."

"What about the FBI?" Stokes looked anxious — this was his first big case.

Rondeau held up a hand. "One step at a time. We'll reach out if we feel the need. Now, NCIC will only take a report if certain criteria are met. Physical or mental disability. So we really need to get that information from a general practitioner. Otherwise, we have to show the family was involuntarily taken, and we do that by the evidence. We also have the resources of the state police and the Safe Return Program. But I think we need to keep this workable, keep it moving." He lowered his hand and addressed the group. "So let's start by finding everything we can about the Kemps. It's gonna be a challenge because we're dealing with the lives and habits of two adults, not just one. Let's get in touch with their friends, family, no matter how far flung. Alright?"

Nods and murmured agreement. There was a palpable excitement in the room. Rondeau felt it, but he also felt uneasy.

"Also, let's get a TRAK bulletin going, right away. I want to see the faces of the Kemps plastered all over the county, the state." He looked at Deputy King, and King nodded. Rondeau added, "This is where we can bring in Ski and the boys, too."

King looked dismayed at the prospect of coordinating with Trooper Ski, but Rondeau knew he'd get it done. Rondeau considered Peter King trustworthy, and he didn't trust most people. He knew the young deputy had aspirations to be an investigator. There might be some resentment there, since Oesch had formed the county's first detective squad and hired two new guys, but King played it off. He had good instincts; Rondeau was glad to have him aboard.

King's partner, Althea Bruin, was a stand-up cop, too. Maybe the sharpest tack in the bunch.

"Deputy Bruin, you're good on the . . . what do you call it?"

She frowned. "The computer?"

"That's right," Rondeau said, and winked. "The thing with the keys and the mousepad. Let's at least reach out to the Missing Persons and Child Exploitation Unit and request the case be listed on the New York State Police Missing Persons website. They may deny the request, but be persistent. And one other thing — Britney, if you could get me going an Entry and Exit Log for the Kemp residence. I want everyone signing in and out. I've spoken with the DA and Judge King and we're good to go." He clapped his hands together. "People, that house is now a potential crime scene. Let's get to work."

* * *

The sheriff closed the door after the rest of them filed out, trapping Rondeau in the room.

Rondeau took a seat at the desk, Oesch stood, arms folded, by the door.

"You think this is the right call?" he asked. It was a vague question, but Rondeau knew what the sheriff was asking; whether their department could handle the case.

Oesch was new. He'd been the undersheriff and primarily responsible for the jail until Dunleavy had stepped down. Oesch took over and was the only one running in the previous fall election. He still seemed to be trying out the shoes. It would take time, but Oesch was earnest. Rondeau had once seen a dog-eared copy of *Enthusiasm Makes the Difference* in the sheriff's office, nonfiction from the 1950s about the power of "positive thinking."

"With respect, Sheriff, this is what you created the squad for. This is why I'm here." He added, "Hopefully, you know, this is all just some big misunderstanding. Some family member or friend will come forward, or the Kemps will just show up again. But, you know, maybe not."

Oesch nodded, and his eyes drifted over the stacks of files and general mess of Rondeau's office. No self-help books here. The only self-help taste Rondeau ever acquired was *The Big Book*, after the shots of Cutty Sark and six packs of Budweiser tallboys had gotten the better of him.

"But you don't think it's overreaching to set up Incident Command?" Oesch asked.

Rondeau shook his head. "Not at all. I think that's just what needs to happen, Sheriff. Pragmatic, basic. Let's physically search for these people."

Oesch rubbed his chin, looking at Rondeau. "So what do you think?"

"At this point?" *Murder-suicide*, Rondeau thought again. But that was just years on the job making him cynical; there was no physical evidence yet something like that had occurred. "It could be anything, really."

"Yeah, could be anything. Well, I'm glad you took the call. And I'm glad you're here."

Rondeau smiled. He knew the sheriff was nervous; a missing person's case could be costly. And the sheriff's office had a history. A couple years before, there had been a case involving a dead teenager. Deputies could investigate crimes, but in Stock County, they primarily ran the jail and worked patrol. The investigation had gone to the state police but Dunleavy, sheriff at the time, wanted to keep one of his deputies involved. The deputy wound up dead. Dunleavy had never been able to forgive himself. Close to retirement anyway — the same baby boomer generation as Swift — Dunleavy resigned, he and the wife sold their house, took the dogs and moved away. Oesch wanted to keep the department's nose clean.

Rondeau realized the sheriff was staring at him. Rondeau had fallen silent, lost in thought. He snapped out of it.

"I'll do my best, Mike."

Oesch made to leave, then stopped. He looked bemused. "You know, Dunleavy retired to Myrtle Beach?"

Rondeau's skin prickled. He'd just been thinking about the former sheriff. "Didn't know that. South Carolina?"

"Yeah. I guess there's an Elvis-themed restaurant there."

"Elvis-themed, huh?"

Oesch nodded, smiling. "I heard Dunleavy takes his wife once a week and always orders his favorite, the *Love Me Tenderloin.*"

Rondeau laughed. Oesch wrapped his knuckles on the door, almost a superstitious gesture. Then he made one last remark. "I want you to know I put in a word for you, with Captain Bouchard."

Oesch was referring to the drone shooting. Bouchard was the state police captain. Since they'd handled the call, it had been theirs for the charging. No criminal charges were being pressed. Oesch was saying he'd had a hand in that. Between the jokes about Dunleavy and the comment on Bouchard, he was trying to bond. Rondeau looked across the small office and said, "Thank you, sir."

"Good luck, Jason. Let's find this family." He closed the door after him.

Rondeau felt a weight slide over his heart. In two years, there'd been nothing as heavy as this. This case could go bad in several ways, and it was all on him.

He spread his hands out over the files and marshaled his focus.

Hopefully Stokes would be quick locating extended family, and Silas would come up with something useful from the family's home. And who knew? Maybe they'd just decided to take a trip — realized how short life could be, and been spontaneous.

That would be nice.

CHAPTER SEVEN / Addison Kemp

Stokes brought Addison Kemp into Rondeau's office. Stokes was excited and presented her like the key witness in a major trial.

Hutchinson Kemp's sister was attractive — in a natural, girl-next-door way. But there was something about her which struck Rondeau right away: the woman was tough.

He offered her the chair on the other side of his desk, sparing Stokes a look, who seemed to be trying to hide himself in between the file cabinets.

She wore jeans and a faded black *Metallica* t-shirt beneath an expensive leather jacket. It wasn't a thrown-together ensemble. Addison had money, Rondeau decided, but she didn't want to *look* like she had money.

"What happened to my brother?"

She also came right to the point.

He shifted in his chair, wincing at the way it squawked. He glanced at Stokes and jerked his eyes at the door, still open. Stokes closed it. "We're going to find out," Rondeau said. "So, you're Hutchison Kemp's biological sister, yes?"

"Correct."

"And you're unmarried?"

"Divorced. I changed back to my maiden name last year."

He nodded, sensing that she didn't like to get personal. But personal it was going to have to get.

"And you live in Indian Lake?"

"I have a house there. Just for the past couple years."

"You don't live there full-time?"

"No."

Stokes pressed his lips together, eyes flashing. He'd given Rondeau Indian Lake as Addison Kemp's sole address.

She was sharp. "Your partner probably found me there because my other residence, in Albany, is still under my married name. I have an LLC under that name and changing it was not an option."

"What's the business?"

She'd had both feet planted, massaging her knuckles. A real tomboy. "I have a cleaning business. Industrial, residential. Mostly industrial."

"Wow, great. Okay. So you divide your time between Albany and Indian Lake." Rondeau pulled out a legal pad from a drawer.

"Something like that."

He looked up at her. He took the pad and set it on the desk, which he had spent five minutes cleaning off in anticipation of their meeting. Now he couldn't find a pen. He searched in the drawer. Addison Kemp leaned across and handed him one. "Take mine."

Green Clean was embossed on the side. "Thanks." He jotted a note about the split residences, asking, "Do we have your contact information for both places?"

"I gave everything to your partner."

He clicked off the pen and set it down.

"Okay. So it's *Ms.* Kemp?"

She nodded. "Addie is fine."

"Addie. Okay. When was the last time you spoke to your brother?"

Her body language changed. She leaned forward and put her elbows on the desk. "I talked to him on the phone fifteen days ago."

"Fifteen?"

"Exactly fifteen days. It was his birthday; I called him up."

"Talk long? How did he seem?"

"He seemed good."

"Yeah?" Rondeau already sensed hesitation again. Things were veering back to the personal. In just a few minutes, right or wrong, he had sized up Addison Kemp: She had money, or she had secrets, or both, and that gave her a general wariness. She preferred facts and specifics to conjectural territory. A business woman, despite fashion choices to the contrary.

"He, you know . . . he was having some trouble."

"He was?"

"Family stuff. Work stuff. Life."

"Life."

"Right." Her eyes danced.

"Ms. Kemp . . . sorry, Addie — anything you can tell us right now, everything, no matter how small the detail, can help us right now. We need to determine—"

"He wouldn't do anything." She shook her head back and forth, mid-length hair slipping across the leather jacket shoulders. "He wouldn't hurt them. Ever. He wouldn't hurt himself. It wasn't that kind of trouble."

"Okay. Good . . ." He felt like she was sending mixed messages. "What kind of trouble, then?"

"I guess . . ." She looked down for a moment. "Trying to juggle family life, trying to juggle a marriage along with a consuming career. A job that . . . you know. He could really lose himself in."

Rondeau leaned back, forgetting about the chair's tendency to squeak. "Let's talk about his work."

Now her face brightened. She smiled for the first time, just a touch of it on her lips. "He's good. I love my brother's movies. Have you seen them?"

Rondeau glanced at Stokes again. It was a kneejerk reaction, the kind of thing you do when you're busted; look for someone to share it with. "Ah, no I don't think so. I'm not a big TV guy."

"*Citizen Farmer* is amazing. Totally put me off of meat. I've been a vegan for three years, one month, twenty-one days. Never looked back. Don't miss it."

Never looked back, Rondeau thought, noting the irony. She never looked back, but knew how long she'd been a vegan, to the day. He could understand. While he wasn't one of them, most people in AA had their sobriety charted to the day, even the hour. He was an outlier, his own date of cessation hazy. He'd relapsed a couple times and stopped keeping track.

"That's great," he said to her, not knowing what else to say. And thinking that even if cow farts were destroying the ozone layer, or whatever, he liked his burger with Swiss cheese and bacon. Side of mayo. "So he's a hard worker? Always got something going?"

"For sure."

"Was he working on something recently?"

She seemed stuck for a moment, and Rondeau realized it might be his phrasing — referring to her brother in the past tense.

Before he could correct himself, Stokes interjected, "New project in the works, right? About waste. All the things we throw away every day." Stokes had done the research.

Addie looked at him. "That's right. At first I was like, 'alright, Hutchie. No one wants to watch a movie about garbage . . .'"

"I would," Stokes said. "I like that kind of stuff."

"Oh, so does he. And he got this great idea . . ."

". . . Put GPS dots on certain refuse items, track them digitally, then show up with the camera crew along the way."

She seemed surprised and pleased that Stokes knew all this. "That's right, that's right . . ."

"Good title, too," Stokes said. "*Nothing Disappears*. I like that."

"I came up with it."

"You did?"

She nodded, pleased with herself. She was suddenly quite happy-go-lucky for someone whose brother, niece, and nephew were missing.

"We were working on the tagline when we spoke last," Addie said. "Some may think that's premature, but in today's market you've got to get your promo going way head of time."

Stokes was a fan. "*There is no throwing 'away'*. It's a good tagline. People toss something they're done with, and it's out of sight, out of mind. But all that plastic ends up floating in an ocean gyre . . ."

"That's exactly right." She gave Stokes a knockout grin.

Rondeau broke back in. "Tough to get that funded then? I assume he has to get funding, right? Get a . . . what-do-you-call-it . . . a producer to put the money in."

"Partly," Addie said. "He's still raising the rest."

Rondeau scratched a fresh note. "How?"

"Crowdfunding," Stokes blurted out. Rondeau speared him with a look. He wanted Addie to answer, not Stokes. Stokes shrank back into the files piled behind him.

Addie bobbed her head in agreement. "That's right. He used a crowd-source platform and, last I checked, had raised two hundred and thirty thousand."

Rondeau whistled. "Is that enough, though? I don't know how much movies cost."

"Well, the big studio movies cost more all the time, but the whole filmmaking world has been democratized by the digital revolution."

She just said something, Rondeau thought, *but I'm not sure what*. He nodded his head like he understood. Maybe what she was saying was that the barrier for entry was lower because cameras and film didn't cost as much as they used to.

"He hired a drone and everything," Addie said, staring off. She was marveling over her enterprising brother while Rondeau felt suddenly riveted to the chair. Here was some confirmation.

"A drone?"

"Well," she hedged, "It's correctly called a quadcopter. The quadcopter has small cameras attached. You can use it to fly over the landfills, get those big sweeping shots." She moved her hands in the air to mimic the aircraft in flight. In the meantime, Rondeau and Stokes traded looks, thinking the same thing: Hutchinson Kemp could be the owner of the quadcopter Millard shot down. Or, at least, it could be relevant.

Rondeau asked, "Addie, any reason you can think of why your brother and his family have disappeared?"

She dropped her hands and slumped back in the seat, as if remembering why they were all there. She looked down and slowly shook her head. "No."

"Does he do this? Has he ever done this? Just pick up with the family and go somewhere, unannounced?"

"I think if you thought that, we wouldn't be here."

She fell silent. They all did.

After a moment passed, Rondeau spoke again. "I need to ask the painful questions now. Okay? You can just give me yes or no answers."

She steeled herself, rolling back her shoulders, sticking out her chin. "Okay."

"Do you know, or do you suspect, your brother was having an affair?"

"No, I don't suspect. He's as monogamous as they come."

"Okay. Has he ever hit his wife, Lily? You said they were having problems . . ."

"No. Absolutely not. I didn't say that, exactly. . ."

"He ever strike either of the kids?"

She looked mortified. "Of course not. No."

"Has he had any financial problems lately? I know we sort of talked about the money . . ."

"No. He was well on his way with the crowdfunding for his film. I put in a bit myself. And he knows if he ever needs anything, he can come to me. My business is doing well. We didn't come from money. Our parents died and didn't leave us much. What we have, me and Hutchie, we've worked hard for."

Hutchie, Rondeau scribbled. And, *Dead Parents*. "I'm sorry to hear about your parents. What happened to them?"

She let out a long breath. "They died in a hit and run. Nine years ago."

"I'm sorry."

The interview went on for another hour. Rondeau covered the Kemp family's medical history (they were waiting to talk to the family physician, but sometimes siblings knew more than the doctors), their previous residences, places they liked to vacation, a list of every friend of her brother's Addie could think of, his wife's friends, where they each went to college. Partway through, Stokes got a call on his cell. He left and didn't return. Rondeau's own phone had been vibrating in his desk drawer. He thanked Addie and told her he'd be in touch, then checked to see fourteen new messages.

He had gone through one whole legal pad, now he took out another. With a fresh cup of coffee he started listening to his voicemails. It was going to be a long night. And really, what his mind kept coming back to — besides the family, those little kids in trouble, or dead — was this documentary the guy had been working on. He'd need a court order to pull data from Kemp's equipment, but felt sure Judge King would push it through. For now, they had the warrant to search the home.

CHAPTER EIGHT / The House

The rain sluiced down the windshield as Rondeau sat in front of the Kemp residence, the color leached by the downpour, everything ashen.

He could see the shapes of the forensics team moving in the house. Britney Silas stood in the window silhouetted by bright lights. Special lights which could illuminate all sorts of things tungsten couldn't. Mopped-up blood. Semen. Boot prints.

He waited for Silas to be ready for him and looked through the "Checkmate" file on Hutchinson Kemp.

Checkmate, a pet favorite of Detective Stokes', was a new comprehensive personal history system. The web program filched through endless digital reams of data on a person, from criminal and court records to social media platforms, sex offender databases, realty information, and more.

Hutchinson Kemp was pretty clean. He had been popped for Driving While Intoxicated at nineteen, which was reduced to Driving While Ability Impaired. He got another one a few years later, and lost his license. He attended the drunk driver program to get it back.

According to some social media information, he was open about it, and considered himself in recovery.

A kindred spirit, Rondeau thought. Another friend to Bill. Or, as they sometimes said in the program, at least "more than a passing acquaintance."

Kemp had collected his share of traffic tickets, none outstanding. He'd been in one barroom scuffle — right around the time of his second DWI. So he was a bit of a scrapper, maybe. At least with a good head of booze on. Rondeau could relate to that.

At one time, Kemp had been barred from entering Canada. Canada had drunk driving laws which were harsher than in the States. Kemp had gone to the Canadian Embassy, jumped through a bunch of hoops, paid a couple thousand bucks, and gotten his right of entry restored. A filmmaker wasn't worth much in the modern world if he couldn't travel to a neighboring country for a shoot. And Kemp had been to quite a few places. He'd taken trips to Guatemala, he'd been to Spain, Portugal, Tunisia, and Jordan.

Rondeau mused over these last two countries. Jordan? That was an interesting place for a filmmaker to go. Yet he didn't see anything in Kemp's filmography involving the countries. Had Jordan been a pleasure trip then, to a resort? What about Tunisia?

Holding the thick Checkmate printout, it crossed his mind: The famous fruit vendor in Tunisia who had set himself on fire in protest of government, touching off the Arab Spring. Could the Kemp disappearance be linked to some type of terrorism? Was Hutchinson Kemp somewhere right now, being held up by chains, being interrogated? For what? His documentary on cattle farms? On household garbage? Going by the missing shifts at the hospital, and the neighbors' last sighting of the Kemps at home, the family had been missing for three days. Yet there'd been no contact from a kidnapper demanding a ransom, no demands from a terrorist group looking to free prisoners or convert everyone to some backwoods religious fundamentalism. If the Kemps were alive, why were they being held?

The front door opened, and Britney Silas leaned out, squinting in the rain. She spotted him and waved him over. They were ready.

* * *

Silas gave Rondeau the guided tour. Some things he already knew from the night before: popcorn bowl downstairs, crayons scattered on the rug. In the kitchen, things were fairly neat, but there were more signs of a hasty departure.

"Coffee prepped and ready to brew," Silas said, touching the stainless steel coffee maker with a gloved hand. Rondeau had slipped on latex gloves, feeling a bit like a man about to go into the operating room. Booties covered his shoes and a net over his hair. "Dishes in the sink," she said.

He looked around the kitchen. "Nice stuff." A brushed chrome stove, cast-iron cookery; even the slotted spoons hanging above the stove looked expensive.

"Here's the history on the house," Silas said. "Property was left to the wife, Lily, nee O'Connell. It was her father's, Patrick O'Connell."

"Was he Jewish?"

"Irish," Silas answered, missing the joke. "The family had this house built five years ago."

Interesting, Rondeau thought, looking around again. They'd kept it modest. The house didn't look like much from the outside — new, but simple. Inside, he could see the craft: rustic hardwood floors, walls and trim painted in earthy tones. The fixtures were brass or wrought iron. Even the electric outlet covers were nice. Orange tags dotted the decor. Silas was logging anything that looked like it had been left unattended, evidence of an unplanned departure, like the coffee maker and sink. Or the mug which had been sitting outside, now bagged and sent to the lab.

She took him through the bedrooms. Their feet crunched over plastic laid over certain areas. Rondeau eyed the teddy bear on the bedroom floor and felt a kind of twist in his stomach. There was an orange tag on the ground next to it, marked "27."

"The closets and drawers are full of clothes," Silas said. "We found empty suitcases. Doesn't look like anyone packed for a trip."

"I want to see his office. His edit studio, or whatever you call it," Rondeau dragged his gaze away from the bear.

Silas led him downstairs. "Cobleskill called me," she said as she went down. Cobleskill was the DA. "She was surprised she hadn't heard from you yet."

Rondeau felt a sting. "Well, there's nothing prosecutorial so far. When there's a villain, she'll be the first to know."

Silas reached the bottom and gave him a look.

Downstairs was an office, a laundry room, a family room. An evidence tech was dusting the TV, which had been turned off. Aside from the office, the floors were concrete. Rondeau looked over the framed pictures in the office. One showed the entire family in the sun. Not a beach resort, though — pine trees in the background — it could've been taken on this very property. The kids were adorable. Healthy-looking baby boy, pink cheeks, in his mother's arms. The girl was by her father, her hair in pigtails.

Other photographs showed Kemp with people Rondeau didn't recognize. He took out his phone and started snapping shots. "We've got all that," Silas said. He took another pic, despite her. He wanted to know who these people were. Like this guy, here, weighing in at probably three hundred pounds and wearing overalls. Kemp had his arm around the farmer, wearing a huge grin. Rondeau would bet this was from the cow documentary.

"Where's all his stuff?" Rondeau glanced at the large oak desk. There were a few papers there, a mason jar of pens and pencils, a couple of balled-up used tissues, but no computer, no big screens, or whatever editors and filmmakers used. Just some square patches where the dust had yet to settle.

"That's the million-dollar question," Silas said. "Here." She held out a smaller, 4x6 photo. "Pulled this from the shelves over there."

It was a candid shot, one taken by the wife, maybe, Kemp sitting at his desk, turned halfway around, that same big grin. The man had large ears. A bit of a funny hair cut the way it was all crazy like that. But boy, did he look content. And behind him at the desk, there were the screens Rondeau had pictured. Two of them side by side, along with a laptop, a computer tower, extra hard drives, and a camera.

He kicked at something on the floor while studying the picture. A cable, not connected to anything.

"Well," he said, "whatever happened, whoever had a hand in it, they took all his gear. So much for the court order to have a peek at Hutchie's stuff."

"Hutchie?" Silas cocked an eyebrow.

"What his sister calls him." Rondeau stood back and crossed his arms. "And you haven't found anything else, equipment-wise?"

She shook her head. "Not a single device. I agree, everything looks like this family left in a big hurry. Or they were taken. But not a phone or tablet was left behind."

He nodded, his interest piqued. What did Hutchinson Kemp have that was so important? Maybe his sister had some of his stuff. A sample, a video, something.

CHAPTER NINE / Hiding in the Shadows

Addison Kemp was scheduled to complete blood and DNA samples in the morning, and to have her phone calls and emails analyzed — all correspondence with Hutchinson pored over by CSI. She had gotten a room at a local motel.

He met her at the Boars Head Inn, the one restaurant in Hazleton. She was drinking a beer at the bar, and she'd changed out of jeans into a pair of slacks, opting for a white blouse that resembled a tuxedo shirt. In fact, as he came up closer upon her, that's exactly what it was. A man's tuxedo shirt.

She took her leather jacket from the back of the stool and they let the hostess lead them to a table. Rondeau was ravenous. He hadn't eaten all day. They discussed the weather and the mountains and things people did in the Adirondacks if they weren't looking for missing families. And then as the food was delivered, the talk came around to the search.

"We've established an Incident Command at the Public Safety Center. If we need to widen out, we'll move over to the civic center, plenty of space there," he assured her.

"How does it work?"

"Search parties go out, form bump lines, use GPS; they scour miles of woods. Deputies go door to door with photos of the m . . . of your family. Troopers assist, and paper the areas outside the county. Websites are up, and your family is listed in a bunch of databases. By tomorrow morning, everyone with a badge from here to Florida and California will know that they're missing."

"And when do you go to the press?" She had ordered another beer and drank it down pretty quick. She knifed into her eggplant dish for the first time. Rondeau was already halfway done with his steak, chewing while he talked, manners be damned. She didn't seem to mind.

"Soon. Typically, there are a few days from the start of the investigation before we provide public information. We can't control what leaks — usually the conference is more to clarify things as it is to put out the word."

"And to congratulate all the law enforcement and volunteers."

He raised his eyebrows at her.

"I've seen some missing persons' press conferences," she said. "Lots of congratulating."

It seemed a challenging remark. He set down his cutlery and decided how to best respond.

"You've seen a lot of missing persons' press conferences?"

"I was, you know, online all afternoon. Looking around."

"Then you know it's a monumental effort. Working round the clock, lots of people involved." Sometimes, he thought, too many. FBI, District Attorneys, press — everybody eager to get in on things. Rondeau liked simplicity. Good old-fashioned investigation.

"Where's your experience coming from?" she asked. "You handled missing persons' cases before?"

Jesus, she was abrasive. Or maybe she was just candid, and he was being oversensitive. "No. But I've liaised with missing persons' cases. I worked with Ninth Street a lot."

"Ninth Street?"

It had slipped out. *So much for thinking before I speak*, Rondeau thought. "Just what I call the FBI. Term of endearment. In the District, and this is late 90s, FBI headquarters was located on Ninth Street. So that's what we called them."

"You were a cop in D.C., huh?"

"A detective. Same as now, yeah." She knew the lingo — people who lived in D.C. often called it the District.

"Why you up here?"

Oh boy. That was a long story. He really wanted to get to the part about her brother's documentary footage. He'd indulge her first. He supposed it was the least he could do.

"My sister got sick. And she passed."

Addie set the beer down, folded her hands. "I'm sorry."

"It was a while ago."

"So you came up here to . . . help her? When she was sick?"

"Yes."

"That was good of you."

He decided to tell Addie the story. For one thing, he was thinking of getting Addie to do a polygraph. Too many red flags in his mind to just take her at face value. Maybe if he shared a little about himself, he'd earn some trust. He explained to her how his sister, Jessy, and her husband, Millard, had finally gotten pregnant with their one child after trying for many years. Jessica had been a later mother — forty-one at the time Gabriel had been conceived, the long-awaited gift. *My geriatric pregnancy*, she would refer to it as, and laugh. Jessy was often laughing, except maybe late in the term, when the pregnancy had encountered problems. She had developed ovarian and cervical cysts. Due to the cysts and other complications, the pregnancy had been an ordeal. Baby Gabriel hadn't made it.

"Oh," Addie said and made a face. "Oh my God. I'm so sorry."

"Millard took it really hard. I mean it was devastating to them both, but my sister . . . she was tough. Kind of like you."

Addie blushed and looked away.

He didn't tell her any more.

"What happened to her?" The question shocked him back into the moment.

"After the baby . . . Jessy was diagnosed with full-blown cancer. It spread quickly."

"I'm really so sorry. Must've been so hard for them. For you."

He nodded and looked around the room, unable to meet her eyes for a moment.

"What about your brother-in-law now?"

He shrugged. "Well, from what little I know about mental health, adults don't usually just slip into delusional personality disorder. Millard experienced an event once in his past, and maybe that set a tone. After Jessy and the baby . . . Millard became really paranoid, I guess. Delusional. I don't know how credible that diagnosis is, like I said, I'm not a—"

"It's *Don Quixote*."

He found her gaze. "How's that?"

"*Don Quixote*? One of the greatest novels ever written?"

He shook his head. "I don't know it."

She glanced away. Then something flickered in her eyes. "What sort of delusions?"

"Oh, I guess you could say 'conspiracy theories.'"

"Like?"

"Mostly the old chestnuts; how President Kennedy was assassinated because he'd signed a bill to empower the

Treasury, and the Federal Reserve killed him. Or, how the CIA funneled seizure money from the crack-cocaine epidemic in Los Angeles during the 1980s to the Contras who were fighting to destabilize Nicaragua."

"I remember that. Wasn't the Iran-Contra scandal about selling weapons to Iran and using the money to fund the Contras? I hadn't heard about the drug-CIA thing. Makes sense to me."

He paused, thinking about his assessment of Addie as someone who was only interested in hard facts. Maybe she was just humoring him, because he detected a lie in her last statement. He really wanted to poly her.

He shrugged again. "Millard's got 'em all under his hat. I think he has what you call a 'persecution complex,' too — he thinks people are following him."

"Really."

Rondeau gave a nod. "He's seen men dressed in black hiding in the shadows. When he stopped driving one night and ran out in the road, ranting and raving at another vehicle he was convinced was following him. He doesn't drive anymore."

"I was gonna say . . ." She turned on a full smile and leaned back. She'd finished her vegan dish, and his steak was long gone, along with the roasted red potatoes with the rosemary garnish, the side of asparagus and cooked carrots. Down the hatch. He put his hands on his stomach, leaning back, too. They held each other's gaze for a moment.

Rondeau said, "Can you tell me about what you saw on your brother's footage?"

"You think he's got shots of planes flying into towers?"

"No, of course not, but . . ."

"I'll do you one better," she said. "You can look at it tonight."

He sat up straighter. "You have footage with you?"

"I thought it was at home, or I would have brought it up myself. I could've sworn he'd mailed me a flash drive. He did, but that was family stuff. The footage he'd sent me — I thought more about it after you called and checked my Vimeo account. He sent me a password-protected video. Eyes-only kind of stuff." She waggled her brows. "Real conspiracy shit, what with landfill workers talking about how fast their trash cells filled up."

It wasn't the first time he'd though that for someone whose brother — and his entire family — were missing for three days, she was quite cavalier. On the other hand, everyone coped with trouble differently. She'd been defensive at times in his office earlier that day. She was divorced, she ran a business, had people counting on her. Maybe it just wasn't her style to show she was upset. Or to even allow herself to get upset in the first place. He could relate to that, too.

"I want to look at it anyway," he said, going for his wallet.

She held out a hand to stop him, pulling out a billfold. "I got it," she said.

"Mine's a tax write-off," he said.

When the waitress came, Rondeau paid the bill. Fifteen minutes later, he was standing outside her hotel room, waiting for her to copy over the footage to a flash drive. She came out of the room, handed it to him, and he wished her goodnight.

He didn't glance back, but he felt sure she stood watching him all the way until he got into his car. Though when he got behind the wheel and looked through the windshield, her door was closed.

CHAPTER TEN / Bar fight

The blow came out of nowhere to Peter King's jaw. It was hard enough that he saw stars, stumbled back a step, and blinked. Here he was again, another fight, and this time he was in the middle of it.

He grabbed John Hayes again and dragged him backwards out of the bar. He realized what had hit him was Hayes's elbow, inadvertently — Hayes was trying to ward off an attack from another man, Brad Rafferty, who was Terry's younger brother.

Trooper Ski hadn't arrested either man that morning. Hayes was still getting into trouble, and Peter felt responsible.

Brad Rafferty advanced on Hayes, his fists up, his face red. Hayes had pissed him off that much — as only Hayes could seem to do when it came to the Rafferty brothers. The rest of the bar customers looked on, eager to watch the fight play out.

"You're a commie pussy," Brad spat. He glowered at Hayes, still following as Peter hauled him away towards the door.

"Get back, sir, stand back," Peter ordered.

Brad stopped and seemed to realize for the first time there was a sheriff's deputy standing there in the bar. Holding onto Hayes, in fact.

"Let him go, let me have him," Brad said. "He's a traitor. Stay out of it, King."

Peter had been on his way home. Aletha was waiting up for him — they even had a date night planned. But he'd gotten the call from the bar, Men on Horses, or, Moh's to the locals. It seemed Hayes couldn't leave well enough alone when it came to the Rafferty brothers. Peter almost wished he hadn't taken the call. Maybe Brad was right. Maybe Hayes needed to be left to the mercy of the mob. But Peter had already passed the buck once.

And Brad didn't seem to be the only one Hayes had upset. Moh's had a dozen customers, mostly male, either curled around the bar or standing in the back by the pool table, and they had that same venom in their eyes. *What did you do now, Hayes? What the hell did you* say *to these people?*

Brad lunged forward. His fists were up again. There was no time to react, to get Hayes out of harm's way. Brad landed a blow smack in the middle of Hayes's nose. Peter had a tight grip on Hayes, but the impact from the punch was still enough to snap the man's head back and into Peter's face. The deputy stumbled and fell against the door, knocking it ajar. Hayes crashed against him and they landed in a heap.

Lying there, momentarily stunned, he could feel the cool night air rushing in. Janis Joplin was crooning in the background.

Come on, come on, come on, come on and take it! Take another little piece of my heart now baby . . .

He shoved Hayes aside. He scrambled to his feet and went for his gun.

He stopped when he saw Brad's expression. In that split second Peter made an assessment: *he's carrying, too.*

Brad had a concealed weapon. In New York you could get a conceal-and-carry permit for your handgun, and they were becoming more popular. School shootings and street violence fueled the vigilantes — arm yourself or be a victim. Apprehension about the government was another justification.

Brad had the stance: feet planted wide, arms hanging. Ready to draw.

You've got to be kidding me. It was like some scene from the Wild West. Only this wasn't the dusty streets of a border town, it was here, now, a mile outside of Hazelton.

Hayes groaned at his feet, still flat on his back in the doorway.

Peter kept his hand on his weapon but didn't pull it. He raised his other hand in a gesture of peace. He held Brad's eye.

"Brad," came a voice. "Brad, that's enough."

The bartender's name was Betty. She'd been working there for twenty years, and the one who'd called the cops.

"Alright," Peter said. "Okay . . . Brad, you've made your point. Stand down."

Brad was unperturbed. "*You* stand down, cop."

Come on, come on, come on and take it! Janis wailed.

Peter didn't budge. If he took a step, made a move, Brad was going to pull.

The seconds rolled by. Janis continued to screech and howl, but her voice was fading. A new song took over; he recognized the opening guitar chords and cymbal crashes of *Radar Love.*

"You're a civil servant," Brad spat. "I pay your salary."

"I'm here responding to a disturbance, Brad. I entered the bar and found you harassing one of the customers. When I tried to remove him, you pursued. Then you knocked me to the ground." He risked a step forward. "I'm well within my rights to arrest you and take you to jail. This is a public place. You have no right-to-defense here."

It was a ridiculous pissing contest. *Either I press this guy, or I back down.* He could send for backup. Dispatch knew he'd taken the call but there would be no one coming to assist unless he requested it. There was a chance that one of the troopers in the area might nose it out on their own, but there was no counting on that.

Better to de-escalate the situation now, get out of here and deal with Brad later. There were a dozen witnesses. Maybe the bartender would agree to a statement about what had happened, even if the majority of the customers would stay silent.

Peter took his hand off the gun. He felt his heart sink. But it was the right move. Wasn't it? To get Hayes out of there, plus take Brad along, would be too hard. He'd have to cuff them both, call in the backup, and it would add hours to his night. Hayes needed to go, and that was that.

"Alright, Brad. We're going to leave. You need to keep calm."

"I am calm."

You fucking asshole, Peter thought. But he realized what he was feeling, already, was regret. He had been humiliated.

"Good," he said. Keeping his eyes on Brad, Peter took a step back. He lowered down to a squat and grabbed Hayes by the shoulder. He shook him; Hayes moaned. "Get up," Peter commanded. He squeezed Hayes's shoulder — hard. Hayes yelped, but it worked. He flailed for a moment, then used the doorframe to stand up.

Peter took one last look around the room, one last look at Brad. There was no denying the smug satisfaction on the man's face. The look pissed him off. For a moment, he imagined rushing Brad, tackling him and beating him to the ground.

Instead, he dragged Hayes out the door and left.

* * *

"What is it with you and these guys, huh?"

Peter took the dark roads. His adrenaline was still rushing. He needed to lash out at something, someone.

Hayes was silent in the backseat.

Instead of going home, Peter was going in the other direction, back to the goddamn jail. He buried the accelerator and sped through the dark, trees blurring past, road dipping and rising. He'd already placed the call that he was coming in. Hayes was going to be locked up for the night, at least.

Hayes was drunk — the fumes filled the car with the smell of sour booze and sweat. Peter hated it. He liked a clean car, a clean life. He understood that Hayes was as human as anyone else, but he wished the man would just go away. Just disappear. He tried to remember a good time in his life, a time before he'd been caretaker to the mentally ill, the criminals, the ignorant; a policeman for the social failings of the world. Not what he had signed up for. He'd wanted to help, and make a difference.

Almost there. The lights of the jail were on the horizon; over the trees, a soft glow. Much as he regretted having to go back there tonight, seeing those lights eased some of the anger twisting through him.

Hayes suddenly laughed. "They think they're free," he said, and broke out in a brief coughing fit. His voice was nasal from his busted nose. Then he resumed, "They think it's the government that's going to come after them. Can you imagine, Pete? Their little pea-shooters against an army. Against armed drones."

Well, Brad Rafferty managed to make quick work of me, Peter thought, feeling a bitter twinge.

Hayes whistled through his clogged nose. There was probably blood in the back of the car, on the seats. Peter would have to scrub it out tonight. Yet another thing to tend to before this long day was over. If he didn't have Althea . . . he didn't know what he would do.

He could feel his heart easing. Another storm had passed. Or he had swallowed it down. He knew he had a

58

temper. Since his youth, people had teased him about it. They said he overcompensated for his small size. In farm country, kids ran on the plus size. But then he'd met Althea, who hadn't grown up in the region. She was his fresh start. The key out of his own cell.

Something occurred to him. He looked in the rear-view mirror, through the metal grate.

"Is that what you were talking about at the bar, Hayes? That people aren't free? That they weren't — Brad and whoever else? I think I saw Joe Fleming there, and Tony Spillane, Nick's nephew . . ."

"They don't want to hear it. No one wants to hear it." Then Hayes grew petulant. "No one wants to hear what I have to say."

"What about earlier today? You giving Terry Rafferty an earful of the same shit? Now you're bleeding again, John, and this time you're going to jail."

Hayes didn't respond, but in the absence Peter felt something change in the air — a subtle difference in the atmosphere. Like Hayes was genuinely, emotionally hurt.

"Why do you say these things, huh? Why get people all riled up?"

"Because I believe in freedom," Hayes said. "Freedom from tyrants."

"And what sort of tyranny are we talking about? You just said going against the government was a joke . . ." Peter's thoughts shifted, already his mind was moving on. He saw this type of thing all the time, anyway — and he didn't blame the cops or the therapists or anyone who dealt with people like Hayes — after a while you stopped really talking to them, you stopped hearing, you just went by the playbook. You said "uh-huh" while they spoke, determined if they were a danger to themselves or others, and you went to bed to start all over again the next day.

"Like what happened to that family," Hayes said.

Peter suddenly slammed on the brakes. His head was buzzing again. He pulled off the road, the tires throwing gravel and dirt.

The cruiser came to a rest and Peter watched Hayes' shape in the mirror, the points of light in the man's eyes. "Say that again?"

"The family. The one that disappeared."

"What about the family? You know something about that, Hayes?" He thought of Maggie, the little girl.

Hayes squeaked through his bludgeoned nose. "I seen the fella couple times. Kemp. Down at the store, with his kids. You know the type — liberal."

"Okay . . . and?"

"You just know something is going to happen to a guy like that."

"That's it?"

Peter waited for more. When Hayes didn't say anything else, Peter got the car moving again, off the shoulder and back onto the road. He drove a bit slower, though, the surge of anger and frustration left behind.

"He pokes around too much," Hayes went on at last. "He looked too close, asked too many questions."

Now it just sounded like the usual jabber. Peter picked up the radio. "Stock County; SCS-14."

"He's a disruption," Hayes said about Kemp.

"Uh-huh."

Over the radio: "Go ahead, 14."

Peter pressed the button. "I am minutes away with John Hayes, en route to the jail, over."

"Copy that, 14, will relay."

Peter hung the radio on the dash. He kept his eyes on the road. "Just an overnight stay, Hayes. A nice bed, a meal in the morning. Could be worse, right?"

"Oh it could be," Hayes said quietly.

CHAPTER ELEVEN / The Footage

Rondeau hung up the phone. County Jail was a good place for a guy like John Hayes to cool his heels for the night; Deputy King had made the right decision. In the morning, Rondeau would call Mental Health and ask for Hayes to be assessed. Deputy King said that Hayes had mentioned the family. Even if Hayes was spouting paranoid bullshit, it all had to be checked out at this point. Rondeau didn't know Hayes like King did — the deputies had direct contact with more people in the county than Rondeau, who had only been here a relatively short time. King said Hayes was a commercial truck driver, sometimes worked for the Highway Department, running a plow in the winter. Other seasons, he was hard up for work. He took to drinking and mouthing off about the government. His antics reminded Rondeau of a more aggressive Millard. King said Hayes had been upsetting the Rafferty brothers, local contractors. Didn't know about what, if anything, besides general politics and opinions.

The Rafferty brothers were possibly the contractors who had built the Kemp home. So there could be a connection there, too, however circuitous, worth keeping an eye on. Deputy King agreed he'd follow up on it the next day. For now, he said, he was going home. Put ice on his eye.

Rondeau swirled the drink in his cup. Apple cider. Best this time of year, when the orchards were bursting with fruit — McIntosh, Cortlands, and more. It was a small pleasure, the cutting, bittersweet taste of it. He almost forgot about everything for a moment.

He set the empty glass on the kitchen counter and walked into the gloomy dining room. The table was covered in papers. He didn't know when the last time he'd used the table to sit down and eat a meal. Most of his meals were eaten in the car, or standing over the sink.

He pushed some of the papers aside until he revealed the "Best Practices Protocol" document he'd handed out that afternoon. He set this aside, too. Next was a thick file. The reporting mechanics on a single missing person were extensive. For a whole family it multiplied. It began with the basics for each person — name, aliases, date of birth, identifying marks, height, weight, gender, race, hair color, and so on. Of course there was the clerical data, too — driver license and social security. Recent photos were obtained. Description of clothing the person was last seen wearing, notable items they may have been carrying. It included their primary care doctor, even their dentist.

Then the same mechanics needed to be run on all available extended family members. Addison Kemp was going to have a fun-filled morning of blood work and DNA samples. She was the sole sibling of Hutchinson Kemp, but Stokes had found more family members for his wife, Lily, who had been contacted. Patrick and Mary O'Connell hadn't seen their daughter in over three months, when they'd been up for a week in the summer. They were retired and lived in South Carolina. Same as Sheriff Dunleavy.

Mary hadn't spoken with Lily for a week. She said that her daughter wasn't a huge Facebook person, so her dormant page hadn't aroused any concern. Then the mother, according to Stokes, who'd spoken to her by phone, had broken down and cried. They were either going to book a flight or drive up. Either way, it would take them some time to arrive.

Social media was its own animal when it came to missing people. Public profiles were fine to access without a warrant, but digging into Hutchinson Kemp's crowdfunding sites would require a sworn affidavit. Tomorrow was Sunday, so the signing would have to happen in Judge King's home.

The Kemp home itself had a profile, a story to tell. There were the contractors, possibly the Raffertys. Then there was the finance. Who paid the mortgage? Money played its role in almost every case. Even the property realtor, the broker; these elements could shed possible light.

So many pieces, he thought, looking over the contents of the table. So much paperwork, so many details.

The big, drafty home creaked and groaned around him. The radiators wafted brittle heat. Upstairs, the bed springs squeaked as Millard rolled over.

Jurisdiction played its usual meddling role in a case like this. Luckily, he'd been the one to file the missing family report, and the Kemps' home fell in county, as well as state, jurisdiction. No one had fought him on it, which was a good thing. He'd done his due diligence and promptly notified the state police. They, in turn, offered their services. If, at any time, he should wish to contact Detective Dana Gates, he was encouraged to do so. Gates had been involved in a high profile case just last year, the same case that wound up landing Connie Leifson a position at the college.

But there was no confirmed abduction. It was still perfectly possible that the Kemp family had left of their own volition. While the records showed they didn't own a second vehicle, they could have walked off somewhere.

There had been a red tricycle in the garage, but no stroller. A family with two young children almost always had a stroller. The search party launched from Incident Command tomorrow would scour the woods surrounding their property, and beyond.

They also could've been picked up, maybe by a friend. Rondeau wouldn't know enough to make the call on how plausible that was until he had a full profile on Hutch Kemp, each of his friends and his co-workers. Lily, too. But there was no unequivocal sign of foul play in the house. Things left undone, yes. Dirty dishes, food left out, and empty suitcases — that was enough to alert suspicion, but not confirm anything. He reiterated to himself: They could have left, freely, for any number of reasons. It could have been related to the documentary film, for all he knew.

He reached to the middle of the table and picked up the small flash drive which Addie had given him.

Rondeau bounced it in his palm for a moment. He considered getting another cup of apple cider from the fridge.

What are you doing, Jay? Are you stalling?

It occurred to him that he was, in fact, procrastinating. Not his style, not at all. Of course he wanted to know what was on the drive.

So? Why are you just standing there?

He didn't know. He decided to stop putting it off, quit telling himself the family was okay, and he walked into the living room.

The glass-faced woodstove was dark inside, and the room was cool. It was that time of year when the sun warmed the house during the day, but the nights grew chilly. The first frost was maybe a week, maybe only days away. If the family was out in the woods somewhere, they wouldn't last long.

He sat on the couch and opened up his laptop on the coffee table. He waited for it to boot up, and stuck in the drive. There were two files on it, both of them called

".mov" files. The first was named *Rushes - Scn 14*. The second, *Bday Misc.*

Addie hadn't told him there were two files. He didn't know what "Rushes" meant, but clicked on it since it was first on the list.

He sat back on the couch to watch, and realized he was scratching himself on the shoulder so hard it was starting to hurt. He took his hands and gripped his knees.

The video played:

Black screen. Then, a voice: "If by your words or actions you threaten corporate profits, you are at the top of the list for domestic terrorism."

An image faded in. An aerial shot, sweeping over rows of vegetables. A barn in the distance. This was a farm. The shot cut to cows grazing, then chickens pecking the dirt.

"We had chickens," a second voice said. A man appeared, leaning against the barn beside a henhouse. Rondeau recognized him — the farmer in the picture from Kemp's office. "We had eight. My wife named them. She called one Carol. Can you imagine that? A chicken named Carol." He laughed, and then the shot went aerial again. Rondeau thought it was the type of footage captured by a drone — or, what Addie had said, a quadcopter with a camera.

But no signs of trash, or waste.

This is the new documentary?

The narrator's voice — Rondeau guessed it was Hutch Kemp's voice — resumed. "You can speak up and you can tell the truth. But you will be guilty. Because if you cause a disruption in the profits of industry, you are guilty under the Patriot Act. Animal rights and environmental activists are the number one domestic terrorism threats according to FBI . . ."

The image cut to more cows, only they weren't grazing in an open field, but squished together in a factory farm. The next few shots were brutal, showing cows knocked on the head, their throats cut, standing udder-deep in their own feces.

"Today, the number one cause of deforestation, global warming, water and air pollution, and human disease is not fossil fuels. It's the meat industry. Yet small, sustainable working farms are finding it difficult to gain a foothold in the food delivery system. Not because the market doesn't demand it — it does. But because the market is rigged."

The screen went black, with the words *SCENE MISSING*. The voice continued. "The agricultural industry is a multi-billion dollar juggernaut with proponents seated in the legislature. Environmental groups are patronized by leading meat industry corporations. Scientific research is bought and paid for. While animal agriculture destroys our planet — and us — it is protected by our very government."

The video abruptly stopped. Rondeau looked and saw it had come to the end — only two and a half minutes in length. That was it. He clicked on it and watched it through again. It hadn't been a glitch, the hundred and fifty seconds composed the entirety of the clip. He sat back for a moment, thinking. That was not the most current film. That clip had been from the previous film, *Citizen Farmer*. Had to be.

Still feeling anxious, he selected the second file, marked *Bday Misc*.

The clip played. Rondeau could tell right away he was looking at the Kemps' house. The shot was shaky — "handheld," he thought they called it — but the image was clean, high resolution, as good as the documentary footage he'd just watched. The scene was Kemp's office. He heard the man's voice, off screen. "Be right up!"

The video cut to the upstairs kitchen. Same handheld style, likely Kemp playing cameraman. Rondeau recognized the woman in the room: Lily. Wearing an apron, putting frosting on a cake.

At her feet, leaping up and down, repeating something Rondeau couldn't quite understand, was a little girl.

Rondeau leaned closer.

Lily turned to the camera, offered a wan smile. "In a minute, honey," she told the girl. Rondeau realized the girl was requesting to lick the frosting off the fork. This was a home movie. He glanced at the time bar below the moving image; about three minutes in length.

Lily dipped the cake towards the lens. *Happy Birthday, Daddy* was written in gooey white script. The rest of the frosting was blue, made to look like waves. A dinghy floated on the water.

The girl was still leaping at the mother's feet.

"I'm just going to give it to her," Lily demurred.

She set the cake on the counter and picked up the wooden fork, tines slicked with frosting.

"Sure, yeah. Go ahead," Hutch said from behind the camera.

Rondeau's ears pricked up. He had never been married, but he'd been in a couple of long-term relationships. He recognized a note of frustration. Maybe the parents argued over the little girl's sugar intake, or something. She looked healthy enough, Rondeau thought. A spry little four year-old.

Had Addie meant to show him this? What was she trying to tell him? See what a happy family my brother has? Or, see that they have problems?

He watched on, through a couple more cuts, until Hutch was following around the second child with the camera. The baby boy was a crawler — a *creeper*, Jessy used to say about kids that age. He was really moving along, the shot trailing in a way reminding Rondeau of *The Shining*.

Then a time jump, because now it was dark outside. The camera aimed at the family's dining-room table. Streamers hung from the chandelier above the table. Balloons bobbed softly against the ceiling, strings gently blowing in a breeze wafting from an open window.

Rondeau waited for the usual off-key rendering of the "happy birthday" song. He lowered his eyes to the timeline. Less than twenty seconds to go. Wasn't going to be much of a birthday video.

Just the hovering decorations, everything quiet, and it ended.

He sat back on the couch, staring at the black screen.

He started to scratch, then stopped himself.

"Huh," he said to the empty room. He sat like that for a moment longer, thinking. He leaned back to the laptop and used the mouse to grab the timeline scrubber and drag it back. Then he watched the whole birthday video over again, as he had done the movie clip. Only he stopped, this time, when Lily turned to Hutch in the kitchen. Wearing her apron, standing over the cake. Turning her head as he came closer, giving him that smile, that look; something in her eyes.

Rondeau paused it there. He looked at Lily Kemp, and she looked back at him. He pressed the key to advance the film until he came to the shot of the dining room table, balloons floating. The windows beyond were dark, indeed, but not entirely. There was a streetlight giving off just a bit of illumination in the distance. Out on the road, near to the trees, it looked like someone was standing there.

Rondeau leaned towards the screen, his pulse racing. It could've been a shadow, something else, but he didn't think so. It was a human silhouette. Like someone was there, watching the house.

SUNDAY

CHAPTER TWELVE / Plans

Peter was eating a hasty breakfast at home when his phone buzzed on the table. He took the call from Rondeau.

"Morning. What's up?"

"Morning. So this is the story for the next couple hours," said Rondeau. "New guy is talking to Lily Kemp's co-workers at the hospital and following up with the doctor's office and bank accounts."

"Sounds good."

"And I'm with Britney Silas. We're doing the Direct Sample Evidence from toothbrushes. That goes to the NMPP and will get uploaded to the DNA database program. But that can take time, so I'm sticking with the sister, Addison Kemp, as she gets poked and prodded. She's volunteered to take a polygraph for us, just to clear up a couple things."

Peter scraped up the last of his eggs and continued listening.

"Search teams have been deployed to the man-made pond behind the Kemp's home, dragging it, scouring the woods around the area. So far, nothing."

"That's too bad. Or I mean, good. Both?"

Rondeau hesitated. "Yeah."

"You want me and Deputy Bruin in on that search?" It was really the sergeant's call.

"No," he answered. "I got something else for you. First of all, how you doing?"

"I'm good to go."

"Face is okay?"

Peter raised a hand and touched the tender spots beneath his eye and along his nose. Swollen there, turning shades of purple. He knew Rondeau's concern was genuine, but couldn't help feeling embarrassed. And angry. *I had a frigging showdown with some cowboy who basically drove me out of the bar. I backed down like some scared kid. Not like an officer of the law.* "I'll heal," he said.

"I spoke to the DA," Rondeau told him. "This is an easy assault charge. Pled out, Brad Rafferty will go away for thirty days or pay a nice fine."

Peter bristled. Of course he could arrest Brad for the previous night's skirmish, but the idea left him sour. For one thing, Peter's father could be the judge who got the case. Peter didn't like that. It might look like nepotism. He didn't know what he really wanted to do with Brad Rafferty yet.

Rondeau let him off the hook and shifted the conversation. "I'd like you to do something for me, if you don't mind."

"Shoot."

"I want you to tell me what you think."

Peter set down his fork and wiped his mouth. He looked for Althea but she was in the shower. He swallowed, prepared a response. "What I think? I think that there's something going on between the Raffertys and

John Hayes. I don't know if it has to do with what we're dealing with, though."

"Well, you know, I wonder about something . . ."

"Yeah?"

"I wonder if the Raffertys were contractors on the Kemp house."

Interesting, Peter thought. It was potentially a way to deal with Brad Rafferty without it looking like payback. "I can find out."

"Good."

Peter could hear coffee burbling in Rondeau's office. Something occurred to him. "You know Nick Spillane?"

"No."

He looked out the window as he spoke. "Spillane recently bought a bit of property in the county, has built a few spec homes and a restaurant that never seems to open. I've seen Rafferty work-trucks at some of the sites. Including the restaurant."

Rondeau was silent. Peter hustled on, "Spillane's nephew was in the bar last night. Spillane was a junk dealer, you know. Big money in that, actually. He's from, Florida, I think, and then he moved up here. Isn't Kemp a filmmaker? And his new movie is about waste, you said?"

"That's right. Maybe junk, whatever that is, factors in."

"Yeah, maybe." Peter didn't know much about documentaries. He knew that Althea watched a bunch of them on Netflix. They seemed to take an issue, sensationalize it, and sell it the same way you sold any other film. It had to be entertaining. Truthful? Perhaps. "Have you seen footage from that film?"

"No. I saw something from another one of his movies. For one thing, all of Kemp's editing equipment is gone. Drives, computer, all the data. You know, if we could find that missing equipment. . ."

"I read you." Peter detected something in Rondeau's voice. He felt the detective was holding something back.

He heard the water in the shower shut off. Althea was finishing up. He still hadn't spoken with her about last night. He'd come in and found her already asleep. She'd gotten out of bed first, made the breakfast, and he'd awoken to her in the bathroom, getting ready. He doubted she'd noticed the mark on his face in the darkness of the bedroom — the sun was only now rising over the mountains.

"Tell me more about what John Hayes said to you in the car," Rondeau asked.

Peter picked up his plate and took it to the sink. Althea was about to come through, en route to the bedroom. He didn't want her to see his face while he was still on the phone. "Sure, yeah. He said he'd seen the Kemp people around the town."

"Okay. What else?"

Peter slipped out the back door of the house, still in his bare feet. The air was cold, his breath plumed out, his feet swishing in the dewy grass.

"Well, and that . . . I don't know . . ."

"What?"

"That Hutchinson Kemp was asking for it, or something."

"Asking for it?"

"Yeah. He called them liberals. Said the guy was poking around where he shouldn't be."

"Was he specific? Did he say anything specific? Did he ever, I don't know, watch them? Walk around outside their house?"

"Hayes? No. I doubt it. He was . . . he was a little gone last night, too. I've known John a long time. Always been a drinker."

"Uh-huh. So he . . ." Rondeau was trying to put it together. "He just shared this with you, this general prescience, and that was it?"

"This general what?"

"This feeling that the Kemps were going to get it."

"Yeah. That's it." Peter felt a touch of regret. Had he been too hasty to offload Hayes? He'd given Rondeau a quick verbal report last night, but he'd been brief, eager to get home.

"Okay," Rondeau said. "I'll follow up with Hayes. I'll talk to him."

"Oh. Okay. Alright."

Peter was about to hang up.

"And Peter, thanks."

"Yeah?"

"Yeah. Be safe out there."

"Will do."

He ended the call and remained standing in the grass for a moment. Then he headed back to the house, to explain to his girlfriend why he looked like he'd been in a boxing match last night.

CHAPTER THIRTEEN / Carmelita's

Peter and Althea pulled up in front of Nick Spillane's restaurant. *Carmelita's* was unfinished and located in the middle of nowhere and nothing. The speed limit was 55 mph. Even if you were starving as you barreled along, you'd probably drive right by, just a blur of cedar siding and an empty parking lot.

There was one small sedan and a huge pick-up truck that said *Rafferty Bros Contracting* on the side of it, in the parking lot. The logo on the truck was a hammer and handsaw forming an X-shape. The bed was loaded with construction supplies. Apparently, the Raffertys worked on Sunday. So much for the day of rest.

Looking out at the empty restaurant, Peter felt something touch him, startled, and realized it was Althea. She took his hand.

He looked around the car, to see if anyone was watching. He and Althea had made an agreement that they remain professional. No public displays of affection. Just two cops, doing the work.

"Hey," she said. "You okay?"

It wasn't easy to keep things compartmentalized like that. Stock County only had a few deputies, and they'd each had their own car until last year. That was when Deputy Alan Cohen had walked into the house in South Plattsburgh and stood over a basement meth lab set to blow.

The explosion had taken Cohen with it. Later on, word came down that he'd been awaiting backup. But the backup hadn't arrived as quickly as Cohen needed — not anyone's fault, the deputies were usually far-flung, only two on shift at a time, maximum — and so Cohen had ventured into the house alone. Since Cohen's death, every shop now carried a deuce — two cops per car. Peter wondered where the extra money was coming from in a bear economy, but budgets weren't his job.

His job was to protect and serve. And now he did it with the love of his life at his side. It wasn't always easy.

She was easy, though — she was about the easiest person to love he'd ever known. He'd never expected to have a relationship like this, to settle in with a steady companion. But then along she'd come, a new deputy for the department, and everything had changed.

She rubbed his hand for just a moment before letting it go. He hadn't responded when she'd asked if he was doing alright. So she answered for him. "Yeah, you're okay, tough guy."

"You ready?"

"Always."

They got out. The morning air was cold, but the sun was out, rising above the tree line. Peter and Althea crossed the dirt parking lot, scuffing up the sand. For a moment everything was quiet. Maybe no one was working on a Sunday after all. Then the squeal of a power drill broke the silence, followed by the pounding of a hammer. The pounding reverberated off the trees surrounding the restaurant. It really was the middle of nowhere out here, with Hazleton about three miles away, New Brighton four miles in the other direction.

Peter knew about suburban sprawl, and businesses opening along the outskirts of developing communities. He didn't think this was what Nick Spillane had in mind — Hazleton and New Brighton were far from developing. Quite the opposite: people were draining away. When Peter attended school in Hazleton, the graduating class had forty-five kids. This year it would be thirteen. Half the residents of Stock County were on some type of disability or welfare. The rest worked in the health field, for the county, or got their income from carpentry or some other trade.

No one came out to greet the two deputies, so they went round the back, where the sounds were coming from. Peter nodded to Althea, who took one way around while he took the other.

He came across piles of construction materials — OSB board, foam insulation, stacks of laminate flooring. A few thousand dollars of materials sitting outside with no cover except for a tarp that had come unhooked from one of its bungee cords and flapped in the breeze. Spillane had some big bucks, that was for sure.

The back of the building was getting an addition. Two-by-four framing shaped out a new room and the beginnings of a deck. Peter saw a carpenter bent over one of the floor joists. Big, long, two-by-six boards ran parallel, suspended over an uneven ground. The carpenter was screwing them into place, power drill whirring in his grip. He stopped and looked at Peter, standing just beyond the framework.

"Morning," the carpenter said, setting aside the drill.

"Morning." Peter hung his hands on his belt. He had to squint in the sunlight.

"Looking for the owner?"

"I am. Is he here?"

The carpenter hesitated, looking at the nice bruise around Peter's eye. The carpenter was in his late forties, wild hair full of sawdust. "Uh, yeah. I mean, no. Well, you mean Nick? Carm is here, though. She's around somewhere. I, ah . . ."

"I'll find her." He appraised the construction. "Looks good."

"Thank you."

Beyond the new framing he saw Althea, near the rear entrance. She was talking to someone inside. As he approached, Althea gestured towards him. "And here is Deputy King."

A shrunken little woman stood in the back door, grey hair in a bun. She wore an apron, a long grey skirt, and a flower-patterned blouse. Her eyes were dark, her complexion olive. She offered Peter a smile, something lurking in her glittering eyes. Something that told him she was a tough cookie.

"Morning, ma'am," Peter said.

The doorway was just a square cut in the plywood, elevated above the ground about two feet. No stairs in place yet.

"This is Carmelita Spillane," Althea said. "This is her restaurant."

"Oh great, great," Peter said. "Doing a lot of work, huh? Looks very nice."

"I was just telling Mrs. Spillane that we were hoping to have a word with her husband, but he's not here."

"Oh? Do we know where he is?" Peter cocked his head to the side.

"Church," Carmelita said. Her voice was deep for such a small person.

"And do you know when he'll be back?"

"Can I help you with something?"

Althea beat him to it. "Just routine, ma'am. We're helping out the investigation into the missing family. Do you know the Kemps?"

Carmelita turned and looked at something inside the restaurant before responding. "No, I'm sorry."

"You've heard about the disappearance, though?"

Carmelita shook her head. "No, no." She had an Italian accent, Peter thought. Subtle, but there. He thought he could see a couple dark hairs on her upper lip quivering in the bright sunlight. One of her eyelids didn't open quite as wide as the other. She was probably seventy-five years old. Maybe eighty.

"Well, it could be possible your husband, or perhaps some of his workers, know who the Kemps are, so that's why we're hoping to talk to him. We want to talk to everyone who saw them last. It helps us get a picture of where the family members were, what they were doing."

"I'm sorry, I don't know," Carmelita said. She seemed distracted, her mind elsewhere. *Maybe she's got something in the oven*, Peter thought.

He stepped closer. "Mrs. Spillane, have you noticed a film crew around? Guys and gals with cameras? Maybe talking to your husband about his business?"

"His business?" The woman's sparkling eyes narrowed. "What business?"

Peter waved a hand. "The restaurant business. Or, I don't know, whatever else your husband was involved with. Buying and selling old iron, glass, paper, cordage, that sort of thing."

Off to the side, the power drill and pounding noises seemed to get louder — the chorus was joined by some other tool, splitting the air with a shrill racket. Carmelita's words were temporarily lost.

"I'm sorry ma'am," Peter said, coming even closer. "Say again?"

"I say, 'what business is it of anyone?'" she shouted, leaning down.

The construction abruptly halted, and Peter heard footsteps through the restaurant. He glanced at Althea. He didn't like what he saw in her eyes, so he looked away.

There was an accusation there, like he was overstepping, being rude. He didn't think he was being rude. He'd been asking some simple questions. A family was missing, for God's sake. You couldn't tiptoe around everyone's feelings.

A man appeared in the doorway behind Carmelita. "What's going on Carm?" He looked out and met eyes with Peter. Brad Rafferty squinted at the cops, then his eyes flashed with recognition. "Oh," he said.

Peter's hand closed around the grip of his gun. His thumb popped the holster thong.

Brad put his arm around the elderly woman. "These police bothering you, Carm?"

"They're talking about Nick. They're asking questions about him."

"We're here because of the missing family, the Kemps, and we—" Althea began.

"She doesn't know anything about that," Brad said. He gave Althea a certain look. Over the past year, Peter had learned to spot that look; he knew what it meant. Brad was measuring Althea, judging her by the color of her skin.

"Why don't you come down from there," Peter said.

Brad wiped his hands on a rag. He dropped the rag on the floor and hopped from the doorway. His boots hit the dirt, pluming up the dust, right in front of Peter.

Althea came closer. Peter held up his hand to her, kept the other on the gun. He could see Brad's belt — nothing holstered there. Maybe there was a weapon strapped to his ankle beneath his work jeans. It was possible there was something within his flannel shirt, but Peter didn't see any bulges, save for the man's physique; Brad was two hundred pounds of solid muscle.

"Okay," he said, close enough for Peter to smell the coffee on his breath, "I'm down."

Peter leaned inches closer. "Turn around. Step to the wall, and put your hands on it. You're under arrest for assaulting John Hayes last night."

"I didn't assault nobody."

"No?" Peter pointed to his face. "I didn't do this shaving."

"I don't know how you got that." He jerked his head toward Althea. "Maybe it was your woman there? She get a bit rough with you?"

Peter reached out, took Brad by the shoulders and spun him around. He shoved and Brad stumbled toward the wall, bracing himself with his hands splayed. A second later Peter was behind him, patting him down. "You have the right to remain silent . . ."

"What's going on?" Carmelita sounded more angry than concerned.

". . . anything you say can be held against you in a court of law. You have the right to an attorney . . ."

He found the weapon. A small .380 in a pocket holster. Peter removed it carefully and handed it to Althea. He kept searching and found a utility tool in Rafferty's back pocket, one with a razor blade. A pack of cigarettes and a Zippo in his flannel shirt. He didn't need to tell Althea to check if the gun was loaded. She already was. "It's a KEL-TEC," she said, "P-3AT. Standard magazine. It's loaded."

Peter finished reading Brad his Miranda warning as he slapped the cuffs on him.

By now, the first carpenter had left his work and was standing beyond the framing. "Hey," he said, but it lacked any authority.

"It's alright, sir." Althea stuck the gun and pocket-carry holster into her pocket.

Peter stepped close to the cuffed Brad, and whispered in his ear. "I thought all morning about how I was going to come back to Moh's tonight, maybe have a little drink with you. But this is just as good," he said. Then he grabbed Brad and yanked him from the wall, shoved him into walking.

He gave Carmelita a quick glance. "Thanks for all your help, ma'am."

And he marched Brad back around the restaurant to the car. Althea got ahead to open the car door. Peter pushed down on Brad's head to help him into the backseat. Brad's eyes rolled up, a smirk curled his lips. "Oh I see," he said. "She yours?"

Peter stepped back and let Althea slam the door on the asshole carpenter.

CHAPTER FOURTEEN / Land-full

Rondeau drove through the countryside towards the landfill. He plucked his cup of coffee from the console holder and took a sip. The car hit a pothole in the road and the coffee slopped down the front of his suit.

"God . . ." he said, swerving. A vehicle coming the other direction blared its horn as he veered over the double yellow. The vehicle passed, its tires biting into the gravely shoulder, as Rondeau corrected his steering and got back on course. ". . . Dammit," he finished.

He put the coffee cup back in the holder. Keeping his eyes on the road he leaned over, popped the glove box and fished around for some napkins. Still swearing under his breath he dabbed at his shirt and tie and tried to assess the damage. There was a nice dark stain forming there. He scrunched the napkins up and chucked them aside. To hell with it.

He urged the car back up to speed.

The day was off to a bad start. For one thing, Rondeau had questioned John Hayes for half an hour but Hayes, bleary-eyed and either hungover or sick, had given away nothing. Whatever he'd been alluding to the previous night — whatever he'd said to King — he wasn't saying it now. And he denied any suggestion that he'd ever loitered outside the Kemps' house, watching them or anything else. Rondeau told him to stay in the area. Hayes articulated his one and only clear phrase during the interview: "Where the fuck else am I gonna go?"

Rondeau had tried to get in to see Addie Kemp before testing and sampling, but he'd been too late. Millard had called, freaking out. He was worried about the drone he'd shot down, about people coming for him. Rondeau assured him that it was going to be alright, but his brother-in-law was really coming unglued. It had taken precious time to calm him down, and it had gummed up the morning.

He was able to reach Addison by phone, though, and ask her why she'd given him those two particular clips. She'd apologized and said she must've given him a clip from the wrong film — the one called *Citizen Farmer*. He asked if she'd seen someone outside the house in the birthday video. She hadn't. Not for the first time, he suspected she was lying — or at least trimming the truth — but until she took the polygraph, it was tough to say. He was revising his list of questions for her as he went along, and the DA was chomping to get involved. It was a mess.

He passed the clip to Silas, told her to have her people seek to enhance the person on the road as best as possible.

Finally, he'd gotten the drone owner's phone number from the state police. He called the number and spoke with a guy name Paul Palmirotto. Yes, Palmirotto said, he worked with Hutch Kemp. On two films, *Citizen Farmer* and the one currently in production, *Nothing Disappears*. Rondeau explained he needed Paul to return for questioning. Paul had started off brusque, ill-tempered.

"Are you kidding? After what happened, I was delayed a whole day. I've got a shoot in Memphis today, and tomorrow in Colorado."

"This is very important, Mr. Palmirotto. Your co-worker . . . your *friend*, Hutch, is missing. His entire family is missing. If I'd known you'd worked on Hutch's films sooner, I would have just . . ."

"I'm very sorry, and very worried. I can come back by mid-week, on Wednesday. Okay? I want to help. But, Jesus. They said the property where my copter was shot down belonged to a detective. Is that you?"

"Yes, very unfortunate. I'm sorry. My brother-in-law . . ."

"Look, I don't care. We'll sort that in court. I've got to go. I'll be back as soon as I can to help . . ."

"Okay. One last thing — the *Nothing Disappears* film, you were shooting around here? Where? Who did you interview?"

Palmirotto sighed irritably. "My schedule is all over. I'll have to check. But for Hutch's film I did one shot. Over at the landfill, in, whaddya call it — Stock County. We had a miserable day. It was raining. Talked to some guy about how fast the shit filled up. That's it."

"What was Hutch's . . . what was his objective for this film?"

"His objective? That people throw things out every day and think they just go away. Nothing goes away."

"And *Citizen Farmer*?" Rondeau recalled the shots sweeping over the pastoral landscape. The factory cows, by contrast, in their filthy stalls. "You said you also worked on . . . Hello?"

The call had been dropped. Further attempts yielded voicemail only. To go any farther, to force Palmirotto to communicate or to pick him up and bring him back to Stock County would require the FBI. Rondeau still wasn't ready to pull that trigger yet.

So since Addison had passed him the wrong film clip, and Palmirotto was unreachable, Rondeau decided to go to the landfill himself. It was good to get away from the office, get off the phone, get *moving*.

The landfill was only open three days a week, Monday, Wednesday and Saturday, so he was unlucky. It was just after nine thirty on Sunday morning, and the gates were closed.

"Shit."

Rondeau piloted the truck around the gates anyway, bouncing over the rough terrain. Branches scraped against the side of the truck. He got back on the road and made his way to where the big weigh-in scales sat next to a small building. He started to drive over the scales when he saw someone emerge from the building, waving his arms. Rondeau rolled down the window. He held out his badge as the old man hobbled over.

"Closed," said the old-timer.

"I know. Detective Rondeau. Just having a look around. I'm investigating a missing family."

"Oh," the old-timer said. He'd heard about it, it seemed. "Alright. Well, drive on through. I'll meet you up there by the bays."

"Thanks, but I'll just . . ."

The old man turned and walked away.

Rondeau stuck his badge back in his coat pocket, the side of his hand brushing the wet coffee stain. He drove ahead to where the land rolled on, ventilation spouts sticking out of the ground like periscopes from submarines. A pillbox building sat beside two deep bays. He parked and got out.

He waited as the old man walked with his bow-legged hobble up the hill, then introduced himself. The man said his named was Wilfred Moore. "They call me Buddy."

"You worked here long, Buddy?"

"Twenty-eight years."

"Twenty-eight years," Rondeau whistled. "Twenty-eight's a long time."

Buddy nodded and brought out a battered pack of smokes. He shook out a bent cigarette and lit up. "So how can I help?"

Rondeau had never been here before. His trash was picked up on Thursdays by a company called Voigt. They provided the bins for rubbish and for zero-sort recycling. Rondeau imagined Kemp sticking a small camera on one of those bins for his documentary.

"You ever see a TV crew out here? A film crew? Going around, getting shots?"

Buddy seemed to straighten his crooked spine, and thrust out his chin. "Oh sure. I talked to 'em."

"Oh, really? When was that?"

"That? That was . . . ." Buddy rolled his eyes to the bright, cloudless sky. "That was about two weeks ago," he said around the dangling cigarette.

"Two weeks ago," Rondeau nodded.

"Oh yah," said Buddy.

"They have a lot of cameras?"

"A lot? Oh, they had the one they took my picture with," he said. "And then they had one floatin' around."

"A quadcopter?"

Buddy looked confused.

"A drone?"

His eyes grew big. "Yeah, oh yah. A drone. Flew it out over the fill."

"How many on the crew?"

"Just two. Guy with the drone, other feller askin' the questions."

"Hutchison Kemp?"

"I can't rightly remember."

Rondeau nodded. So far it all lined up, name or no. "This a big landfill here?" He glanced around, wondering how it worked, who was in charge. He had Eric Stokes, among various other assignments, looking into how landfills operated, and who was ultimately responsible for the three major ones in the county.

"This is five cells," Buddy said, with a distinguished note of pride.

"Five cells?"

"Cell number one filled up in the first year we was opened."

"Really. How big is a cell?"

"Five acres."

"So this is a twenty-five acre landfill?" Rondeau's eyes scanned the terrain. There were the rolling hills with the spouts, and also mountains of various rubbish types. The low sun blazed through his view, but he could make out a pile that looked like household appliances, another that was mostly wood products, a third that was a mound of twisted metal. He thought like a filmmaker, flying the drone along in between the piles, banking through the mountains of trash, getting the most sensational shots. *My God*, the unsuspecting viewer would say, breathless, *just look at all that garbage!*

"Yep, twenty-five acres." Buddy confirmed.

"How long was a cell supposed to last?"

"Oh . . ." Buddy dragged and the smoke drifted up from his cigarette. "We 'spected first one would give us three years."

"Three years, really. And it was full in a year."

"Oh yah."

"So these," Rondeau swept the hand holding his notebook, "are all filled up, or what?"

"Yep. All full. None of the stuff stays here anymore."

Rondeau turned around and looked into the bays. They were actually just huge funnels, emptying into containers that would get hauled away by rigs. "Where does it go?"

"Right now? Glens Falls."

He jotted a note, thinking, *nothing disappears*. "So this isn't an active landfill anymore?"

"Nope. Transfer Station."

"To Glens Falls."

"Yep."

"And that's just household waste, right? What about other stuff? Toxic things?"

"Well, your paint cans and your chemicals can go to the Highway Department for disposal 'bout twice a year. They usually send out a flier, we post it here. Otherwise, the big companies and that, I don't know what they do. They don't come here, though, that's for sure. We're just a little operation."

"And you told all this, about the transferring, to the guys filming."

"Oh yeah."

Rondeau put on a smile. "Fun? Being in a movie?"

Buddy was matter-of-fact. "I don't give a shit," he said.

Rondeau laughed. He started to put away his notebook and paused. "Does this place make any money, Buddy?"

Buddy squinted. He seemed deep in thought for a second. "*Make* money? No, I don't think so. It's all taxpayer-funded."

"Well, thanks for your help, sir. I'm going to have a look around, alright?" Rondeau made to leave.

Buddy nodded and pointed at Rondeau's chest. "Wife knows a great way to get out them stains with bakin' soda," he said. Then he turned and wobbled back to where he'd come from. Rondeau walked away, pulling his suit coat closed.

He headed up towards the mountains of waste. It was a huge spread, and it took him fifteen minutes just to wind through the piles. Dozens of old refrigerators, stoves, toilets, bicycles, microwaves, metal girders, tufts of insulation. A bulldozer sat unmoving on the rim of a deep pit of detritus. The cold wind soughed through, tugging at his clothes.

His own property was beginning to look a bit like this. He was reminded of Millard, last day as a transit cop, finding the severed head in the subway. He gazed at the bulldozer for a minute, thinking — thought not really wanting to — of how easy it would be to bury a family of four in a place like this.

CHAPTER FIFTEEN / Two Roads

He met with Eric Stokes an hour later, back at his office. Rondeau eyed the coffee maker on the small counter like it was an enemy, foregoing a fresh cup, much as he wanted one. He draped his coat over the back of the chair. Stokes sat nearby, watching and waiting patiently as Rondeau moved to a tiny closet and unbuttoned his stained shirt.

He laid the shirt over a file cabinet and pulled a fresh one from the closet.

"Whoa," Stokes said from behind him. "When did you get those?"

Rondeau paused, keeping his back turned to the other detective. He pulled on the shirt and began to button it up before answering.

"D.C.," he said.

"What caliber?"

"Three-seventy-fives." He turned around and fastened his cuffs, then looked Stokes in the eye.

"Damn," Stokes said, staring, as if he could see the scars through the shirt.

Rondeau sat down across from him. He spent a moment arranging things on his desk, feeling a bit exposed. "So, got anything to add to the landfill angle? I didn't get much."

"Well," Stokes said, sounding pleased with himself. He dropped some papers on the desk and traced his finger down a list. "A landfill is a pretty meticulously engineered depression in the ground. Unlike the old 'dumps' of the past, it's a complicated system designed to protect groundwater from contamination. Landfills take years of planning and development and require a significant investment. You've got excavation, excess materials, rock trenches, two feet of clay. It takes a sheepsfoot roller to pack the clay and—"

Rondeau waved a hand. "Skip all that. Go back to 'investment.' Who makes the investment?"

"Ah, the township, I guess."

"The township and not the county?"

"Think so."

"Well, I want you to *know* so," Rondeau said.

Stokes gave him a look. He seemed to be deciding for himself whether to take Rondeau's sudden attitude head on, or just ride it out. To his credit the new guy didn't just roll over.

"You wake up on the wrong side of the bed?" Stokes asked.

"Kemp's sister, I think, is lying to me. She told me she had footage from Kemp's film and ended up giving me some other project of his along with a home movie."

"So, let's poly her."

"I plan to. I need you to talk to Cobleskill, though." Cobleskill was the eager DA. "Tell her it's sensitive. I want Addison feeling like this is just routine."

Stokes gave him a quizzical look. "Anything interesting on the home video?"

Rondeau thought about the expression on Lily Kemp's face. The glimpse of something in her eyes, implacable but undeniably *there* for those few seconds. And the mystery person outside the house on the road.

"I've got CSI checking out a few frames of video where it looks like someone outside, watching the house."

Stokes' mouth hung open.

"I doubt it will give us much. It's blurry, far off, not even a hint of a face."

Stokes nodded. "So the other clip — it was from what other movie? *Citizen Farmer*?"

There was something in the way he asked. "You've seen it?"

"Watched the whole thing last night." His eyes got big and he bobbed his head some more. "Pretty interesting stuff."

"Yeah?" Rondeau stared off. He should have watched it, too, but he had no internet at his house.

"Makes you want to be a vegan. Basically says that everything from climate change to resource wars, plus all sorts of illnesses — all attributable to factory farming."

Rondeau considered Addison Kemp's vegan meal at the restaurant. He refocused. "Alright. Here's my Christmas wish list. You ready? Voigt. That's the company who picks up trash round the county. I want a contact person there. I want to get in touch with Glens Falls, find out if Hutch filmed or interviewed at the landfill there. I want Paul Palmirotto hounded daily — hourly — to get his ass back here. Here's the number." Rondeau pushed his pad across the desk to Stokes. "I want to look into Addison Kemp's ex-husband, too. Guy she has the cleaning business with."

"Anything else?" Stokes looked up from writing.

Rondeau pawed at his chin, thinking. "Well, we've got no way of knowing where any of these 'GPS dots' of Kemp's led, do we? For his trash film?"

"It's pretty new tech. We'd need to have the code for each dot in order to locate them. Unless we find that in his stuff, we'd only be guessing."

"Okay. Well, let's look until we find the codes."

"That it?"

"No, that's not it, that's not ever it. But it's enough for now."

Stokes looked sympathetic. He held his ground when needed, but was genuinely compassionate, and smart. That was the new guy. Dammit if Rondeau didn't like him.

Then Stokes' expression changed.

"What?" Rondeau barked.

"Deputies King and Bruin picked up the guy this morning who may have assaulted John Hayes last night."

"Yeah, he assaulted King, too. It's Brad Rafferty — I thought Peter might play it cool with him. Guess not. When?"

"Early. About two hours ago."

"He's here?"

"He's here," Stokes nodded. "And get this — Rafferty works for Nick Spillane."

Rondeau's mind leapt to make the connection he'd been dubious about before. Maybe Spillane owned fleets of those containers that hauled waste from used-up landfills to the next ready site.

He stood up, fumbled for his suit jacket and slipped it on. "Let's find out everything about Spillane," he said. "Let's find out if that old coot has money invested in the area, in the landfill, in any of the equipment that transports the rubbish, anything."

"You got it . . ." Stokes seemed caught on an idea. "What about this other film, though? You think there's anything to it? I mean, trash, okay, but, you know, maybe this *Citizen Farmer* movie . . . I mean, you think Kemp pissed off some big players? The meat industry is gigantic. And to say they're well-connected is an understatement."

It had certainly crossed Rondeau's mind. He'd even wondered if Addison had shown him the clip not as a mistake, but to say something. Yet he felt resistance to this idea. They had the waste angle, for now.

Rondeau grasped the doorknob. "I'm going to talk to this Brad character. I'll get it sorted."

CHAPTER SIXTEEN / A Warning

In the parking lot halfway between the department offices and the jail, Rondeau's phone buzzed in his pocket.

The incoming call read *Unlisted*.

"Hello?"

"Detective Jason Rondeau."

"Speaking. Who is this?"

There was a pause. "Detective Rondeau, this is your first and only warning." The voice sounded strange. Modified to be deeper. "Shut down operations and immediately cease investigation into the missing Kemp family."

Rondeau's heart pounded. He scanned the parking lot looking for someone, anyone. This could be the beginning of some kind of negotiation. He saw a woman walking from her car on the far end of the parking lot, head down: Mindy, from accounting. Rondeau snapped his fingers in the air, twice. Mindy didn't notice and kept walking.

"Who is this?" he said into the phone. "Get me some proof of life that—"

"If you do not comply with these instructions, we will be forced to retaliate."

Rondeau lowered his arm. This wasn't a person speaking through a voice modulator. The quality was excellent, with tone and inflection almost human, but there was no longer any doubt: this was a computer-generated voice.

Still, he couldn't help it. "Retaliate how?"

"You have twenty-four hours to dismantle Incident Command, to shred any and all documents pertaining to this case and destroy all forensic evidence."

"This is . . ." Rondeau began. Mindy was almost inside the office. "Hey!" he called over. At last he grabbed her attention.

"Twenty-four hours," the voice repeated.

"Hey!"

Mindy mistook Rondeau's gesture. She smiled and waved. He motioned for her to come over. She appeared confused, then moved in his direction, scowling and glancing around.

Rondeau waited for the voice to resume. After a few seconds, he took the phone from his ear and glanced at the screen. The call had ended.

"Jesus Christ," he muttered. His heart was really slamming. He held the phone out in front of him like it was contaminated. He was still staring at it, thinking, when Mindy reached him.

"Detective? Something I can—"

He held up both hands, one holding the phone. "Stop," he said. His thoughts were running in several directions. One of those routes challenged him not to involve anyone else at this point. Keep it contained. "Sorry," he said, and dropped his arms. He tried to put on a warm smile. "My mistake, Mindy."

"It's *Cindy.*"

She folded her arms in front of her, purse dangling from her wrist.

"Cindy, right, of course. False alarm."

She continued to stand there and frown.

If you do not comply with these instructions, we will be forced to retaliate.

Who talked like that? Or, moreover, who programmed a computer to talk like that? It was an odd form of military talk, or some kind of terror group. He needed a forensic linguist, maybe. If only he'd been fast enough to record the incoming call.

He stared at the phone.

Destroy all forensic evidence.

Was it a bluff? A hardball overture for hostage negotiations?

Maybe, but it sounded like the kidnappers didn't want to negotiate anything. It wasn't a profit crime, or a crime to achieve political aims. A message like that sounded more like murder. Like the Kemps were gone.

Then why would they communicate? Was he close to discovering something? He had to be.

Mindy — or, Cindy, rather — turned and walked back towards the office, shaking her head as she went.

Rondeau stayed grafted to the spot. Hutchinson Kemp's editing gear had been taken — when the TV and other valuables remained — that was obviously something. It indicated that what Kemp was working on had a definite role to play. Either his current film, *Nothing Disappears*, or the last one, *Citizen Farmer*.

One thing was certain, the message confirmed foul play. And that the perpetrators were at least sophisticated enough to place a phone call to the lead detective via computer. Any attempt to determine the call's origin would likely find its route bounced all over the internet, untraceable.

Why reveal their sophistication? Why not let the cops chase their tails for a few days, maybe even weeks, let the case grow cold? It hadn't even been designated a high risk disappearance yet.

It would be now.

You have twenty-four hours.

There was nothing in the handbook for this. Nothing in the pages of the Best Practices Protocol that touched on the subject of *Perpetrators Place Computer-Generated, Highly Threatening Phone Call*. This wasn't in any playbook, really, anywhere, for a detective with the local Sheriff's Department. This was federal territory.

Rondeau suddenly headed toward his truck, parked at the far end of the lot. He slipped his phone into his pocket. He was very aware of it there, the weight bouncing against his chest with his quick steps, like it was now a live explosive, ticking off a countdown.

He didn't trust Ninth Street. And it wasn't just his brother in-law, prattling on about government corruption and end times — but because he'd seen some things first-hand. Things he hadn't shared with anyone, lest he be tossed into the same crackpot category as his late sister's husband. Things that led to catching a couple of bullets in his midsection and shoulder, if you wanted to get right to the meat of it.

That was hard to slough off. Harder when the threat clearly indicated that ramping up the investigation from here would only result in . . .

Retaliation.

Whatever that meant.

Rondeau walked faster, the problem circling in his mind. Maybe he didn't know what to do about it just yet, but his gut was informing him on a few moves. And he trusted his gut. His gut had scar tissue, and scar tissue was tougher than regular tissue. Millard had taught him that.

CHAPTER SEVENTEEN / Conspiracies

"Here are some facts for you today," Millard said, riding shotgun. Rondeau sped through the countryside. He had an idea where he wanted to stash his brother-in-law for a few hours. He'd picked him up from the house. He couldn't leave him alone now, not the way he'd been behaving lately, not after the threatening phone call.

He'd tried Connie Leifson twice, but she either wasn't back from her trip yet, or just not answering. He would do the next best thing: go to her parents. Millard would be near the Kemp home where Rondeau planned to do some more exploring. CSI had gone over most everything by now, with their lights and dustings and potions, and he could be alone.

"Not now, Millard."

The big man stunk of being in bed half the day — body odor and bad breath. Rondeau cracked both front windows and cranked up the heat. The wind thundered through the gaps.

"This year," Millard carried on regardless, "the US Government will appropriate over a hundred and fifty billion dollars into the 'black budget.' The Pentagon has misplaced trillions of dollars, you know. And bank fraud, like the mortgage fraud of 2008? Cost taxpayers hundreds of billions. But people complain about welfare."

Rondeau was trying to think, and Millard was irritating him more than usual. Debating with the man was pointless and he usually avoided it. But they had five miles before they got to the Leifsons. It may not have been the best idea, it may have been taking advantage, but he felt he had no other choice at the moment. He needed to stash Millard. He needed an hour — just one free hour — to think, focus, and decide how to respond to the call.

"Mill, people are pissed at welfare because the ones who feel the pinch are hardly better off themselves. The just-better-than-poor have to subsidize the poor. And—"

"That's not true." Millard fiddled with his fingers, picking at the hangnails. He carried a tin of hand sanitizer which he rubbed religiously on his palms, usually dark with oil grease. "We doubly subsidize the corporations when we—"

"Let me finish. The Pentagon didn't 'lose' the money. They lost track of the accounting. There's a big difference there, Mill."

Millard was undeterred. "There are nine hundred US military bases around the world. Most are placed near oil-rich countries. Libya is a failed state after we invaded, since they were trying to establish their own currency, the dinar, and move away from the petrodollar . . ."

"Stop, Millard. I can't right now. I need to think."

Rondeau glared out at the road, willing the houses to show up faster. Another three miles and they'd be there. *You have twenty-four hours.*

One day. To tear it all down. Right. Walk into the sheriff's office and explain to Oesch that a computer voice told him they had to fold up their tent. Sorry, call off the search, torch the lab, the computer voice warned me there would be "retaliation" otherwise. Oesch would want to alert the feds. And maybe it was the right move. Maybe it was the *only* move. But what if . . . ?

I just want to see something. I just want to see something first. I want to get my head right. I need a minute.

Millard surged on with his speech. "We have alternative fuel, we have alternative food sources. But they're not as profitable. So we get fuel oil and factory-farmed animals. Meanwhile, the battle for resources is turning into a third world war." He turned and looked at Rondeau. "Did you know that it was Rockefeller who was behind Prohibition? Ford had made cars that could run on alcohol but Rockefeller thought it would ruin oil profits."

"Okay, Mill, we're almost there."

"Think of all the things that have happened that most people don't know about, or they outright deny! Everything shaped in the name of profit. We lose history, we lose the soil, we lose—"

"Millard, shut up." Rondeau took an anxious breath. "First of all, Ford was a capitalist. He was planning on making a profit on cars, alcohol-fueled or not. And maybe another capitalist headed him off at the pass so he could make his own money." Now Rondeau turned and met the wounded look Millard was giving him. "Or maybe that story is just conspiracy bullshit," he said.

Millard shrunk against the door and Rondeau felt a pang of guilt. He also felt hypocritical. Didn't he have his own pet conspiracy theory tucked away? Only it didn't feel like a theory. It felt like the burning punches of gunshots, the kind he often relived in dreams.

They'd called it a "friendly fire accident." Sure, and all the paperwork was done up, and everyone went through extensive interviews and came out smelling like roses. These things happen. Casualty of the job. The price of the badge and the gun — sometimes you took one for the team in the heat of battle. The FBI had managed to live down the incident, no problem. But for Rondeau, it hadn't been so easy. A year later, he'd left town, never to return.

He could recall the exact moment his vehicle crossed the Potomac on his way north. Sweet relief.

"'Conspiracy' is a legal term," Millard said in a small voice. "Just means more than one person planning a crime . . ."

"Alright, you win."

Rondeau's phone buzzed. The surprise of it almost caused him to lose grip on the wheel. *How things have changed*, part of him observed wryly, *usually Millard is the paranoid wreck and you're the cool cucumber.*

He opted to pull off the road. They were within a mile of their destination, but he didn't want to miss the call. Or drive into a ditch, answering it.

He fumbled for the phone. His heart eased when the screen showed it was his office calling.

"Stokes?"

"Yes, sir. Stokes here. Got something for you on Addie's ex-husband. Gerry — with a 'G' — Matheson. Company is called *Green Clean*. I swear — where is the imagination these days?"

The name Matheson sounded familiar. But it might've just been one of those names. "Okay, do me a favor. Field this one. Give Matheson a call. Feel him out. Just following up, ask how long they were together, if he met the Kemps, how well he knew them."

"You got it. How did it go with Brad Rafferty?"

"I didn't talk to him."

"You didn't . . . ?"

"Something came up."

Stokes hesitated. "Anything I can do?"

Rondeau closed his eyes. He scratched at his shoulder, then his chest. He thought of Millard picking at his fingertips and he forced himself to stop. He opened his eyes. "Stay reachable, okay? I'll be back in touch soon."

"You got it. I, ah . . ."

"Any other calls to the office?"

"Silas called. You were right; nothing useable on that video. Could've been someone out walking. We'll never know."

It was disappointing. Rondeau began to speak, but Stokes hurried on. "And, well we're fielding about ten tips an hour on the missing family. Word is definitely out. Press has been calling for statements, wondering when we're going to hold the conference . . ."

Rondeau frowned. "Screw the press. And those calls are supposed to rout to the volunteers at Incident Command."

"I know. But lot of the older people still have the department on speed dial. They didn't even see the ad, they're just trying to be good citizens. So far the troopers have responded to a couple of deer sightings and two kids playing *Minecraft* in the woods, or something. And a lot of people just talking about 'suspicious activity,' lending their expertise to—"

"I got it, I got it."

Another pause. Rondeau wanted to hang up. Things were spilling over the edge.

"You alright, boss?"

"I'm fine."

"You haven't called me 'new guy' once."

"Well, you're initiated now." Rondeau looked into the woods. No Kemps out there, not drowned in their backyard pond, not lost on an ill-equipped family hike. Probably not slain at the hands of the father, either. Those things happened, but not to this family, Rondeau didn't think. Not anymore.

"Stay reachable," he repeated and hung up. He dropped the car into gear and pulled back onto the road. He wasn't checking his mirrors and a truck blared its horn as it veered around him. Once he'd gained the speed limit, the Kemp home came into view.

"You've got a lot of balls in the air," Millard said.

"Quiet."

Rondeau watched the Kemp home as they blew past, then slowed and turned into the Leifsons' driveway shortly after. The little Prius was there. Good, they were home. He was struck again by the wrongness of his behavior — Jessy would not approve. He should have called first. But he'd been afraid it would be easier for the Leifsons to kindly refuse over the phone. Maybe make up an excuse. Anyone would. Who wanted a lunatic hanging out in their home?

"What're we doing here?"

Rondeau looked at his brother-in-law. 'Lunatic' was harsh. He wasn't a lunatic, he just had nobody. The ideas rolled around in his head, no place to go. And unless he had his Winnie and was on his own property and you flew overhead with drones, Millard was harmless as a boy. He could get loud and worked up, but he was not violent.

You can't do this.

No. He couldn't. It wasn't fair to anyone. He would have to just keep Millard with him. Let him sit in the car. As long as he was here, though, he decided to check on the Leifsons and make sure they were okay, see if they'd heard from Connie.

"Sit tight." He got out and walked up to the door. He checked his clothes, brushed some lint off his jacket, and knocked.

A moment later, the door opened and Rondeau's smile faded.

Mrs. Leifson stood in the doorway. Her eyes were red, glimmering with tears.

Rondeau didn't know how to respond at first. "Mrs. Leifson, I . . . is everything alright? What happened? Is Henry okay?"

"I'm right here," came Henry's baritone voice. The man shuffled into view behind his frail wife.

Rondeau struggled for words. "Henry . . ."

"Connie's been in an accident," Henry Leifson said.

CHAPTER EIGHTEEN / Shadow Men

A light rain was falling as he drove back to the Kemps, and there was even a double rainbow in the sky. The effect was surreal. Rondeau felt dazed. Millard sat beside him, but for once his brother-in-law was quiet.

Car accident, Henry Leifson had said. *Just after the ferry.*

Connie had been in Vermont. Rondeau had gotten more details from Stokes: she'd been pulling out of the Lake Champlain ferry lot when an eastbound vehicle had slammed into Connie's small car, impacting on the driver's side, doing significant damage to the vehicle, and to her.

The driver of the vehicle was still an unknown subject, or "unsub." He'd been behind the wheel of a large pick-up truck. He was whisked away to Fletcher Allen Hospital in Burlington, along with Connie. The state police were handling it.

Rondeau pulled into the Kemps' driveway. There was a County Sheriff's vehicle parked by the road. Rondeau aligned the drivers' sides as Deputy Borden rolled down the window.

"Detective," Borden said. "How we doing?"

"Good. Okay." He took the clipboard Borden handed him and scribbled his name, the date and time. He handed the entry log back to Borden. The deputy took it, and then sneezed loudly. The deputy nodded at the house. "You got one tech in there right now, I think. Lemieux."

"Thanks," said Rondeau. He pulled behind the Kemps' Subaru. There was nothing he could do for Connie right now. She was in critical condition. The accident had happened just a half hour before Rondeau had arrived at the Leifsons. It had occurred precisely while he was standing in the parking lot at the sheriff's offices, listening to a computerized voice warning him to drop the case.

You have twenty-four hours.

Rondeau got out of his car, still hazy. He had to focus. Nothing he could do for Connie, he kept reassuring himself. The hospital needed to care for her. No one other than immediate family would be allowed to see her, not even a cop, unless he claimed it was part of his investigation. And was it? Had the phone call hinted at something in the offing? Was this part of the warning?

Rondeau dropped his head between his shoulders, leaning on the Chevy.

Even the Leifsons were waiting to see Connie, he reasoned. Even her parents were being patient. Imagine that — your only child (and Connie, far as Rondeau knew, was an only) was all mangled up by a brutal car accident and you had to sit tight until you got the call to come see her.

He looked in the direction of the Leifson house. He could only see part of it — the autumnal trees blocked his view. But it wouldn't be long before Henry Leifson would say "enough waiting," pack his wife into the car and make the hour trip to Burlington regardless. Rondeau felt the same way.

What had Connie been doing? Why the mysterious trip away for a couple of days? She hadn't been under any obligation to tell him.

He looked at his brother-in-law through the windshield: his big body, flannel shirt, and dirty pants. Millard was putting on more sanitizer, looking back at the deputy's car with a dour expression.

The best thing he could do now was continue to work the Kemp case. If it connected to Connie's accident, he'd discover it by figuring out what happened to the missing family. Or, he would learn who the unsub was as soon as the state police had the info. Probably it was unrelated. Probably it was just an unfortunate coincidence.

It was hard, though, not to link it, after a computer voice had threatened you over the phone.

He walked around the Subaru, the Kemp family vehicle. A modern station wagon, with two child seats in back, one big, one smaller. He stooped and cupped his hands to better see inside. Britney Silas and her CSI team had already scoured the car, and he'd looked at the report. Nothing much to tell. He could see a bit of paper trash strewn about on the floor. In the back, a couple of children's books. A plastic toy that was some kind of miniature princess. He circled the vehicle. In the back hatch, a couple of plastic shopping bags, empty. All of this had been logged and recorded. A man's belt, for some reason, near the bags. A piece of ribbon that could have been a severed balloon string, or package wrapping. And two pieces of plastic, as if broken off from some larger item.

Rondeau looked over the vehicle at the house. The windows reflected the colorful trees. He thought he caught movement of the tech inside. CSI had done trace analysis on the vehicle, and matched fingerprints with those found in the home. Lily Kemp's prints were on file with the hospital. Both Hutch's prints and Lily's prints were found in the vehicle, along with three other sets. Two were determined to be the children's, as they matched prints in the home found on toys, on the child's highchair. One set of prints was still being cross-referenced. Cross-referencing prints could take days.

Addison Kemp's prints had been found in the home — just a partial, located on the medicine cabinet in the bathroom. CSI worked logically, starting with the most obvious places, things people frequently touched, such as doorknobs and cabinetry and bureaus. They dusted remote controls and computer keyboards.

Kemp's keyboard was gone, of course. There hadn't been a computer found in the entire house.

Aside from Addison Kemp's prints, there were three other unmatched sets. Including those found in the vehicle. So whoever had been in the Subaru had not necessarily been in the house. Could have been anyone — someone Lily had given a ride to at work, or maybe one of Hutch's colleagues. Maybe the drone operator, Paul Palmirotto.

One family, one registered vehicle. At least that made things a little bit easier.

Rondeau left the vehicle and headed to the house. He'd been pining all morning to get another look. Alone, undistracted. Letting things reveal themselves. Police tape fluttered in the breeze, stretched across the front door. He was distracted, now, though, big time.

"I told her about them," Millard said.

Rondeau stopped halfway between the Subaru and the house. Millard had gotten out of the truck and was standing beside it.

"Millard, just wait for me. Get back in the truck and w . . . You talking about Connie?"

Millard was embarrassed, nervous, or both. He looked away. "Yeah. I told Connie about them."

"About *who*, Mill? About *who*, exactly?" There was a sharp edge to his tone, but he couldn't help it.

"I told her about the shadow men."

"The shadow men." Rondeau followed Millard's gaze. The rainbows were still there, fading. Misty raindrops glittered in the sun.

"Sometimes they're called the zero ring men."

Rondeau took a deep breath. Part of him wanted to reach out and throttle his brother-in-law. Shake him back and forth, jiggle loose whatever insanity had battened on to him when Jessy died.

"What did you say to Connie, Millard?"

"That they're untouchable. Very high up."

"High up?"

Millard said nothing, but his eyes betrayed the answer.

"Millard," Rondeau said patiently, *"I'm* the government, buddy. Okay? Does that mean I'm one of these shadow men?"

"No." He winced, as if Rondeau's question was absurd. "Of course you're not. You're not thinking of it the right way." Millard broke eye contact. "Forget it. I'll wait for you. I'm tired. I know how you feel about me, you know." He moved to sit back down in the car.

Rondeau took a step closer. "Did you tell her something about the Kemps?"

"How would I tell her about the Kemps? I haven't seen her in a month."

"I'm just trying to figure out what you're talking about, okay? Connie's hurt. She was in a car accident. And you just told me—"

"I told her that they watch," Millard said. He straightened his back defiantly. "They watch me. I'm on a list. For things I've done, things I've seen." He pointed at the Kemp house. "And they were too. He was."

"Why?"

"Why? Jay, it's all around you, man — if you disrupt industry, you're a national security threat."

There it was, Rondeau thought. The old canard that if you were big business, you were in bed with the government. We were all doomed unless we shopped and consumed GMO food and took our poisonous vaccines. Chemtrails were sprinkling brain-altering particulates from the sky. Global warming was a hoax cooked up by liberal groups who want everyone to buy green products and revitalize inland cities because the coasts were going to be washed away. The Supreme Court was ruling on gay marriage to reduce population growth. Racial equality was a plot to advance communist interests. It went on and on.

"Okay," he said to Millard. "Alright."

"You don't believe me."

"Well, Millard, it's not that . . ."

"Jay?"

"Yeah?"

Millard's scowl had faded. He wore an earnest expression that Rondeau had never seen before. Like a little boy.

"Do you think I'm real?"

It was a heartrending question. The man doubted his own existence. "Of course I do. Now, look. I need to go inside . . ."

Millard sank back into the vehicle without another word. Rondeau hesitated, stuck in limbo. "Millard, it's not that I don't believe you. I believe you believe these things. And you know what? You're probably right about some of things you say. I . . . I have my own reasons to doubt government agencies sometimes. And you know that."

He scratched his scars as he stood by the truck. "But I need specifics, buddy. I'm running an investigation here. A missing family, you know? They need my help. Maybe they were abducted. I think they were. But I need hard evidence. If this has something to do with the government, I need facts. So, I'm going to go inside. Okay?"

Millard was in a full pout now, slumped in his seat. "Alright." It was barely audible. Then, "You'll never get anything, though. Not with them."

Rondeau let it go and started to close the door, but the rain was almost finished now. He left the truck door open so Millard wouldn't be closed in.

He headed to the house again. His phone rang. It was Stokes. Rondeau moved into the house, snapping apart the police tape as he answered. "What have you got?"

"Just letting you know, Voigt sent me all of their data. Glens Falls landfill is closed. I talked to Oesch and the searches are going strong. Captain Bouchard with the staties said we've papered all the way down to New York City. We can tap the video cameras at the Canadian border, but we need the feds for that. I think Oesch is still waiting on your call . . . are we bringing in the feds, Rondeau?"

He looked around the house. It stank of chemicals, like a CSI crew had been working for thirty hours straight. "I just need a little time. Tell Oesch to give me just a little time and then I'll . . . and then I'll know."

"Ten-four. Everything okay?"

The question irked him. "You keep asking me. Well, I got Connie Leifson, my friend, in a car accident. I got my brother-in-law sitting outside and—"

"What? You're breaking up, I think . . ."

Rondeau glanced at the phone. Spotty coverage in the house. "For God's sake . . ." Rondeau said, and ended the call.

Enough. He found the box of gloves by the door, and snapped on a pair. It was time to go to work.

CHAPTER NINETEEN / Something in the Basement

Rondeau moved through the house as the shadows deepened, the day darkening in the windows. There was a trove of evidence, but nothing helpful. Signs that a family lived there, sat on the couch, toggled the remote control, cooked in the kitchen, slept in the beds. And then, two sets of unknown prints.

Rondeau was sure the prints wouldn't belong to an abductor. Even the most mundane of criminals knew to wear gloves.

There was no landline in the house, no messages to check. The parents' cell phones were gone. The abductors had taken all of Hutch's work, along with every other data store. It was a thorough job. Smooth, quiet, leaving nothing to chance.

Neighbors liked the family. Not a single interviewee ostensibly harbored ill-will towards the Kemps, or knew of anyone who did. The Kemps might have been considered "outsiders," since they'd only lived in the region for five years (Kemp was originally from New York City and Lily from Saratoga), but otherwise the family was considered respectable. Only John Hayes, in his offhand way, seemed to think they'd been headed for disaster.

And maybe Millard, who thought *everyone* was headed for disaster.

Few people even knew what Hutchinson Kemp did for a living. They thought he was self-employed or perhaps a writer.

Lily Kemp had been with the community hospital for two years. Colleagues commended her hard work and pleasant attitude. They were worried about her.

Before working as a nurse, Lily had completed her training while pregnant with her first, the daughter named Magdalena.

Magdalena, Rondeau thought. *Not your everyday Catholic name.* In the old days, you might have found out about a family from their church, but the Kemps didn't belong to one.

He looked out at the maple trees. He thought of the family in the evening, the kids running around, the parents chatting over a glass of wine. He thought of the home video, the figure standing out by the road, watching.

How did you take an entire family? You'd need a few able bodies. How did you steal a child, kicking and screaming, from her bed?

The place was remote. But at night voices carried. You could hear the wind in the trees. A dog might bark a mile away, and the sound would travel. That's how it was at his house, and he lived in a pretty isolated part of the area, too.

He could make out the vehicles in the driveway from where he was. Where had the abductors parked? It was not a place you walked, unless they'd come through the woods. But with a family of four in tow, in the dark, the woods would be chancy. You'd need a van or a large SUV.

Still standing by the window, he took out his notebook and jotted down a few notes. He circled: *Big vehicle, unmarked.*

And it had probably happened at night. Lily Kemp's shifts were mostly daytime. There was a nursery at the hospital where the baby boy, William sometimes went. Or, the hospital had told them, little William stayed home with Hutch. The girl, Maggie, attended a part-time private preschool along with Peter King's niece. Stokes had checked in with the school — Maggie's last day had been the previous Tuesday. No one there thought Maggie or the parents had been behaving unusually, though they'd been growing concerned about the girl's increasing absences.

He held onto his notebook, staring into the dark. He imagined the crying kids. The parents terrified. They'd be fighting for dear life. Knocking over a lamp, leaving some kind of drag marks, finger smudges on the wall, something. Kemp wasn't necessarily a big man — forensics had him at five foot ten, a hundred and fifty pounds, but that was enough. If your family was in danger, you were going to be a force to be reckoned with.

But, nothing. No traces of a struggle. It was meant to look like the family just disappeared into thin air.

Nothing disappears.

They had been sedated, he decided. The only way you took two parents and their children without signs of a struggle was if they were unconscious. But how did you do that?

Rondeau descended to the basement. To get the best picture of a man, if his laptop and files were gone, you checked out his basement.

The basement was half remodeled. In the finished section, he saw the bowl of popcorn. Bits of that popcorn had been bagged and taken to the lab. He walked to the part of the basement which was still plain concrete. He checked out the boiler — in good condition. There was a work bench with neatly arranged tools. He found a pack of cigarettes, with a few left inside. He sniffed them.

There was a door that opened onto the side yard. He stepped out. A small roof covered the entryway. On the ground was a tin can with a few cigarette butts inside.

This was where Hutchinson Kemp came to smoke, Rondeau concluded.

It occurred to him that if you have kids, and you're pushing forty, and you're wife's a nurse, and you're a "very nice" family — how does the father get in his vice? Answer, he sneaks out the side door. Probably he's not trying to conceal it from his wife — she'd smell it on him — but he's being respectful to her and keeping out of the kids' sight.

And if you were an abductor who'd been watching him for a while, learning his habits, you knew he probably had a smoke to end the day. He's watching TV, eating his popcorn, wife and kids have gone to bed, maybe. Then he steps out, lights up . . .

And that's where you got him.

Rondeau paused, thinking, *maybe you chloroformed him?*

You had to get behind someone for that. Hutch might've taken a couple of steps out from beneath the awning . . . and that's when they pounced. *And wrapped a cloth around his mouth.* Or, maybe they'd stuck him with something. Plunged a syringe into his carotid. A few frantic pumps of his heart, and he collapsed.

Rondeau crouched and ran his fingers through the grass beside the entryway, hoping for a syringe, something forensics could have overlooked. What did you inject a man with that would take him down in a few seconds? He wrote the question in his pad.

He drifted back inside. Perhaps just one of the captors goes upstairs into the wife's room. It's dark. She senses someone enter the room, but of course she just assumes it's her husband. She mumbles and rolls over. That's when the captor gets into bed right beside her. The bed springs creak. She murmurs again, "Good night, honey," and he reaches out and clamps a hand over her mouth. As she struggles, he sticks her with the same stuff.

The husband and wife are now incapacitated. The children will be a cinch.

Rondeau felt something cold pass through him and tried to shake the gruesome vision. He knew he was right, or at least punching around the center of the bag. He stopped by the tool bench, eyes lingering over the hammer and drill, the coiled extension cord, and a stack of manuals.

Kemp was the sort who liked to keep his instruction manuals on hand. He was tidy and organized. Rondeau blew some dust off the stack and went through them. Not just tool manuals, but kitchen appliances, too: a manual for a Cuisinart, one for an expensive food processor from the Culinary Institute. He slid them off the stack one after another, and paused when he came to a large envelope.

He hesitated. An envelope, brown and worn, the kind tied with a string. He unwound it, slid the papers carefully out, so as not to tear anything, and flicked on the overhead fluorescent.

There were handwritten notes, and a couple of computer printouts. The notes referred to something called "cradle to grave." He'd heard the term before, in business contexts. Kemp — presumably — had written: *From creation through disposal, throughout the life cycle. Unsustainability. Also: responsibility for dealing with hazardous waste and product performance.*

He flipped to the next page.

Manifest System. Pollution control in which hazardous waste material is identified and traced from its production, treatment, transportation, and final disposal through a series of documents called "manifests."

It sounded a bit like a synopsis for the new film Kemp was working on. Rondeau checked, but none of the notes were dated. He moved on. *Uniform Hazardous Waste Manifest. EPA and DOT required.*

Environmental Protection Agency and Department of Transportation; those were the acronyms.

All generators who transport hazardous waste for off-site treatment, recycling, or storage disposal. Apparently there were Federal regulations to use this form — EPA Form 8700-22 — for any interstate and intrastate transportation of hazardous waste.

He gripped the pages, considering. This felt a little bit like a plant. If Kemp's abductors were as professional and thorough as they seemed, why this oversight? These forms made it look like Kemp might've stumbled upon some federal law issues in his documentary, *Nothing Disappears*. But grouping the paperwork with instruction manuals would be odd.

There was more, though.

A website printout on the Jordan Valley. More notes and a brief, printed travelogue on Tunisia, which caught his eye.

Then, the final page. Very short, consisting only of two words — *Zedekiah's Cave*. He didn't know what that was.

He took these last few papers, folded and put them in his inner pocket. The rest he replaced in the envelope. As he wound the string closed, his phone buzzed, giving him a start. For one terrifying moment, he was sure it would be the computer voice telling him time was up.

It was his office. Had it been an hour already? Jesus. It was Stokes, but the connection was spotty again. They couldn't make heads or tails of what the other was saying. Rondeau hung up. He realized his brother-in-law had been sitting in the truck all of this time. Time to check on him.

* * *

Back in the driveway, he tried Stokes at the office. The connection was better out here. "Stokes, I want to know everything that could knock a man out, incapacitate him in seconds."

"Including a right cross from Brad Rafferty?"

"Pill, powder, liquid. What do you do if you want to completely sedate a man in a matter of seconds?"

"Got it. What are you—?"

"Also, let's get word to Incident Command, any calls coming in, ask if people have seen an unmarked van or a big SUV in town last week. Maybe even with tinted windows."

"Jesus. Yeah, okay."

Rondeau placed the envelope on the hood of the Chevy and looked at it. "I've got something for Peter King. Have him get with Brit Silas, sign out an envelope I found in the house. It will be with Deputy Borden. Tell him to build it into his dealings with the Rafferty brothers and Spillane."

Stokes was silent, likely writing it all down. "Okay, roger . . . What are you up to?"

"I'm going to see Connie, talk to the unsub if he wakes up."

"Whoa. Okay. You think what happened to Connie is . . . ?"

"I don't know."

Rondeau hung up. He got in the truck and looked over at Millard, sitting on the passenger side. He could feel the papers folded up against his chest. "Strap in," he said. "Here we go."

CHAPTER TWENTY / Infected

Connie Leifson looked dead. About as dead as anyone Rondeau had seen since Jessy.

Jessy had been emaciated. Eaten away by the cancer. Connie was still *full*, if that was the right way to put it, while Jessy had been *empty*. Half of Connie's head was wrapped in a huge bandage. Her arm and shoulder were in a cast. Her left leg was raised, pinned with steel rods. She barely looked human from where Rondeau stood in the hallway, peering through the glass. Then the doctor pulled the curtain across and Connie disappeared.

The doctor explained the extent of her injuries to Rondeau as they walked slowly through the ICU unit. Millard trailed behind silently, wringing his hands.

"Her brain has had quite a shock," the doctor said. "The swelling has put her into a coma."

A coma, Rondeau thought. *Three days ago this woman was teaching her Friday class. Today she's in a coma.*

The prognosis was bleak. "With this type of traumatic brain injury," the doctor went on, "you can never really predict the outcome. But we can see from her brain scan that there is minimal activity. Even the basic involuntary functions — some of them — are incapacitated."

That was doc-talk to say she was excreting waste into a bag, intubated, with a machine doing her breathing.

"We're prepping her for surgery to alleviate some of the swelling. You can wait, if you like, but it could be a while."

Rondeau thanked the doctor and excused himself when his phone rang. He motioned for Millard to follow and moved to a quiet spot, at the far end of the hall. He stared out the window at the University of Vermont campus as he took the call.

Stokes was on the line. "You with Connie?"

"Yeah."

"How is she?"

"Not good."

Stokes was cautious. "How are *you* doing?"

"Told you to stop asking me that. I'm fine." Rondeau scratched his chest, then his beard stubble — he hadn't shaved in two days.

That's not all that's itching you.

(You have twenty-four hours)

He glanced at the clock hanging above the nurse's station. The call from the computerized voice had come in three hours ago. Twenty-one to go.

"You seen the teenage driver yet?" asked Stokes.

"Not yet, just got here. What've you got for me on the sedatives?"

"Yep, okay. And the winner is . . . etorphine hydrochloride."

"That's the most potent?"

"It's what Dexter uses."

"Who?" Rondeau stuck his finger in his ear. There was some commotion on the floor, people talking loudly down by the nurse's station.

"The serial killer guy? *Dexter?* The TV show?"

"I don't know it."

119

"Okay. Sorry."

Two nurses moved quickly from the nurse's station, concerned looks on their faces. Something somewhere was beeping.

Stokes continued, "There's also pentothal, but I think the etorphine is most potent. They knock out elephants with that shit. It's an opioid, but we're talking up to eighty-thousand times more potent than morphine as an analgesic. Uhm, synthesized by Bentley & Hardy in 1963 . . ."

Rondeau kept watch on the activity down the hall. There was a sense of urgency in the air. But it wasn't originating from Connie's room. The nurses turned the corner down a second hallway.

"How do you get it?" He barked at Stokes. He didn't mean to be so harsh, but his adrenaline was starting to crank. He scratched at his chest some more.

"It's only approved for veterinary use. Zoos and stuff, game wardens, that sort of thing."

"But other people can get their hands on it."

"Sure. It's possible. Anything's possible on the web nowadays. You got . . ."

But Rondeau was lowering the phone. The doctor took off running in the direction the nurses had gone, stethoscope flying over his shoulder.

Rondeau turned to Millard and gave him a fierce look. "Stay here," he said.

Then he bolted after the doctor.

* * *

The patient on the bed was bucking and thrashing. It took four nurses and an orderly to keep him down. The door to the emergency room was open, staff rushing in and out. Rondeau stood back, watching the chaos.

The patient arched his back. His eyelids fluttered, his eyes rolled back to the whites. He was frothing at the mouth, bubbling on his lips, foamy white strands of drool.

120

Millard crowded in behind Rondeau. He'd told Millard to stay put, but Millard had joined him anyway.

Rondeau caught the attention of a nurse hustling out of the room. "What's going on?"

She looked him up and down.

"I'm a detective," he said.

"He's having a seizure."

"Any idea why?"

"Excuse me."

She jogged away, clearing the view to the room. Rondeau stared in. An orderly and a nurse placed a bit in the patient's mouth and he chomped down on it. His head whipped back and forth. Someone gave him an injection. Then he stilled, his eyes rolled back, and he glared across the room. Right at Rondeau.

The door closed a moment later, shutting him out.

"That's not good," Millard said behind him.

"Shhh," Rondeau said, holding his hand up. "Stay here." He was treating Millard like a baby, or a dog. Rondeau hurried after the nurse. Two more orderlies ran past in the other direction.

He found her at the nurse's station, rattling through some cabinets. "Can you tell me what's going on?"

She glanced at him, her eyes briefly falling to his holstered weapon. "Is this part of an investigation?"

"Yes," he said, though he wasn't sure how, yet.

"He's in septic shock."

"You mean infected? With what?"

"You'll have to talk to the doctor."

Rondeau opened his mouth to respond when someone interrupted. "Detective?"

Dana Gates, with the state police BCI, was standing in the hallway, a concerned look on her face. Rondeau realized there was tension in the air — his fault. The nurse hustled past him.

Rondeau shook it off. He offered Dana Gates a wan smile. He hadn't met her before, but knew her by reputation. She'd been the lead detective on a serial killer case the previous year. They shook hands. Gates had short hair and was fit like a yoga instructor beneath her conservative pantsuit ensemble.

"They told me you were up here in ICU," Gates said. "I've been down in the emergency room interviewing the driver."

She scanned the curtained windows to the ICU rooms. "The vic is in one of these?" Her eyes landed on Rondeau. "She's a personal friend of yours?"

Rondeau nodded. He felt his pulse easing. Suddenly he remembered Millard, and looked around for him. His brother-in-law wasn't in the hallway. Millard hated hospitals. But if there was anywhere for him to wander safely, this was it.

Gates was watching him. "You want to talk?"

CHAPTER TWENTY-ONE / The Past Catches Up

The waiting room outside the ICU was comfortable, with cushioned chairs and large windows. Rondeau watched the wind shear the leaves from the trees as Gates talked.

"Driver is an eighteen-year-old," she said. "Took his father's truck without asking. Maybe had some sort of a tiff with him. They found THC in the kid's urine, alcohol in his blood."

"Okay," Rondeau said. So that was that, maybe.

"What's the word on Ms. Leifson?"

"She's critical. They're prepping her for surgery. Pretty extensive injuries. To her head, her neck. It sounds like the kind of thing where she could be paralyzed."

"I'm sorry to hear it." Gates had a neatly folded handkerchief she used to periodically dab at her eye. He saw she had some scars around it.

"Yeah, thanks." He couldn't get the infected patient out of his mind. It was sticking for some reason, the idea of an infected person with contaminated blood. Stokes said Kemp's film, *Citizen Farmer*, dealt with animal-borne diseases from the meat industry. He regarded Gates. "You're pretty sure this was just an accident?"

"What are you thinking? Our missing family — *your* missing family case — we've got some intersection between that and this?"

"I don't know. What I'd like, if you can do me a huge favor, is to keep me in the loop on it."

"Of course."

"I mean, what we know is that the truck is registered in the name Meyers, and that's the young driver's father, that checks out. And he's coming in hot, way hot, doing close to thirty miles an hour to the ferry lot when he impacts with Ms. Lieberman."

"Leifson."

"Yes, Leifson. Sorry."

"Anything interesting at the scene? I came straight here, over the bridge."

Gates hesitated. "Well, there are some jurisdictional prickers. I put CSI on crash reconstruction, even though we've already got the data from the vehicle computers — every now and again reconstruction can tell us things the computers can't, but the computers are pretty reliable. Everything from how fast the cars were going to when the brakes were applied."

"Were they?"

Gates gave him a probing look. "Yes. The driver applied the brakes in the last few seconds."

"How many seconds? Maybe it was just an involuntary action? Maybe he . . . ?"

"Meant to ram her? I'll try to find out, Detective Rondeau. That's what my job is. But I got a late start. I've been fielding overflow calls on your Kemp case all morning."

Rondeau knew Gates was a tough investigator. She'd been through hell on the college killer case. She'd gotten glass in her face — that was why her eye was messed up. "I'm sorry, I'm not implying anything."

"Lots of calls going through BCI get redirected up here," she explained anyway. "Depending on their origin.

Not all calls go to Incident Command, unfortunately. There's a shortfall."

"I understand." Stokes had reported similarly. "Anything solid?"

"We follow up everything we can. Some of these, though, like the one we got just this morning . . . I mean, the things people come up with, right?"

Rondeau felt a flutter in his chest. "Tell me."

"Oh, ah, just that the whole thing, you know, has to do with the Indian Lake Project."

The name of the place tolled familiar; Indian Lake was where Addison Kemp had a business and a second home. "I don't know what that is — the Indian Lake Project."

"Ah, yeah — you're not a native, right? Okay, so, this Indian Lake Project theory is about secret CIA drug testing."

"I see."

Gates elaborated. "Indian Lake is supposedly one of the sites where the CIA did the experiments in the 70s. They used orphaned children, or so the more sinister versions go." Gates seemed disgusted by the idea. "Some people think the experiments are ongoing. And Indian Lake is a main site."

Whether or not the story was nonsense, the fact that it connected Addison Kemp was enough to crank Rondeau's heart rate some more. "Someone following that one up?"

"We're stretched thin, Detective. This one didn't even make it to triage. You know how it goes; most people think these conspiracies are as ridiculous as a faked moon landing."

All the manpower is on the search, he thought. *And it's a waste. We're not going to find the family that way.*

He stood up a little too quickly. He suddenly needed to find Millard. He stuck out his hand and Gates shook it, without getting up.

"Thank you, Detective Gates. I'll be in touch." He hurried out of the waiting room.

* * *

He found Millard in the cafeteria, gobbling down peanut butter sandwiches. Rondeau took a chair. He had no appetite. He waited while Millard ate, thinking again how his brother-in-law seemed calmer, while he was on edge.

The clock was ticking. Connie's accident may not have had anything to do with the missing family, but he couldn't get the sick patient out of his mind. Vague suspicions and a random caller claiming the Indian Lake Project had something to do with the Kemps weren't reasonable grounds for ignoring protocol.

He knew it wasn't right to be so wary of the government, the FBI. It wasn't fair to the Kemp family. It wasn't fair to any of his fellow investigators, keeping them out of the loop on something as important as that phone call four hours ago. Not only was it unfair, it was, really, kind of insane. It wasn't the workings of a rational mind, was it?

No. And certainly not all FBI were corrupt, either. Christ, throwing an entire federal agency into one category because of an isolated incident — that was what paranoiacs did.

He looked across the table at Millard, still chasing after the crumbs on his plate, oblivious to anything else for the moment.

Rondeau pulled up the contact number for the department. He would speak directly to Sheriff Oesch. He'd put it to him. He'd explain what had happened, the threat, and why he'd hesitated . . .

But what was he going to say? That he'd kept something as important as this to himself because of what had happened years ago? He had the bullet wounds to prove his experiences were true, but what had ever come of it? Had there been any indictments? No. Business had gone on as usual at Ninth Street. They'd closed the case after ruling it was friendly fire.

126

"Hit me with it, Millard," Rondeau suddenly said. He put away his phone and watched his brother-in-law. Millard was drinking a small carton of milk. He set it down, wiped his mouth with the back of his hand.

"Do what?"

"Give me all you got. Go ahead. You've got an open forum here. Tell me everything. Start with what you know about CIA drug testing."

Millard just blinked, as if this was a put-on. Rondeau nodded encouragement. "Okay," Millard said. "You got it." He looked around the cafeteria for a moment. Then his eyes landed back on Rondeau. "MK-ULTRA. In the 1970s the CIA gave American citizens LSD, mescaline, and other drugs. The idea was to develop enhanced interrogation tactics. Mind-control the enemy. And this has been admitted; proven."

"How would the FBI get involved?"

"Easy. The CIA is not a domestic organization. You want to keep something secret — and they did, keep this secret, for decades — you bring in the FBI to create cover."

Rondeau gazed off, rubbing his jaw. "Yeah . . . I don't know."

"You don't know? Look, I'm crazy, right? That's what people need to believe in order to sleep at night. Fine. But if you had claimed in 1972 that a burglary at the Watergate Hotel was part of a secret plot for White House officials to illegally spy on Nixon's political opponents during reelection, you'd be part of the tinfoil hat crowd, right?"

"I guess." Millard could definitely be eloquent when he wanted to be.

"Let's start with the FBI and Whitey Bulger."

Rondeau made a buzzer sound and swiped a hand through the air, ushering the idea along.

"What?" Millard pouted.

"Been there, done that. Whether or not Bulger was an informant, we'll never know."

"He wasn't. No way. He was—"

"What else you got? *Come on*, Mill. This is it. Give me a solid, credible reason not to trust the feds."

They were drawing some looks from the other people in the cafeteria, but Rondeau didn't care.

"J. Edgar Hoover," Millard started again. He hesitated, watching Rondeau.

"Yeah, yeah, and Hoover blackmailed people in government to stay head of the FBI, and at the same time he was blackmailed by the mafia to stay off their backs. Try again."

"Well, if you're gonna . . ."

"Don't be so sensitive. Come on."

Millard frowned, but continued anyway. He couldn't resist a willing audience.

"The FBI kept data for years on any and all federal employees thought to be homosexual."

"That's true. Not a conspiracy. I want something darker. Deeper."

"For decades, the CIA and the FBI employed and protected at least a thousand Nazis, using them as spies and later shielding them from prosecution."

"Now we're getting somewhere. More."

Millard searched the table with his eyes. Rondeau knew he was putting his brother-in-law on the spot, which was a shitty thing to do. He felt that adrenaline still bubbling through him, like a pot on the stove, and he couldn't dial down the heat.

Millard landed on something. "If you're an environmental activist, or an animal rights activist, you're on top of the FBI domestic terrorist watch list."

Rondeau snapped his fingers in the air and then pointed at Millard. "I like that. I like that one. I've heard it before. Why is that the case, you think?"

"Because if you disrupt the economy, you're jeopardizing national security."

It was almost note for note what the narrator in the movie clip had said. "But, why?"

Millard shifted in his chair, his eyes roving. "Because our economy is our power."

"Why would environmental activists or animal rights activists disrupt the economy?"

"You get people thinking global warming comes from burning fossil fuels, maybe people slack off the fossil fuels. Or, they think global warming comes from industrial farming, they stop buying the meat."

"I doubt it."

"Even a little bit, and the industry takes a hit. Billions of dollars lost."

"Fair enough." But, what? Kemp's documentaries had environmentalist leanings and the FBI didn't like it? So they'd — what? Swooped in and abducted his family? It was too much of a stretch, and Rondeau knew it.

Millard raised his thick eyebrows. "I mean, then there's what happened to you, Jason. If you want a reason not to trust the feds, I think it's right in your past, staring you in the face: The Valentine Killer."

The name hit him like a punch to the gut. Rondeau flashed back to his days with the District. A man had shot up a shopping mall, killing fifteen people on Valentine's Day. The killer had left a note at the scene, claiming he would attack again on the next holiday. The Bureau had taken over the investigation, using forensic experts to examine the note, and use the information to track the killer.

But, they'd gotten it wrong. At least, in Rondeau's view, they'd misinterpreted the note, and went after the wrong person. The Bureau targeted a mentally ill man with a record — though nothing close to homicide.

Two more holidays had arrived with two more mass shootings and the killer eluding capture. They had wanted him bad. Rondeau demanded to be on the frontlines when the Bureau took down their subject of choice, and they'd agreed. The lead agent for the Bureau was Lee Angstrom, and Angstrom didn't like Rondeau, didn't like this District cop who was only supposed to be observing, but kept insisting that they had the wrong guy. Angstrom insisted they had forensic evidence to link the suspect. As they closed in for his capture, shortly before the Fourth of July that same year, things got messy. They'd surprised the schizophrenic man at the shipyard where he worked, and he'd tried to run. In the crossfire, Rondeau had taken two bullets in the chest — from an FBI agent. Of course it was even worse if it had happened in pursuit of the wrong man.

He'd been the hospital for a month. During his stay, he'd been visited by a man named Dominic Whitehall. Whitehall claimed to have evidence of further crime lab tampering by the FBI. But Whitehall disappeared soon after, and once Rondeau was released, he got the hell out of there.

And now here he was, a detective with the Sheriff's Department for a backwoods county in upstate, New York. His first big case, a missing family, and prudence dictated he call in the feds; he'd been contacted by the ostensible perpetrators. But Millard was right. His past was holding him back.

* * *

Rondeau tracked down Connie's doctor. He was just about to go into surgery when Rondeau caught him and convinced him to step into the break room. An orderly was cleaning up the morning's coffee grinds and empty donut boxes.

"Will you excuse us?"

He saw the look in Rondeau's eyes and left without a word. The doctor raised his hands. "Detective, I assure you, we're going to do everything for Ms. Leifson."

"I know you are."

"We're attempting emergency intracranial surgery, which can be dangerous for comatose patients, but we're very confident."

"Thank you."

"If you'll excuse me . . ."

Rondeau caught the doctor by the elbow. "I need to know about the infected patient. It's important."

The doctor appeared confused for a moment. He glanced at his arm and Rondeau removed the hand. "He has an intense bacterial infection. He's got pneumonia, and his bloodstream is contaminated."

"Have you seen more of this? Anything else like this, recently?"

The doctor searched Rondeau's eyes. "Yes."

"What is it? What causes it?"

"Microbial infection. We're dosing him with some strong antibiotics; we'll see if he responds."

"What about other patients? Are they responding?"

"No. Best case, bacteria like this are susceptible to colistin, what we consider a last resort antibiotic. But this is a tough genetic mutation . . . plasmids that move freely from one bacterial strain to another turn them into what we call 'superbugs.' And colistin, unfortunately, has been overused."

"On patients?"

The doctor had sadness hovering in his eyes. Rondeau didn't like what he saw there. "On livestock. The short version is, Detective, we've used up all of our antibiotics on animals. Diseases like this MCR-1 microbial infection are basically untreatable until we have a new drug. Now please, I have to go and operate on your friend."

CHAPTER TWENTY-TWO / Indian Lake

Indian Lake was in Hamilton County, the least populated county in New York State. It made Stock County look like a teeming metropolis. Hamilton was the first place Rondeau had looked for a job after he'd left the District. He'd wanted to get as far away from society as possible and still make a living. But Hamilton had no detective squad. One sheriff, three deputies, and a two-cell jail was the extent of local law enforcement.

It was so out of the way that his cell phone wasn't getting a signal. He rolled over the roads, with Millard riding shotgun, the both of them silent for much of the drive. Close now — just a few miles out.

Finally Millard spoke. "What are we doing here?"

"Following a lead."

"What about the woman? Ally?"

"Addie. Addison Kemp. She's still with forensics. I'll get back to her."

"I'm worried about you."

Rondeau faced the road again. Nothing but trees, winding road. They'd passed through Long Lake and Blue Mountain Lake. Nice places, wild and unspoiled. A little bit of tourism helped sustain the communities, but for the most part people were back-to-the-landers who hunted and trapped, chopped firewood, lived basically. There were some vacation houses too. He envisioned them all getting sick, turning septic like the patient at Fletcher Allen.

"Come on," Millard goaded. "Tell me what's going on. Who am I gonna talk to?"

"Are you kidding?" Rondeau said. "You talk to everyone."

"I do not." Millard folded his arms and stared out the window. They were passing by a lake, wind-chopped and battleship grey. Softly, he added, "No one listens to me or believes me anyway."

He had a point there. "I listen," Rondeau said.

Millard shifted in his seat. His enthusiasm was palpable.

"First of all," Rondeau admitted, "I don't trust Addison Kemp. For someone whose brother and his entire family went missing . . . I don't know. She's hiding something. Then she tells me she's got footage he's working on, but gives me the wrong clip. For a supposedly successful business owner and all that, hard to believe she'd make such a critical mistake."

"Maybe she wanted you to see something," Millard said.

Rondeau cut him a look. "She also never said anything about this Indian Lake conspiracy."

"She was being careful."

The first buildings were showing down the road; they were coming into the small town of Indian Lake. Millard elaborated on the idea. "She could be compromised. She could know exactly what happened to her family, but she has to protect them."

They passed a construction site with two large cranes and a green school bus. The road bisected white-painted houses, a gas station, a grocery, and the Indian Lake School — a small brick building which probably housed all the grades in one school. The GPS had only been working intermittently. The route forked, Rondeau took a turn, and the GPS died.

"Terrible what happens to a family like that," Millard said. "You take this nice, happy family . . ."

"We don't know they were happy."

Millard looked over. "Why?"

"People just assume," Rondeau said. He was thinking of the home video, those few frames where Lily Kemp looked at her husband, who was operating the camera. He remembered her eyes. Emoting a kind of pain, or longing. Could've been normal marriage strain, but it could've been because her husband was poking a sleeping bear.

Already the buildings were thinning out as they headed out the other side of town. They reached a dirt road. The sign read: *Private Drive*. Rondeau made the turn.

The truck bounced over the rugged terrain, and Rondeau suddenly blurted it out to his brother-in-law. He told him about the call from that morning while he was outside the jail. He told him about the ultimatum. "Now we've got eighteen hours," he explained. "And goddammit if I'm not seriously considering calling them." He meant the Bureau. Old Ninth Street.

"Oh no," Millard said immediately. "You don't want to do that." The big man jiggled in the seat as they bounced along the rocky road.

"No, no," Millard repeated. "If this is what I think it is, I can promise you: you bring them in with what you know, and it's bad for you, Jason." He stared. "We're better off on our own."

* * *

Rondeau swung the truck door shut. The slam echoed in the forest. The house sat on a rise, trees all around on three sides with a sloping, tangled yard. The two wheel ruts heading up towards the house barely passed for a road.

"We'll walk from here," Rondeau said.

"We should have brought something to eat." Millard dragged his fingers across his flannelled belly.

"You just ate."

Christ, this place was backwoods. Was anyone home? They left the truck and moved up the rugged trail meant to be a road. Rondeau didn't see any vehicles up there.

What are you doing, Jay? Jessy's voice, her ghostly image surfacing in his mind's eye. She stood by the old gaslight stove. Stirring one of her magnificent stews in the large cast-iron pot. He could almost smell it; garlic and earthy spices — a hint of saffron. *You really think this is the best thing, Jay?*

No, he didn't think this was the best thing. He didn't know what the best thing was, that was the problem. Normally, decisions came easy. A quick analysis followed by a choice, often the lesser of two evils.

But Addison Kemp's betrayal spoke volumes: *Be careful. Go it alone, get to the bottom of it.*

He continued up along the path, Millard breathing heavy behind him.

The lawn was covered with fallen leaves and cairns of rocks. The house itself seemed in okay shape. A side building was not, the center strut between the two bays listed so the building tipped left.

The screen door squeaked open on the porch. "Hello?" A woman stood there in rugged clothing; work pants and a sweater. She was holding a shotgun.

"Hello," Rondeau called over. He stopped in his tracks. Behind him, Millard stopped, too.

Rondeau held up his hands and introduced himself. "You placed a call this morning? You said you had information on the missing family case we have going up there?"

She held the shotgun like someone who knew how to use one, her hands on the stock and the barrel. It was unsurprising for someone in a place like this, far off the beaten path. He attempted levity. "We mean you no harm."

The woman had a good vantage from the porch, a view of the whole overgrown yard. Rondeau imagined her blasting away at rabbits, or aiming at the heads of big fall turkeys. Maybe cops, too. But then, she'd been the one to call the police.

She set the gun on the porch and came down the steps, dusting off her hands. They met by the corner of the house. Up close, he could see the grey in her hair, the lines around her eyes and mouth. She was around sixty.

"Sorry," she said, giving his hand a firm pump. "Don't get a lot of visitors. And when I do, it's not usually the kind I like to entertain. I'm Tamika Levitt."

"You called the state troopers?"

"Yes, I did."

She instantly struck Rondeau as someone who'd spent much of her life contending with people who didn't like what she had to say — or didn't believe it. Rondeau thought Millard could relate. So could he.

"I just read about the missing family in the paper this morning," she said.

"What about them made you think that their disappearance had something to do with . . . ?"

"With the CIA torturing people with experimental drugs?"

A wind eddied up the slope towards the house, rustling the trees, making a hushing, hissing sound as more leaves fell. She gave Rondeau a long look, defiance shining in her grey eyes. "It's better if I just show you," she said.

CHAPTER TWENTY-THREE / The Box

He left Millard in the sitting room of Tamika's house, browsing stacks of periodicals. The house was crammed with piles of magazines, newspapers, and books. He wondered if she had internet out here, or she got all of her information from print. She was moving quickly, leading him towards the back of the house.

He glimpsed another room, that looked like a den, with packed floor-to-ceiling bookshelves. They hurried through a huge, ranch-style kitchen in the back. They exited via a small rear porch, and then were crunching through the leaves, headed into the woods.

Tamika was talking the whole time. "My family built this place in 1898. That's four generations back; I'm fifth generation. We have eighty acres of property, abutting state land on three sides. That forever-wild land goes on for miles. So you can understand it took decades before my brother ever found the box."

He had to hustle to keep up with her. At least it was keeping him warm — it was cold out, the day waning.

He didn't mind the woods, but he would never say he was exactly at home in them. He wasn't a hunter.

Tamika looked over her shoulder. "You're not from around here, are you? Not an Adirondacker?"

"No, I'm not," he panted. "My father was military." He saw his breath puffing from his lips. *This is fucking nuts.* "After Fort Bragg, he worked for the Pentagon."

"Really? Then you're not a stranger to state secrets."

I could write a book on them, he thought. What he said was, "Depends on which ones."

"Well, this one is legit. Trust me."

Rondeau glanced back — he couldn't see the house anymore. Even the path seemed to disappear as they moved deeper into the woods. They were in the middle of nowhere, Tamika plowing onwards. The further they went, the more doubt he felt. Everything was wrong about this. He was lead detective on a missing family case, and he was a hundred miles and three counties away from the Kemp home, trailing a mad old woman through the woods. He was about to tell Tamika he needed to turn around, urgent business, sorry, when she finally stopped. She pointed to a hole in the ground slightly smaller than would fit a coffin.

"This is where my brother found it. Documents, photos, all related to the ILP."

"The Indian Lake Project." He peered down into the darkness. "How did he find it?"

"Hunted a lot out here. Followed deer trails. His favorite ridge is just over there." She nodded at a thicket. The doubt continued to beat an alarm in the back of his mind. Wasting valuable time like this when the clock was ticking. Still, there had to be something. He'd trusted his instincts this far.

"He just started digging one day?"

Tamika gave him that persecuted look.

"Ma'am," he said, "I'm under a lot of pressure to find a family who's missing. I don't want to leave any stone unturned, even . . ."

"Even a ridiculous conspiracy theory?" She cocked an eyebrow. "My brother sat for hours when he hunted. He came to know every rock, every tree. He would tell me he would sit so still, so silent, that the animals would forget he was there. The birds would begin to sing, the squirrels would resume their business. He became part of it." She gestured to the spot. "And this is where he was sitting when he noticed something out of the ordinary. The bare earth here, where this hole is. Something that looked out of place. Partially buried, sticking out of the ground."

"Then why the big hole?"

"He excavated all around the box to see what else might be there. But it was just the box. Dropped, maybe. Or placed there in the hopes someone would find it someday."

"Where is it now?"

Tamika turned to Rondeau again. "It's safe."

"It's not here? Is it at your house?"

"Mr. Rondeau. My brother tried to bring this to the public in the best way he knew how. He was cautious, but he wanted people to know. Can you imagine the response he got? Either people thought he was nuts, or they thought he just wanted attention."

Rondeau felt the sting of guilt. He knew the feeling of being shunned for speaking what you believed was the truth.

"And the threats started coming. The phone would ring, two, three times a night. No one would be there. Sometimes he saw people moving around outside of the house, watching."

"Where is your brother now?"

She looked at him, as if he should already know. And, Rondeau felt, maybe he did.

"Dead," Tamika said.

"I'm sorry to hear that." He didn't press for details. Instead he sought the connection. "Now help me to understand why you think any of this has to do with the missing family."

Her eyes locked on him. "People go missing round here all the time. Forest rangers and search parties are out regularly, seems to me. But many never get found. Sure, people get lost, there are six million acres in the Adirondack Park. But when I read about the missing family this morning, I saw where it said the man, the father, was a filmmaker."

The press were certainly making hay. Rondeau waited. He stepped from one foot to the other, trying to get his circulation going. He wished he'd brought a warmer jacket.

"There was a filmmaking group up around here about a year ago. And then again a couple weeks ago. They were in the woods."

That made him stand still.

"And," Tamika said, "their name: Kemp. Addison Kemp is my neighbor — or, what you'd call a neighbor, even though she's a couple miles away, over on the next property. Her property is where the entrance is."

"The entrance . . ."

"To the underground facility."

* * *

He moved back towards Tamika's house, in the lead now, half walking, half running. He took out his phone as he made his way through the woods. He had six missed calls — he'd been too numb to feel the phone's vibration. He went into the settings to put the ringer on. As he fiddled with it, his foot caught a root and he fell forward, the phone flying from his grip.

Tamika helped him up. "You okay? Mr. Rondeau?"

He got to his feet and nodded. "Lost my phone."

The two of them bent down and swept their hands through the leaves. He needed to talk to Addison Kemp right away — he had all he needed to confront her, all the right questions for the polygraph. If there was any truth to this, she was the key to it. Her behavior, the wrong

140

footage, and now she'd omitted mentioning her brother was filming out here.

"Dammit," Rondeau said, staring into the leaves.

"Here," Tamika said, holding up his phone. "Got it."

They got moving again. He kept a better watch on his footing as he scrolled through his data to find Addison Kemp's cell phone number. He tapped the screen to call her. He didn't notice the icon for service had a strike through it again until the call failed to connect.

He couldn't catch a break.

"You have a landline at the house?"

"I do." She was the one panting now, trying to keep up. Rondeau no longer felt tired. He no longer felt cold. He broke into a full run.

CHAPTER TWENTY-FOUR / Addison Kemp's House

Rondeau's Chevy bumped over the dirt road out of Tamika Levitt's property. Millard was squished against the door, Tamika in the middle. She braced herself, a palm flat against the ceiling, and said, "Whoa, daddy."

"Sorry." Rondeau wrestled with the wheel and got them back onto the main route. He roared up to speed until Tamika said, "There, right there."

Another dirt road marked *Private Drive*.

"How far does this one go back?"

"Farther than mine."

Wonderful. Didn't these people ever think to pave anything? Probably would ruin the *rustic* vibe, he figured. Or, it was too expensive. He only cared because it was slowing him down. And because he was furious.

Addison Kemp had already been cleared from the hospital. Her blood and tissue samples were on their way to the lab in Albany. She wasn't answering her cell. Brit Silas said she'd thought the woman was headed back to the motel, but a deputy had swung around to find her car gone.

He'd blown it.

Rondeau barreled onto the new dirt road, already going twenty miles an hour, wheels chirping as they took the turn. He felt like things were slipping through his fingers. He blamed himself for every questionable decision, and yet here he was — the mailbox blurred past, *Kemp* on the side of it. He pushed the truck to thirty as they climbed a steep, rocky section of the road. The incline was severe; Rondeau had to downshift. The tires spun as the truck lurched forward, keeping the momentum going.

"Ever come out here?" he asked Tamika.

"I've been to Addie's a couple times, yeah."

"And the two of you have spoken about the underground facility?"

"We have. But it's not something that comes up a lot."

"What was the context when it last came up? How long ago?"

"That she didn't think much of it. If it got her a deal on the house, so be it. Her plot is thirty-eight acres, and the entrance is on state land beyond that. She wouldn't be able to find it if she tried."

Rondeau snapped a look at her. "Then how are we going to find it?"

"What do you think was in the box? A map."

"Where is the map now?"

Tamika tapped her forehead. "Right here." She dropped her hand and scowled. "Ain't you gonna call somebody? Backup, and that?"

Rondeau returned his eyes to the road. He swerved to avoid a sizeable rock. The trees brushed against the vehicle, branches screeched, like nails on a chalkboard. "We have just so much in the way of resources," he told Tamika.

She was silent for a moment, then said, "With all due respect, Mr. Rondeau . . ."

"Detective."

"Detective Rondeau, I saw in the paper you've got five hundred people searching for this missing family."

"Mostly volunteers," he said. "Civilians. I can't take law enforcement for every whim of the investigation."

"Whim? I'm sorry, but, I'm pegging you as the guy in charge. You wouldn't have come all the way down here yourself, you wouldn't be pounding up this road like you're going to bust an axle if you didn't think this had something to do with it."

Of course it was on his mind, constantly, he should call in every law enforcement aid in the state available to him . . . but then have it all turn out to be bunk? He'd be "Ricochet Rondeau" all over again, disgraced for leading a wild goose chase.

"Ms. Levitt, maybe we want to keep it to ourselves until we get confirmation."

She turned and looked out the windshield, gripping the dashboard to keep herself steady. "Your father raised you right," she said, surprising him.

"We're only a lingering illusion of what we once were," Millard blurted out. It was the first time he'd spoken since leaving Tamika Levitt's home. "Endless national debt, devalued dollar, oil-backed currency in a geopolitical and military fight we're losing."

Rondeau didn't look over, didn't shush his brother-in-law, even though he didn't want to hear it.

Tamika did. She chimed right in and gave a knowing nod. "That's right. This, this right here, this is the deep state," she said. "Where big business and national security meet. And people go missing, and people die."

Millard, pleased to have a like mind around, eagerly agreed, "Any other thinking is delusional."

Ironic, for Millard to call anyone delusional, Rondeau thought.

Rondeau asked Tamika, "You said you only saw the film team here once?"

"That's right. But they could've been here more."

"How did you see them? I mean, you and Addison Kemp are each pretty fucking secluded." The profanity slipped out as he cranked the wheel to take another bend. This bad road was grinding on him. But, thank God — he thought he saw a clearing up ahead.

"I hunt," she said, "just like my brother. First time, I heard the little film crew from half a mile away. Second time, I saw their drone flying around."

It wasn't the first time it occurred to him that Paul Palmirotto's drone had been flying over his property just a couple days before, when the Kemps had already been missing. What was Palmirotto doing if Hutchinson Kemp wasn't even around? Maybe Palmirotto wasn't only working for Kemp.

Millard rambled on, "NSA spying, covert wars to destabilize Russia, CIA black ops; it's what the Cold War was about, what the Iraq War was about — resources and power. This is what happens when you challenge the deep state. They blackmail farmers into using their seeds, poison that organic restaurant chain with E.coli. They send in a special team, get the job done."

Shadow men, Rondeau thought, despite himself.

The house came into view. The road leveled off and was lined with slender birch trees. Rondeau eased the truck along, admiring what he saw. A three-story Adirondack-style mansion. Coffee brown siding, dark green roofs, a huge porch pillared with cedar logs, a stone chimney scraping the sky. He rolled to a stop and put the truck in Park.

He killed the engine. Everything fell silent, and was still.

* * *

"We've got to go in right up here," Tamika said. Rondeau stood beside her at the edge of the woods.

He stared into the impenetrable wall of short blue spruce. "You're kidding. There's no trail, nothing?"

"Well, not for a few miles."

"And you've seen this place? You've been there?"

She looked at him with her stony grey eyes. "You kidding? Think I want to die like my brother?"

He blinked at her, struck one final time by the absurdity of the whole thing. Was he really going to go charging through the woods again with this woman he'd just met? If this was such a heavily guarded secret, the site would be protected. He was so far out of his element, he found it hard to think straight. What was he running on? What was driving him? Instead of thinking it through, he was just reacting. Maybe the woman standing there in front of him with her doughy face and half-lidded expression wasn't what she seemed. If she was so worried, why take the risk now? Maybe this was all a trap, to lure him in.

Rondeau walked past Tamika Levitt, and started back towards Addison Kemp's giant summer home.

"Detective . . . ?"

He left her behind. His father had taught him all about subterfuge and misdirection. His father had liaised with CIA officials, top FBI people; he'd understood the confidence game. After he'd died, Rondeau picked up where he'd left off. Once you knew the patterns and signs, they were all around you. He'd seen the corruption in the FBI first-hand. When they couldn't get the real perp, or had someone to protect, they'd fabricate another. Public image depended on it. Pensions depended on it. The machine had to keep chugging along. Even if you had to get dirty — real dirty — in order to get there.

Rondeau stopped walking when Addison Kemp's home came back into view. Off to the side of it, the Chevy sat empty. His brother-in-law had gone AWOL again.

Millard, where are you?

There was a sound behind him; the quick scuffle of feet. Someone battened onto him before he could turn around. He felt a sting in his neck. He reached back, clawing at the attacker, but the poison worked fast. His knees buckled, his legs gave, he dropped to the ground like a sack of mail.

And then black.

CHAPTER TWENTY-FIVE / Getting Connected

Deputy Peter King looked at his beautiful girlfriend as she spoke.

"Maybe you're not looking for a career change to mental health," Althea said. She closed the locker and walked towards him across the deputies' break room. "Maybe you're going to make detective." She tapped the envelope from Rondeau with her nail, then slipped her arms around Peter's waist and leaned her head against his neck.

The jail was quiet. Deputy Borden had taken sick leave, and Kenzie was busy at the front desk. It was Monday, a slow day. People were still getting on their feet after the weekend.

She reached up and touched the bruises on his face. She was smart, kind, beautiful and strong. She handled a gun like she'd done it all her life. She protected the vulnerable. He, in turn, would protect her.

"I want to marry you," he said softly.

Althea pushed back from him. She looked up with wide eyes, blinked and glanced around. Her demeanor seemed to ask: *Are you kidding me? You're proposing in* here?

It wasn't the most romantic place in the world.

"I mean it," he said. "I don't care. I'll get down on one knee somewhere with coconuts and palm trees—"

"You know I don't care about any of that—"

"But I just want you to know that I plan to marry you. I'll ask you as many times as I have to—"

"In as many nasty places as you can find, apparently."

It made him laugh, and he pulled her closer. They held each other tightly for a moment. Peter gazed through the one-way glass, which overlooked the central area of the jail.

"I want to talk to him."

She searched his eyes. "Brad Rafferty? You think that's such a good idea? Boy, you're full of all sorts of risky proposals today. Ask me to be your wife, question an inmate without a lawyer . . ."

"He doesn't have to say anything he doesn't want to."

"What are you going to talk to him about?"

Peter shrugged and glanced at the envelope she was holding. "His work. His boss, Nick Spillane. The missing Kemp family."

"Uh-huh. You making some leaps there?"

"Maybe."

Her look tightened. "Peter . . . lots of sidestepping procedure these days . . ."

He gave her a kiss on the lips, something he never did when they were on duty. "I'll catch up with you in a few," he said. He walked out of the locker room clipping his belt around his waist, settling the weight of his gun around his hips.

The county jail consisted of three housing areas known as "pods," laid out with the public area in the center. There was a separate wing for adolescents, but in the main jail were one women's pod and two men's pods.

The doors to the cells were open. Inmates hung out on their bunks or milled around in their orange jumpsuits, wearing Velcro sneakers. They played cards, watched TV, or just did time.

A nearby set of metal doors led to four special cells with a mattress and a toilet in each. It was the on-watch area, where volatile inmates could be monitored twenty-four hours a day.

Brad Rafferty was in here. Rafferty had come in hot the day before and had only gotten hotter. In a few hours Rafferty would meet with his lawyer. But for now, he was fair game.

A deputy sat at the on-watch desk. He looked terrible, like he had the flu. Something was going around, anyway. He glanced up from his phone as Peter approached.

"Morning," Peter said. "How's our special guest?" Brad Rafferty was currently the only inmate on watch. Peter could see him through the reinforced glass door to his cell. Brad glared back.

"He got quiet a little while ago," the deputy responded, and blew his nose.

Still looking at Brad, Peter asked. "What did County Mental Health say?"

"He's not suicidal. He's been fine with the rest of us." The deputy winked. "I think the only one he's really mad at is you." The deputy pressed a button on the nearby console and a buzzer sounded as the doors to Brad's cell opened.

Peter stepped into the doorway. He took a moment, letting Brad adjust to his presence. "How you doing this morning?"

"Fuck you." Brad kept his eyes on the wall.

Peter nodded. "I understand your frustration."

Brad cut him a hard look. "Any day, King. Talk to me any day outside of here."

"Right, I just need to take off my badge and my gun, huh?" Peter looked down at his uniform. "You should be grateful I'm wearing this. This is why you don't have a couple of holes in you right now."

Easy, he thought to himself. *Easy now.*

"Any day . . ." Brad said, redirecting his rage back to the wall. "You fucking faggot."

"Is that how you talked to John Hayes the other night? You say things like that to him? Why'd you get so upset at him?"

"Your little buddy shouldn't have been running his mouth."

Peter hooked his thumbs into the waistband of his pants. "You don't believe in free speech?"

"I believe in the right-to-have-your-ass-kicked for your speech."

"What do you care what Hayes says, Brad?"

Brad's head slowly rotated back, his eyes poisonous. He clutched the mattress, digging in his fingernails. "We got enough liberal assholes overrunning us, trying to turn us communist. You probably like that, huh?"

"Did he say something about your boss?"

"My *boss*? I'm my boss, King. Not like you in your little outfit there, answering to your superiors. Shoveling shit for your dad, the big judge. I answer to no one."

"Your client, then. Spillane. Did Hayes say something about Spillane?"

"The fuck do you care? What is this? I called my lawyer. You can't talk to me. Go finger your black girlfriend."

Pete nodded again, looking down, wanting to stride across the room and put Brad Rafferty into the wall. "Okay. You talk to your lawyer, and figure out how you're going to get out of assaulting a police officer . . ."

"A police officer? That what you call yourself? What's next, King? You and her gonna adopt a couple of Muslim babies?"

Stay easy. "I just want to know why you're protecting Spillane."

"I don't know what you're talking about."

"I'm talking about how Nick Spillane has bought up property all over town, and is building restaurants and spec homes like money is no object. I'm curious; he made all that money moving junk around, or whatever? He's been up here, what, five, six years? Semi-retired, that sort of thing?"

Brad held Peter's eye. His upper lip twitched with hate. "Why don't you ask him yourself?"

"I plan to. I just thought I'd come over here and we'd talk, first. Man to man. Because I'm the one pressing charges against you. And you can either do time and pay a lot of money to your lawyer and in court fees and everything else, or, we can just talk. I can make it a lot of time, Brad, I can push real hard — you know that. How much money you got put away? You got enough to cover all the legal costs, make up for all the time you won't be out there, losing work?"

He could see Brad wanted the same thing Peter did — to wrap his hands around the other man's neck and squeeze. The tension was palpable; Peter's hearing sang with the adrenaline.

Then it subsided as Brad's eyes drifted for a second. "Waste," he said at last. "Not just junk. He moved hazardous waste. Owned five trucking companies who managed it. All up and down the coast. You don't know shit, King."

"Maybe not. And for all this time he's been up here, he made any investments?"

"How should I know?"

"Spillane seem like a good guy to you, Brad?"

"I told you, I don't know what you're talking about."

Peter heard a commotion behind him. Voices echoing in the hallway feeding into the on-watch area, the clanging of keys, the scuttle of footsteps. A moment later, the door opened and Sergeant Fransen appeared, a pinched look on his face. On his heels, a small man in a charcoal grey suit, carrying a briefcase. Rafferty's lawyer was early.

Peter returned his attention to Brad, hurrying. "Here they come. What do you want me to say to the DA? Or to Judge King? You know exactly what I'm talking about."

Brad's face bloomed red. But, he caved. "Spillane is old school. You understand?" Brad lowered his voice and looked nervous for the first time in recent memory. "He's *connected*, you get it? And Hayes wants out."

"Hey," Fransen called, hurrying over. "Excuse me, *Deputy* . . ."

"Connected how?" But Peter thought he already knew.

Brad turned his head away, as if ashamed.

Peter spun around just in time to greet Fransen and the lawyer. "Counselor," he said, "good morning."

"Deputy King," the lawyer panted, "You know this is . . ."

"Exemplary inmate," Peter said. He cleared the door. "Just a real, solid guy."

He walked away and caught the eye of Sergeant Fransen. Fransen was livid. Peter strode away, but the sergeant soon caught up.

* * *

The clouds smothered the sky in a grey paste. Wind scattered the leaves around the jail complex.

Althea was waiting for him in the parking lot, sitting in the idling cruiser. She got out as he approached and circled to the passenger side. He stopped her, raising a hand. "You drive," he said.

She raised an eyebrow as she buttoned the top of his uniform. "How did that go?"

"Good," he said.

It was warm inside the vehicle, the vents blasting heat. The deputies pulled on their seatbelts. Peter was carrying a small, zipped, leather folder that he set on his lap.

"I saw Fransen talking to you," Althea pressed. She got the cruiser rolling out of the lot, turned onto the road and headed toward New Brighton.

"Yeah, he's not too happy with me."

For the missing family investigation, Fransen was in the field, working the specialized division that operated Incident Command. But as the sergeant sheriff, he was also a line-level supervisor, and policed the activities of the jail, and his deputies.

"For one thing, he wants my paperwork," Peter said. He was referring to discharging his firearm the previous morning. Any time a cop fired a gun, it raised questions. Interviews and plenty of forms followed. "Apparently Hayes's wife called and lodged a complaint, too."

"That woman? Her? Complain?"

"Yeah, who'd have thunk it." He knew it had been the wrong thing, though. It had exacerbated aggression between him and the Rafferty brothers. You couldn't go around squeezing rounds into the air because you were frustrated, any more than you could beat up an inmate, disgusting as Brad Rafferty was. Peter was working hard to manage his emotions. Because there was more to the Rafferty story than everyday domestic squabbles, and now he thought he had an idea what all their fighting was about. Even if it had meant getting into a bit more trouble, talking to Brad Rafferty without his attorney present.

"You're doing alright, Deputy," Althea said, surprising him. He looked over at her. She kept her eyes on the road, her hands at ten and two. She was wary of him pushing procedural limits, but she had his back. "I wouldn't suggest making a habit of it, though."

He looked back out the window. "I'm reformed as of this moment."

"So, where we going? Spillane? *Carmelita's* again?"

"Roger that." He unzipped the leather folder balanced on his knees and pulled out the papers.

"What've we got?"

"You mean you didn't peek?" He held up a sheet. "EPA Form 8700-22 and 22A."

"That's from the Kemp house?"

"Partly. The rest I pulled off of the EPA website."

"So, what, now we're federal agents?"

"We just want Spillane to take us through one of these forms. Fill them out for what his trucks used to carry. Ask if he's still in the business, in anyway. Then maybe Rondeau will take it federal."

"Rondeau? Stokes said he's MIA. Oesch is worried. Have you talked to him?"

"No, but it's still early. He'll show himself. You know how he's quirky."

"Quirky? He's a liability."

Peter watched the houses as they drove out of town. Maybe she was right. Rondeau had been strange on the phone. Like he was concealing something.

Althea switched back to the topic at hand. "You think Spillane is going to cooperate?"

"Not really. But that's not entirely what we're interested in."

"What're we interested in?"

"To find out if Spillane is connected."

"Connected?"

He looked at Althea again and for the first time felt the stirrings of fear. He suppressed it.

"To find out if he's *made*," Peter said.

"Oh." She piloted the cruiser over the hills. Here the roads broke out into rolling countryside, old barns, horse paddocks. Everything taking on that ashen, late-autumn look. "You mean mafia," she said.

"Yeah. I mean mafia."

CHAPTER TWENTY-SIX / Cooler Heads Prevail

Althea steered the cruiser off the road and onto the dirt parking lot of Carmelita's Restaurant. Bits of rock crackled beneath the tires. She parked and got out. Peter stayed in the vehicle. He set aside the paperwork and pulled out his weapon, a Smith & Wesson M&P9 Duty Pistol. The gun was one of the changes Oesch had made when he'd taken the helm, switching from the Beretta 9mm to the M&P9 as department standard. "Just like they use in L.A.," he'd said.

Althea popped the trunk. Peter glimpsed her in the side mirror, pulling on a black winter coat with a fur-lined hood.

He ejected the magazine from the gun, checked the rounds and the chamber, and slapped the mag back home. He peered out at the restaurant. No sign of construction this afternoon.

But the front door opened, and the little woman they called "Carm" came out.

Peter exited the vehicle, holstering his weapon, framing a smile for her. He then ducked back into the cruiser and grabbed the papers.

"You again," she said.

"Good morning, ma'am," Althea said. "Cold one today, huh?"

"Nick's not here."

"Well, ma'am," Althea said, "that's unfortunate. We really need to speak with him. But maybe you can help us?"

"I don't know what I can do for you. You already arrested one of my workers. What do you want now?"

Peter handed Althea the EPA forms. At the same time, he heard a noise from behind the building. Maybe there were workers there, after all. He walked away. "Be right back."

"Where you going?" Carm groused.

"Just standard security, ma'am," Althea said. "Can I have you take a look at these?"

Peter rounded the outside of the large restaurant, passing the plywood, insulation rolls, shingles and tools. He stopped when he saw the truck. Yesterday, the contractor's pick-up had been out in front. Now it was most of the way around to the back. Peter drew his gun. Maybe it was an overreaction, but he was done taking chances. He heard murmuring coming from out of sight, then a burst of laughter. He passed the truck and a group of men came into view.

They were gathered in a circle, drinking coffee and smoking. Two were sitting on overturned buckets, two standing. One of them was Terry Rafferty. Terry hadn't been there the day before.

Terry stood up as Peter approached slowly. Peter held up a hand. "No need to be alarmed, gentlemen."

"Well, look who it is," Terry said. As if the words were a command, the other men fell in beside him, in a row.

Peter stopped a few yards from the four workers. There was nothing back here but a field, the evergreen trees and mountains beyond.

Peter kept his hand out, as if warning the men back. "Yep, me again. A family is still missing, I'm still part of the investigation."

"What do you want?" Terry Rafferty's words were icy.

"I'd like to know who each of you are. Terry, I know you. Sir? What's your name?" Peter recognized him from the bar, but wanted to be sure.

"Joe," the man said.

"Joe Fleming?" Peter took a few steps closer. "Let me see all your IDs. Take them out, toss them over to me. Anybody carrying?"

Terry glared at Peter. "No. We're not armed, Deputy." He was even bigger than Brad. At least six foot two, Peter thought, and two hundred and twenty pounds.

The men grumbled and looked at one another and dug in their pockets, except for Terry. "You got a real fucking attitude," he said around his false teeth. "Don't you? *King?*"

"Let's not turn this into a bad morning, okay?"

"Is that a threat? You gonna arrest us? What? You and your bitch partner?"

Peter froze. He'd been calm up until then, but now his heart knocked against his ribs.

Terry took a threatening step forward. "How about it, King? Let's hear the truth at last. You splitting that dark oak, or what?"

Peter put both hands on the gun. "Down on your knees. Hands on your head." He took another step closer, within spitting distance now.

He heard Althea's voice behind him. "Alright, alright," she said. Peter kept the gun on Terry, dropped a chin to his shoulder, and watched Althea approach. She was smiling. "Okay, guys. This is getting out of hand."

"Thea, stay there."

Althea kept coming until she was next to Peter. "It's all good," she said. "Carm has taken the paper work, and she's going to call Nick, get him on his way here. That's all this is, guys. Some routine paperwork. Let's dial down the testosterone." She examined their IDs.

"Why you picking on Nick?" Joe Fleming asked.

Althea put her hands on her hips. "You guys do any waste removal for Mr. Spillane? Any of you drive truck?" She singled out one of the men. "You, sir? You're Nick's nephew. You drive for your uncle?"

The men didn't reply. Terry Rafferty's gaze shifted back and forth from Peter to Althea, his upper lip peeled back in a snarl. Peter imagined him taking a spill from his bike all those years ago, his face grating across the pavement at fifty miles an hour. Then getting up and driving himself to the hospital with his teeth left behind on the road.

"You know how this goes, guys," Althea said, handing them back their IDs. "You see two cops here. But there's more of us. You can work with us today, get out in front of this thing, or you can play it hard and we just keep coming. Only more of us next time."

One of the men, smaller than the others, put up his hand, as if in school. "I drive for Spillane," he said.

"Alright, good," Althea nodded. Okay, so she was handling it. Not bad so far. But Terry was still volatile. Peter kept his gun on the man. "That makes one of you," Althea said. "Anybody else?"

Joe Fleming looked at the others, as if hoping to draw support, then admitted, "I drive, too. We're both licensed commercial drivers."

"What do you transport?"

The men wore hangdog expressions now, like boys caught stealing.

"You know," Fleming said. "Waste."

"From where?"

"Ah, shit. From all over. The hospital, um, Upstate Biotech . . ."

"Shut up," Terry snapped.

Althea kept going. "So you wouldn't say Mr. Spillane is retired? He's still pretty active in the waste disposal business?"

Fleming glanced nervously at Terry and didn't respond.

"Okay, guys. Here's what I want you to do. I want you to think real hard about something. About how, if Mr. Spillane is doing anything outside of proper handling methods, how you're each liable for that. You're independent contractors, right? Carry insurance?"

Three of them nodded. Terry and Peter stayed locked in their standoff. Nearby in the trees, a crow let out a loud caw and then took flight from a tall pine. Then Peter heard the familiar grinding of dirt and rocks as a vehicle rolled into the front parking lot. Someone else had arrived.

"Here's how this works," Althea continued. "You talk to us, you each give us a statement. If you were unaware of any violation of the method codes, now's your chance. When this thing comes out, if Mr. Spillane is liable for breaking any laws — and these are *federal* laws, as well as state laws, gentlemen, so we're talking about U.S. Attorney's Office — you look cooperative."

Footsteps approached from behind. Peter risked another quick look over his shoulder. Trooper Ski came round the corner.

Althea finished her spiel. "*Or*, she said, you can choose not to cooperate, and we'll take you into the department, get your statement that way."

"You mean arrest us," Terry said.

Althea locked on him. "You want to give us a reason, yeah. We can do it that way."

"Arrested is not charged," Joe Fleming said in a low voice to Terry.

"They charged my brother," Terry growled back.

Trooper Ski neared. "Morning." He spoke directly to the deputies as he stepped between them. "How's everything here, guys?"

Peter lowered his gun, holding Terry's eye. "It's a beautiful morning," he answered. He holstered his weapon.

"How about it, gentlemen?" Althea asked. "Hop in our vehicles for a minute, warm up a bit? Put a few words down on paper, and then you can get back to work?"

The three of them behind Terry Rafferty muttered to one another, but they began filing out, walking past the cops. Ski stepped over to Joe Fleming, put an arm around his shoulders. "What do you say, sir?"

The two men were physical equals. Joe shrugged off Ski's arm and walked ahead. Althea turned to follow and Peter caught her by the forearm.

Peter could see it in her eyes — apology and justification, sharing the space.

"I called Ski," she said.

"I figured. Good move. Carm really go inside to call Nick?"

"Oh yeah — she's pissed. Says they're going to sue the department. Loss of business, and so on."

Peter looked up at the huge half-built restaurant. "This place is on track to open by, what, the year 2050?"

Althea looked relieved that he was joking around. "Whatever gets Spillane here. Let's give Fleming and Rafferty to Ski. We'll take Nick's nephew, Tony, and the little guy."

"And we're just going to talk to them."

She started around towards the dirt parking lot. "Yes, talk. It's what people do."

He called after her. "Hey."

She stopped at the corner of the building and turned.

"This is pretty big," Peter said. "Spillane cheats or avoids his EPA forms, maybe worse, and this Kemp guy who's making his film about trash, waste, whatever, maybe he gets too close. Then his family goes missing."

"I know," she said. And she disappeared around the corner.

CHAPTER TWENTY-SEVEN / Showdown

Peter followed them around the unfinished restaurant, thinking. They would need search warrants for Spillane's restaurant, his multiple homes, his office, his trucks. But if these independent contractors didn't spill it right now, go on record, there wasn't really anything to charge them with, and so no grounds for search and seizure. Rondeau finding some paperwork on trucking manifests in Kemp's basement was not enough.

Something definitely seemed amiss, though. Spillane was clearly laundering dirty money with his giant restaurant. His workers acted shifty. John Hayes wanted out of something in a big way.

Peter could hear the doors of the cruiser and Trooper Ski's SUV being opened. If the contractors got in the vehicles and confessed, the deputies could hand prosecutors the written statements and Judge King would sign the warrants and Spillane's properties would be searched. Anything related to the missing family would come out. Perhaps they would find Kemp's computer equipment?

But where the hell was Rondeau? Althea was right about him being a loose cannon . . .

Peter heard screaming.

He froze for a second, then ran around to the front of the restaurant, pulling his weapon. He stopped at the corner.

Terry Rafferty had Althea in a choke hold, dragging her across the parking lot, her boots digging ruts in the dirt.

"Hey!" He didn't move, aiming his gun. Trooper Ski had taken aim, too, positioned in front of his SUV.

The three contractors scattered in all directions, one disappearing behind the restaurant. Trooper Ski shouted after them, ordering them to stop, but Peter ignored them. He looked down his gunsight at Terry's head.

Althea gagged and flailed. Terry was trying to choke her out as he walked backwards. Peter didn't have a clear shot, not even close — Althea was right in the line of fire. He needed to get closer. He walked towards her and Terry.

"Let her go!"

"You keep back or I'm gonna break her neck," Terry snapped. His face was red with rage. Peter felt his own anger roiling, mixed with fear. He stopped, but kept his gun on Rafferty. *Stay still. I'm going to put one between his eyes.*

That was dangerous, to say the least. Althea was a good shot, he was an adequate marksman, at best. Even from ten yards, he might squeeze off a round and only hit his girlfriend.

My wife, he thought wildly, *that's my future wife.*

"Let her go," he repeated. "Let her go, Terry, or I'm going to shoot."

"Fuck you."

Terry kept moving backwards. Where was he going? How did he think he could get out of this?

Peter heard an engine roar to life from the rear of the restaurant. He didn't risk a glance. "Ski!" he yelled. "Back of the house!"

Ski didn't respond. Peter was so focused on Althea he hadn't registered the sound of a scuffle. He glanced over and saw Ski fighting with one of the contractors. Joe Fleming had Ski in a headlock and was grasping for the firearm Ski had in his fist. Ski fired into the ground. Peter didn't know whether it was intentionally or accidentally.

This is crazy. This is fucking crazy. How is this happening?

The men separated. Fleming landed a punch square on the side of the trooper's head. Fleming lunged for the weapon again, and this time managed to grab it. Ski recovered quickly from the blow and seized Fleming by the arms. They fought over the gun, kicking at each other, tottering back until they both slammed against the side of the SUV in a metallic crash.

Peter returned his full attention to Althea. *Do something, man! Do something . . .*

He walked towards Terry, regardless of the warning. He slid his finger against the trigger.

The truck appeared from the far side of the restaurant. Gleaming white, extended cab, biggest size they came. It tore across the dirt lot on a cloud of boiling dust and the driver slammed on the breaks. For a moment, Terry and Althea were lost in a dust storm.

"Stop!" Peter had lost the shot completely; he was determined to get Terry in his sights again, and this time he would not hesitate. He heard the men shouting to each other — "Get in, get her in!" — and then saw their shapes as the dust settled. Terry was still behind Althea, hauling her around to the passenger side of the vehicle. They were at the back of the truck. Peter had his second chance. He lined up the sights and slowly let his breath out.

He fired, at the last second deciding not to aim directly at Terry, but just off to the side. The bullet punched into the tailgate, and it worked. Terry jumped, and Althea made a quick move. She planted her feet firmly, swung a leg around behind Terry and then jerked back, throwing him off balance. He slammed against the bumper. Althea spun, threw a fist, and smashed him in the nose.

Terry yelped. He covered his nose with his hands. Althea hit him again, in the ribs; two rapid-fire punches that knocked the wind out of him. Terry doubled over, howling.

Peter was only a few feet away. He could fire again, shoot Terry Rafferty; just take him out. Didn't have to be fatal, but he could put him down. Only, he was distracted by the truck's driver. The window was coming down, and Peter saw the tip of a rifle barrel. A split second later, the flash of gunfire as the driver pulled the trigger.

Peter felt the bullet tug the air beside his head. The shot had missed him by inches. He dropped to the ground and returned fire, pulling the trigger five, six, seven times. The explosions of the rounds were deafening; the bullets tore holes in the side of the truck, but the vehicle leapt forward, tires spinning, churning up dirt in a huge plume.

More shots followed — Trooper Ski was walking forward, gun extended, blasting at the fleeing vehicle. Peter couldn't see Joe Fleming at first, but then he peered beneath the cruiser. Fleming was on the ground, his face turned in Peter's direction, his eyes wide and mouth open. Dead.

Ski kept firing as the big truck ripped out of the dirt parking lot and onto the macadam, where the tires smoked as the rubber sheared away.

"The tires!" Peter called. "Shoot the tires!"

He turned to where Althea had been behind the truck. The wind dispersed the dust and he saw her on her knees.

He sprang to his feet and ran to her, ready to blast Terry as soon as he caught sight of him. But he didn't see the man.

Ski yelled. "Son of a *bitch*!"

Peter looked up at the last second before the truck disappeared around a bend in the road. In that final moment, Terry popped his head up from the back. He'd managed to hop in before the driver had teared away.

The threat over, Peter slipped the gun into his holster and dropped to his knees. He took Althea into his arms. She was coughing, gagging, touching her neck where Terry Rafferty had choked her. Peter yelled to Ski: "In the house — see about the old woman!" He meant both see if she was alright, and see if she was getting her own weapon, and going to be a problem, too.

He cradled Althea in his arms, smoothing back her hair. This wasn't something he'd expected. Terry and his brother Brad were armed and violent, but attacking multiple police officers like this? Trying to take Althea hostage? It upped the stakes in ways Peter hadn't really thought possible.

Ski snapped the radio from his belt and shouted into it. He put out the call for emergency services and for more troopers to respond to the scene. Peter kept a hold of Althea until she seemed to regain her breath.

"Got that guy good," she said.

Peter pulled her close. One thing was clear, this wasn't just about EPA forms and violation of method codes for hazard waste transportation. No one in their right minds went up against sheriff's deputies and a state trooper for what would likely amount to no more than loss of commercial driving licenses or fines. The only thing that made any sense was that this went deeper and worse. It involved the missing family, for sure. Either that, or the world had just gone completely nuts.

"You got him," he said to Althea. "Yeah, you got him, babe."

He looked beneath the vehicles. Joe Fleming was there, still dead as dead got.

That could have been Thea. But it wasn't. She'd made it through, just. No more playing cowboy, from now on. It was time for the U.S. Attorney, it was time for the FBI. These sons of bitches had to go d—

Peter tensed and pulled his gun again as a vehicle approached. It turned into the parking lot — a late model Town Car. Peter left Althea and strode toward it, pointing the M&P9 at the windshield. "Get your hands where I can see them!" He bellowed. "Get them up!"

The old man complied. He had white hair, a face like a catcher's mitt, glinting eyes. Peter came up alongside the driver door, aimed the gun through the glass, popped the handle.

"Get out of the car, Spillane," he said. "You're under arrest."

CHAPTER TWENTY-EIGHT / Protection

Peter and Althea paraded Nick Spillane into the county jail, the staff gaping as they led him toward Booking, where Deputy Kenzie took over.

Althea needed the infirmary — she was banged up but she'd refused an ambulance ride, insisting she stay with Peter.

He sent her on her way to the doc as Detective Stokes hurried over.

"What are we charging him with?" Stokes asked, jerking his eyes around.

"I don't know. Take your pick. Spillane's workers tried to kill Deputy Bruin and/or take her hostage. We can start there."

"This is crazy," Stokes said. "Just absolutely nuts. Trooper Ski shot someone?" His voice was breathy.

Peter nodded. "Joe Fleming is dead." And the sergeant and the lieutenant were stark raving mad over it.

Peter headed down the hall to the office where the men were gathered, already glaring at him as he stepped in. Stokes followed, and closed the door.

"Please," Sergeant Fransen said, "explain this one."

Peter got right to it. "Detective Rondeau asked me to follow a lead on manifest documents for waste transportation."

Fransen sneered. "So you made the unilateral decision to show up with your gun out. Then all hell breaks loose."

"With respect, sir. We had things very calm. Deputy Bruin had the men volunteer to sit and talk with us and provide statements. Soon as we had something, we were coming right to you, right to the DA. The aggression came from them, not us."

"I find that hard to take at face value, King. When you've been running around shooting your gun in the air, questioning inmates without their attorney present."

"Jerry . . ." Oesch began.

"Shut up, Mike." Sergeant Jerry Fransen aimed a finger at the sheriff. "I've been here nineteen years. I've never seen such soft control of the department. This is egregious. Your detectives and deputies are running around like unsupervised children."

Peter didn't like how the remarks wounded Oesch. Peter approached the desk and stared down at the sergeant.

"This was my call. No *way* were those contractors going to say a word with the District Attorney and a parade of cops showing up. They'd lawyer up and shut up. We didn't have anything to take them in on. Go ahead and call Internal Affairs, do whatever you got to do. In the meantime, we've got Spillane, and we need to hear from him."

Fransen boiled. "You're not a *detective*, King. That's why we formed a detective *squad*." He jammed a look at Stokes. "Where the fuck is Rondeau, and why isn't he answering his phone?"

Stokes was already trying to reach him, holding the phone to his ear. "Voicemail," he said. His eyes were shining with excitement.

Fransen redirected his ire at King. "You want to question him? Spillane already asked for wit sec."

"When? I just brought him in."

"His wife called while you were en route. Says neither of them are going to say another word without the feds here."

Spillane wanted protection — more, he wanted immunity. He was going to sing about something, something big, but he was only going to give it to the feds.

Stokes stepped out of the room, talking into his phone, leaving Rondeau a message. Peter could hear him in the hallway. They were all silent for a moment — Peter, Fransen, Oesch, Lieutenant Rumsey — eavesdropping.

"Rondeau, Jesus Christ. I've been trying you for hours. Listen, King and Bruin went out to Spillane's restaurant. They . . . oh man . . . Joe Fleming is dead. Everyone is out looking for Terry Rafferty. Then Spillane showed up and they took Nick into custody. He didn't even ask for a lawyer — he says, get this: he wants federal wit sec . . ." Stokes' voice faded as he walked away down the hall.

Peter caught Fransen's eye again. Fransen seemed to have lost some of his venom. He waved his hands in the air.

"Look, Mike, I'm sorry," Fransen said to the sheriff. "But this is out of our hands now, and out of our jurisdiction. It's my job to deliver the bad news, okay? We question him now, and they'll have all our jobs; they'll crumple this department like a piece of paper. Carmelita Spillane says Nick is going to give it all up. This whole thing goes federal."

"Spillane is in with the mafia," Peter said. "He's organized crime."

"Maybe so, maybe so. But, you're off this, King. You've displayed nothing but bad—"

Oesch broke in for the first time. "That's not your call, Jerry. This is my deputy. More to the point, we've got a missing family. If Spillane is part of the Kemp disappearance — if the two intersect — we need to know right now. FBI or no, we're going to talk to him. Right now."

Oesch took King by the shoulder and the two men left the room.

* * *

Spillane was in Booking. Peter and the sheriff entered the interview room and closed the door. Oesch remained standing, while Peter fiddled with a camera on a tripod. Camera set up, he started recording.

Spillane's old, wrinkled face was set and determined. He pointed a bent finger at the camera. "I'm not saying anything with that on."

Peter glanced at Oesch, who nodded. Peter pretended to click it off.

"I know what you want to ask me," Spillane said, "but only after I'm in federal custody, I'm gonna tell you where that family is."

Peter felt chills all over. His mind raced, but he tried to rein in the emotions and ask the right questions.

"Fine. We'll do that. You don't have to give a location until the FBI is here. They're close — be here less than an hour. But just answer me some basic questions, alright? Can you do that?"

Spillane stared back. He looked like someone who had lived a hard life. He was worn and tough, but there was something beneath the surface.

"Are they in danger? Is this time-sensitive?"

"I've got a lawyer that handles federal matters."

"I understand that. Hutchinson Kemp was doing a documentary film and stumbled onto your illegal waste dumping. So you and your associates came in and took the family. Made them disappear. This isn't about you, this is about the family." He imagined Maggie, playing at the preschool his nephew attended.

171

A nerve twitched beneath one of Spillane's baggy eyes. He was silent. After a few seconds, he looked away.

Peter leaned in. "Mr. Spillane — just tell us: are they alive?"

Spillane slowly looked back. "I don't know. Maybe."

Peter was fast to his feet. He stepped out of the room with Oesch and spoke hurriedly. "Feds can't get here soon enough. If he really knows where they are . . ."

Oesch nodded. Then he looked worried. "Dammit. Why did Rondeau disappear? Where is he?"

CHAPTER TWENTY-NINE / Breakdown

In the darkness, in the nothingness, like the bottom of a
well, he put out his hands and felt along a cold concrete
wall. He was enclosed. Pitch blackness. The smell of damp.

His clothes were gone. His hands scrabbled over the
floor for his phone, wallet, lighter — all gone. Only his
underpants remained.

He waited for his eyes to adjust, but there was
nothing. No scant light. For all he knew, it was airtight. He
might suffocate.

"Hello? Help!" His voice didn't carry beyond the
enclosure, his words soaked up. He tried again anyway.
"Someone answer me! Millard? Levitt?"

He got to his feet, in a squat. He slowly stood, his
hands above his head. He wasn't able to unfurl completely
— the ceiling was there, his fingers pressed against it. The
holding space was only five feet high, maybe five feet wide.
A cube in the ground.

He felt the panic welling up, and suppressed it.
Whatever this was, he bet the Kemps had gone through
the same thing. And he really didn't think they were dead.
Maybe it was just gut instinct, but it felt like the truth.

Hard to say why — maybe because he didn't think the CIA just did away with people. They were more resourceful than that. Everyone had a use. Whether it was as an asset or as a subject of experiment, you kept people around as long as they continued to pay out. That was what his father had said once. You only died when you outlived your usefulness. That was the nature of things.

He moved around on his bare feet, stooped over, checking every inch of the wall, probing with his fingertips, regulating his breathing, thinking practically. They'd put him in here, after all. If there was a way in, there was a way out.

The purpose of this was psychological. It had to be. This was torture. There were much more efficient ways to kill people. In a box like this, it could take days. The average human could go about seventy-two hours before dying of thirst. But there was limited air. Maybe a tiny bit of oxygen was coming in through the ceiling. Oxygen deprivation or carbon dioxide poisoning could precede dehydration. But how would anyone outside be able to tell? There were no cameras in here, he felt, as he kept smoothing his hands along, rotating as he hunched over. You'd just have to wait long enough. What was the logic in that?

This was a test. Put a person in here, let them think they're going to die, then release them after a good time, hit them with questions. A normal person would tell you anything after that. Threatened with going back in the box? No thank you. I was the second gunman on the grassy knoll. Can I go home?

Rondeau felt surprisingly good despite the situation. Crazily, he felt downright *giddy*. He'd done it. He'd followed his instincts, followed the leads, and here he was in the lion's den. There was no doubt that whomever had placed him here had abducted the Kemp family. The only questions were in the details — had Millard been corrupted somehow? He doubted it, but, then, Millard had been pushing him about like the wind. Rondeau wasn't so easily led, but Millard had an influence over him, he had to admit that.

Tamika Levitt? Maybe the call to the police was meant to lure him? Set him up and let him walk into this trap? She'd been standing right nearby when he was dosed. It could have been her . . . she could have called in with her hot tip, knowing it would reach Rondeau. But, how? It was only chance Dana Gates had been at the hospital, that they'd had a conversation. Right?

Millard and Tamika didn't really matter though. Not at present. What mattered most was going on out there now, without him. It was the same thing as what had gone down in the District — someone else was made to take the fall for a crime. In this case, probably Nick Spillane would take the hit. Who knew what they threatened him with — maybe he was an asset they'd had all along. Make it all look like some mafia operation. When in reality it was the government. Working with some major industry. Just like Millard always said. The deep state.

Rondeau stopped moving for a minute, stopped rubbing his hands on the wall. A thought crossed his mind which shut down some of the elation he was feeling. He sank to his knees, feeling a kind of despair grip him. Not because of this prison he was in, not because he felt afraid, but because he lived in a world where things like this happened.

And then a voice spoke in his head.

You realize this is all a bunch of complete horseshit.

It was Jessy. No-nonsense Jessy. Never much one for indulging the reality of black bag operations, underground conspiracies.

It's not. He replied.

You're losing it, Ricochet. This is the kind of stuff we've been trying to keep away from.

Don't call me that.

This is called psychosis.

175

In the nothingness, in the blackness, a light began to grow. Just a dot — the kind of dot that remained on the old TV sets when you shut them off. It grew to about the size of a quarter. He turned his head and the dot followed along with his eye movements.

A person can't tell what's real from what's imaginary. A delusion.

The dot split into four, then six, then more. Each new point a different color. They elongated out, turning into beams that tracked towards him, as though he were moving through a colorful tunnel, a subway ride with streaking colors. They came faster and faster, and more copiously; every color of the spectrum shooting past, as if he were gaining speed.

Rondeau struck the wall beside him. "Let me out!" His thoughts were becoming scrambled. He felt the panic spiral up as it dawned on him: *They drugged me.*

He fell back onto his ass and braced himself against the wall. He gritted his teeth and yelled — the way a person yells on a roller coaster. His skin began to crawl, as if he were moving for real, through physical space, the wind rippling his flesh. He let go of the wall and he itched. He was always so itchy — this felt like his usual irritation dialed up to ten. His skin was alive, writhing with bugs. His bones seemed to vibrate, his muscles spasmed. Rondeau threw his head back as the worst of it came on. He opened his mouth to scream.

You itch because of your scars, Ricochet Rondeau.

Don't call me that! Ever. You hear me? You're torturing me. This is torture.

This is not torture. This is only happening in your mind.

He let out a roar, soaked up by the thick walls, by the earth entombing him.

CHAPTER THIRTY / FBI Debrief

Peter King sat across from a dozen people in the large interview room at the jail. He recognized most of them. The mayor, town supervisor, District Attorney Elena Cobleskill, Oesch, Fransen, Sheriff's Lieutenant Rumsey, and Deputy Stokes. Internal Affairs were present due to the officer-involved shooting. He noted that there was no representative of the state police.

Oesch introduced two of the other three remaining people. "These are Special Agents Jackson and McDonough."

"Hello," Althea said. She was seated next to Peter on the same side of the table. She'd changed into sweatpants and a hooded sweatshirt, which concealed some of the bruising around her neck, but Peter could still see it.

He looked at the final person in the room, standing against the back wall. This man was dressed in a charcoal suit, his eyes hidden behind tinted glasses. No one introduced him.

One of the FBI agents, Jackson, thirty-something, with a bright blonde crew cut, leaned forward and clasped his hands together. His voice was nasal, like he had a cold.

"First of all, Deputies, we want to thank you. You've done tremendous work here, above and beyond."

Peter doubted the Internal Affairs agents seated nearby shared in precisely that sentiment. IA had a mountain of paperwork to get started on with King and Bruin. He imagined a similar bureaucratic fate befalling Trooper Ski.

He nodded his acknowledgment of the obligatory gratitude. Above and beyond? He didn't really think so. Lucky, maybe. Risky, for sure.

"Mr. Spillane has offered us complete cooperation," Jackson said. "We've moved him off-site and two of my fellow agents are meeting with him at state police headquarters now."

That explained why none of the staties were there, Peter decided. Why draw it out, though? Why not get Spillane to disclose the location where the Kemps were being kept right away?

"But we wanted to debrief you here," Jackson went on, "rather than move the two of you all over the place and lose time. We can relay what you give us to our agents currently assisting the state police."

What a clusterfuck, Peter thought. It made no sense. No wonder Rondeau was so skittish about the feds.

"I'm not sure what I can give you," he said. "You know what we know, at this point."

"Please indulge me," Jackson said with a wan smile. For someone who looked so young, he conducted himself like a seasoned agent.

"Well, first was a domestic disturbance involving Terry Rafferty and John Hayes, on Hayes's property. That was Friday. On Saturday night, I received a call from dispatch that there was another altercation, this time between Hayes and Terry's brother Brad . . ."

Jackson broke his focus and leaned over to the agent beside him. They whispered to one another. Peter waited. He caught Eric Stokes' eyes for a moment. Then Jackson returned his attention and stared across the large table. "Please, go on. You were assaulted by Brad Rafferty . . ."

"Correct. And then, next morning, Sunday, I found Brad at Spillane's restaurant and wrapped him up."

"Wrapped him up?"

Peter shifted. He had some bruising along his right leg, and his shoulder hurt. "I arrested him and brought him in."

"For the altercation with you at the bar."

"Yes. So, I talked to Brad. I asked him about Spillane. I've explained all of this to Sergeant Fransen — shouldn't we be focused on the family?"

"What originally brought Spillane to your attention?"

Peter sighed. "Detective Rondeau. He asked me to look into it."

"Uh-huh. I see. And where is Detective Rondeau now?" Jackson looked around at the others flanking him, particularly Oesch. As Oesch made excuses, Peter looked back at Stokes. Stokes widened his eyes and raised his shoulders in a subtle shrug. Jackson raised his hand to quiet Oesch, who was rattling off something about Rondeau being a bit unorthodox.

Jackson gave a quick, dismissive shake of the head. "That will keep. For now, I'll tell you: we've been following Mr. Spillane for two years, since he moved north."

"Why?"

Jackson shot Peter a look that conveyed such a question was inappropriate. Peter didn't give a shit.

"That's a confidential matter, Deputy King."

Peter felt like rolling his eyes. He felt the slightest touch on his elbow. Althea winked and her lips curled into a half-smile. She was telling him to cool it.

He took a beat. "Okay. I mean, I got the manifest documents from Rondeau. Then Brad said Spillane was connected, so . . ."

Jackson held up a hand. He murmured to McDonough again. Peter glanced at the unidentified man at the back of the room. The man turned and knocked on the door to leave. The door opened and he stepped out.

Jackson and McDonough looked ready to go. Jackson tapped the table with his fingers, and rose. McDonough followed suit. "Thank you so much, again, Deputies."

"That's it?"

"That's all we need, yes, thank you. This is a federal case now."

"What about the family?"

Jackson was turning away; he stopped, came slowly back around. All eyes were on him and Peter. Oesch looked like he wanted to crawl out of his skin.

"We're confident that Mr. Spillane will describe the location of the family. It's in his interest now." Jackson fully turned, knuckled down onto the table, leaning in. "Mr. Spillane is elderly. He doesn't care to spend his remaining years behind bars, to die in jail. And he's concerned for his nephew, Tony."

"Did he abduct them?"

Jackson shared a look with McDonough, who nodded slightly. Jackson said to Peter, "We believe the family was taken by associates of Mr. Spillane. Associates invested in him, who stood to lose money if their corruption was unveiled. The US Attorney will allege unlawful transportation of unregistered hazardous waste, failure to produce the proper method documents, health code violations, and possibly the elimination of evidence, in several racketeering cases."

"Bodies," Peter said, hanging on the agent's last words. "Elimination of evidence — you mean they were dumping bodies, getting rid of criminal evidence, using the trucks."

"In some cases, we believe so. In other cases, they may have been simply avoiding government fees."

"I want to go."

"I'm sorry?"

Peter stood up. "I got to Spillane — my partner and I did. I've been thinking about that family, those little kids, night and day. I want to be there when we find them."

Oesch spoke up, "Deputy King, we're all grateful for your actions. You and Deputy Bruin. Really, we . . ."

Jackson paid no attention to Oesch. "Alright," he said to Peter.

Peter felt a rush. He looked down at Althea beside him. He didn't see his enthusiasm reflected back. Her face filled with sorrow, and she shook her head. She didn't want to; she couldn't.

"Let's do it," he said.

CHAPTER THIRTY-ONE / En Route

He rode in a motorcade of three dark SUVs, red emergency lights jittering on the dashboard. Jackson drove, pressing over the speed limit, hunched against the wheel. His body language suggested he was unfamiliar with the routes of the Adirondacks, the windy, hilly roads. Like he might get seasick.

Peter was glad to be free. No one had wanted to let him leave; not Sheriff Oesch, and certainly not Internal Affairs. "I've got a month of meetings and forms and evals to look forward to," he told Jackson.

"Tell me more about Detective Rondeau," Jackson said, turning a bit green.

"Rondeau?" Peter chose his words carefully. "I haven't met a lot of detectives; he's our first. I remember there was a little bit of controversy when Oesch hired him; some of the staff said he had a checkered past, something like that. Oesch seemed to want him anyway; he had an excellent clearance rate. But, you must know more than I do."

He wondered why the agent was interested. This was a major moment for the investigation. They were about to find the missing family and capture a piece of organized crime at the same time. But, Jackson had pulled his federal authority and gotten Peter out of there; if he was interested in Rondeau, and that was why he'd spared Peter from IA grilling, so be it.

"Detective Rondeau was on the job in Washington D.C. for ten years," Jackson said. "There was a mass murderer and we were involved. Killer was tracked to a location, a shipyard outside of the city. Big containers all around, creating alleyways and blind spots. There was a shootout, and Rondeau took a couple of hits; two in the torso." Jackson touched his chest.

"I didn't know that." Peter watched the road blasting at them as Agent Jackson urged the SUV to higher speeds.

"Rondeau didn't let it go. He alleged the shooting was intentional. That we — the FBI — wanted him out the way because we'd forged the evidence on the perp. That we didn't have the right man, or were protecting the real perp and had faked forensics to build a case and nab this other guy."

"Did you?"

Jackson spared a sideways glance. "Do you always say exactly what's on your mind, Deputy King? The ensuing investigation proved otherwise, and DCI found that the bullets had ricocheted off some of the large containers."

Peter absorbed the information quietly. While it was hard to think of anything besides the Kemp family, the Rondeau thing invaded his mind. He became defensive, feeling like he needed to speak up on his colleague's behalf. "Rondeau's a good detective. But when you're life is law enforcement, when you work as much as we do, go through as much as we do, it's a lot of stress . . ."

Jackson wasn't listening. He put his finger to the side of his head. There was a thin wire snaking into to his ear. Then he rolled his wrist and spoke into his cuff. "Clear, twenty-two. We are en route. Traveling with Deputy Peter King." Then he suddenly slowed the car and took the shoulder. Without a word, he opened the door and got out. He retched into the stiff, brown grass.

Peter's phone rang. He was expecting Althea, checking up on him, but it was Stokes.

"Peter. A woman named Tamika Levitt called the state police yesterday." Stokes sounded out of breath.

"Okay . . . ?"

"She originally called the hotline and spoke to Detective Gates. That's how I found out, just now. Levitt claimed she had information on the Kemp family. Rondeau went down to investigate."

"Where?"

"Indian Lake."

Peter looked out the window. "That's fifty miles from here." They'd passed Pottersville about fifteen minutes earlier, where a bumpy backroad led to Indian Lake. He'd taken the trip a few times over the years. "What did she say when she first called?"

"She thought the missing family had to do with something . . . ah, some black budget operation."

It was hard to gauge over the phone whether Stokes believed it or not. "Interesting. Well, what does she say now?"

"Nothing. I've tried her five times in the past hour. No answer at her home, no cell phone. But, Peter . . . her place neighbors Addison Kemp's house."

"No shit?" Peter caught a touch of Stokes' excitement. "So are we sending someone down there to check it out?"

"I called the troopers. They said they sent two men."

"Good."

"You know where you're going yet?"

"No. Headed south on 87. Past Pottersville."

"Let me know when you know, okay?"

"Yeah."

"Hey — good luck. Be careful."

Peter hung up. As he watched Jackson pulling himself together out in the cold, he wondered if he'd misjudged Detective Rondeau. Over the past two years, he'd come to know the man as odd, a bit of a mess, with the habit of spilling coffee on himself. Rondeau scratched a lot, like he had an allergy or eczema. And his office looked like a refuge for paperwork from the last century, even though he was in charge of a small squad in a rural area . . .

But, heading off on a lead like this on his own? Was he hiding something, or just wanting to play the hero? There were rumors, too, that Rondeau was a binge-drinker, and Deputy Kenzie said he'd seen the detective talk to himself. Then there was the drone shooting. Everyone was wringing their hands over that one; Oesch was planning to have a serious talk with Rondeau. But, then the missing family case had come along, and it all got swept aside.

Now this about Rondeau's past, taking fire during a showdown with a killer, and blaming the FBI. Running off on his own to chase down a lead. Maybe it was the connection to Addison Kemp he was investigating, or maybe he was completely nuts.

CHAPTER THIRTY-TWO / Ricochet Rondeau

Time had lost all meaning. His physical boundaries had dissolved. Rondeau was adrift in a sea of consciousness, every corner of his psyche laid bare for vicious introspection. The past and the present collided. He was in the shipyard, moving through shadowy corridors. The gun fire rattled around him, coming from all directions. He took the hits to his chest again and again, on an endless loop. *Ricochet Rondeau, Ricochet Rondeau* echoed like a crowd chanting, reverberating off the corrugated steel.

The shipyard became his house, rows of containers turned into gloomy rooms, everything covered in years of dust. Rondeau drifted through them, a ghost. Blood fell in a trail he left behind, as if from his shipyard wounds. *Ricochet Rondeau Ricochet Rondeau* . . . the words echoed through the drafty house. He rose up the stairs to where Jessy lay bedridden, withering away like some kind of dying plant, desiccated by thirst, her bones protruding through her skin, nothing but sinew and hanging flesh.

On the bedside table, a framed picture of a husband and wife. Only he was in the picture, smiling, next to Jessy, instead of Millard.

The picture rapidly aged, turning a dull yellow. The edges curled until the glass shattered.

Rondeau's eyes fluttered. Something was happening. Heavy wood scraping against stone. A moment later, blinding light, light as brilliant as heaven, bathing him. Sand pattering down.

Hands reached in and hoisted him out of the tomb. They carried him away, his head lolling, dried froth on his lips. He'd strained so much in his prison that his muscles felt like jelly. His thoughts continued to leak in all directions. He was on a gurney, being loaded into the ambulance. He was a pall-bearer, carrying the casket down the steps of the church. He was in the casket, his arms folded across his bleeding chest.

There was a sound like metal dragging over rocks. He was positioned in a chair. Ropes cinched across his ribs. Hands tied behind his back. His chin lay on his chest, he could feel the drool slipping from his mouth. Was this really happening? He tried to open his eyes but it was still bright — less so, better here, but still difficult.

"Here's what's going to happen, Detective." The voice had the computerized timbre from the phone call, only further distorted. He couldn't hear properly. He tried to look around but couldn't lift his head. He had no muscle control. He was dimly aware he'd urinated on himself.

"We're going to release the family," the inhuman voice declared.

The family, he thought. *The family*. The idea bled out in his mind, like *Ricochet Rondeau*, a mental litany stretching to oblivion.

You have twenty-four hours. That brought him back. Time had most certainly run out. He hadn't pulled the plug on the investigation, or even conveyed to anyone the terrorizing message. He'd called their bluff, then? These ideas brought him further under control, and he managed to pull his head back, plant his feet firmly and sit upright.

His vision was over-bright and starry, like looking through a prism. Colors chased the edges of his sight lines. He could make out three figures, standing in formation. They looked like soldiers; shoulder-width stance, arms behind their backs.

A ten-hut! His father's words emanated out of his mental depths. Corporal George Rondeau. One of the many who had died on September 11. His father had been part of a major internal team that had been investigating securities fraud. Their entire command structure had been wiped out on that day, their headquarters taking the brunt of Pentagon's damage. George Rondeau, who had served in the army for twenty years, stationed at Fort Bragg, risen to the rank of corporal, then taken a desk job at last. Killed in the attacks.

Rondeau mumbled something, but his lips felt numb. He wasn't able to speak. He stared at the figures in front of him, their bodies shimmering with quicksilver, then turned his head. His neck creaked. His entire body was sore, muscles knotted, freezing pain in his joints. There were two empty chairs beside him. He looked down to the floor beneath the chairs. Stains there, like blood.

"Detective Rondeau, do you know where you are?"

A modulated voice used in sophisticated interrogations. Subjects were placed in a room, in front of a giant mirror. Behind the one-way glass, operatives and interrogators would monitor heart rate, vocal stress levels, body temperature. But this was no such room. This was more like a cave.

Zedekiah's Cave, he thought.

He tried to respond, but what came out was garbled and unintelligible. He licked his dry lips, swallowed, and tried again. "Innnian lek."

"You think you're at Indian Lake?"

He slowly turned his head back. His jaw felt like it wanted to lock up on him. "Yes."

"Detective Rondeau, are you aware of your psychiatric problems?"

Where was the family? Had they just said that they were going to release the family? How much time had he lost? A day? More?

"You have an organic degenerative condition," said the voice. Despite the deep distortion, it sounded female. Rondeau thought it was the person in front who was speaking, though it was hard to make out a face. Much was lost to the mirage, the rest obscured by backlighting, but the figure was curvier than male.

"No," Rondeau slurred.

She produced paper from behind her back and tilted her head, as if reading. "Detective, I have a complete work-up on you. We know all about you. It's amazing you're still in law enforcement. But I suspect you've kept some of this secret, have you not?"

"Where the fummly?"

"They'll be released soon. After our conversation."

"Why?"

"Why the conversation? Or why are we releasing the family? Detective, we're not animals."

Rondeau took a breath, pushed out his chest. He felt drunk — he sounded drunk. Had he been drinking? Bourbon in the apple cider? Jim Beam at night while working the case? His body weakened, his mind sluggish. He made every effort to speak clearly, forming the words carefully. The consonants felt like blocks in his mouth. "This about my father."

"Why would this be about your father?"

"What he knew."

"Are you saying you think that the disappearance of the Kemp family has something to do with your father, and so, you? That's rather narcissistic, Detective. Wouldn't you say?"

"Let me see." He spat to the side. "The family."

"Detective, in your delusional state you believe we have somehow orchestrated all of this in order to get to you, yes? Aside from it being so elaborate, when we could have just come for you directly — what would we gain?"

Rondeau thought of the recent crimes in the region: a thirteen-year-old boy, murdered; a serial killer at a college campus. The Sheriff's Department needed investigators to handle the rise in major crimes, so he had joined their first detective squad. For a rural area, there was a dark underworld at work. It was the perfect part of the country for criminals to work in anonymity. Drugs, prison breaks, internet crimes, mafia.

And it was the perfect environment for off-the-books government ops. Private security groups, CIA, working together.

"You don't have an answer," the woman said. "That's usually how it goes with paranoia."

While she laughed in that distorted voice, Rondeau took the opportunity to look around. The lights were dazzling, but he thought he saw additional tripods, bearing speakers. His captor was wearing a microphone which hooked into a sound system. At least that part wasn't in his head.

"Besides," she said, "we could do any number of things. Make it look like you committed suicide. Stage a murder. But, again, these would be great lengths for us to go to in order to satisfy your delusion."

"You . . . will kill me then."

The woman snapped on a pair of gloves. "Well now," she said, "there are things worse than death. And better for us." She waved a hand in the air, and one of the others handed her a small package.

"You gave me something. What you give me?" He thought of the patient on the hospital bed, septic and dying. But he didn't think he was sick. He squinted in the blinding light, trying to see his captor's face.

"It's called 25-I."

25-I? That was a powerful hallucinogen. A brain-scrambler. Used by high-tech security firms and government agencies during interrogations.

She leaned in, and he noted the angular cheekbones, the blond hair drawn back into a tight bun. The woman in black fatigues looked impossibly like Connie Leifson.

He heard a firearm racked, a bullet loaded. The woman moved toward him with a syringe.

CHAPTER THIRTY-THREE / Bluestone

The door snapped open and Jackson returned to the driver's seat, purged, at least for the time being.

"You alright?" Peter asked.

Jackson eyed Peter's phone as Peter slipped it back in his pocket. "Yeah, I don't know. I must've caught something. Anything important?" He meant the call. He must've seen Peter talking.

"Just the little woman checking on me." The lie surprised him — it had slipped out easily. Right or wrong, he felt protective of Rondeau.

They got going again, coming up on the interstate. "I hope this family is alive," Peter said. "I hope those kids are okay." He had another thought. "You ready to tell me where we're going now?"

"Ulster County."

"Ulster County?"

"Bluestone quarry."

Peter thought it through. There were several stone quarries in the state. Bluestone was no longer an active site.

He tried to reason through why the mob would take the Kemp family there, why that would be the location

Spillane gave them. "Bluestone's been shut down for decades," he said to Jackson. "It's all new-growth there now, along the Hudson River; it's a park. I drove through there this spring. Little trees, wide open views."

Jackson pinned the needle at eight-five miles an hour. He looked pale and grim. "New York State hemorrhaged labor in the 1930s thanks to the Workmen's Compensation Act. Quarries used a lot of off-season farm workers, but the farms were shutting down. When the quarries were abandoned, states took over the land. Lots of people hated that, blamed industrial farming, which was really getting underway. It went on for years. Last quarry was disposed of in 1990."

"You know a lot about it."

Jackson cut him a look. His eyes were bloodshot. "Bluestone used to mine feldspathic sandstone. You get smooth, thin slabs out of that, good for sidewalks. New York City is covered with it. It's fine-grained, evenly bedded, easy to process."

"Is that right?"

Jackson took the ramp to merge onto the interstate. They passed three state trooper vehicles — two cruisers, one van — followed by an ambulance, all lights blazing, waiting to fall in behind them. A temporary traffic funnel had been set up — fire police keeping traffic in the left lane so that the vehicles had an unimpeded route. Peter tried to see if he recognized anyone in the bright yellow jackets. The afternoon was dark, a cold rain stirring in the air.

Jackson brought the SUV up to interstate-speed, the convoy following, the lights twirling, engines roaring. The press was somewhere back there, too, Peter was sure of it. Trailing them down to the Bluestone quarry, eager to get the scoop of the year.

"Still not sure why they'd take the family there," Peter said. But his mind was working on it. An abandoned quarry, under state jurisdiction, was probably off most people's radar. A park ranger might occasionally patrol, looking for vagrants or dead wildlife, but it would be mostly left alone.

"Like I said," Jackson explained, "the FBI has been watching Spillane for years. We knew he was still active. We knew he was transporting hazardous waste."

It made even more sense to Peter. "Some of the new dump sites are abandoned quarries."

"Right. You've got these rock formations, you've got composition that holds up under chemical stress. Like certain waste materials. Forming a natural container, no seepage into the groundwater, no contamination of the rivers or the lakes."

"It just sits there."

Jackson moved into the left lane now that they'd gotten beyond the orange cones and flashing signs. "I'm not an expert. But I guess that's the idea. I've investigated one of the sites before. It's not pretty, and in stinks like the dead, but, it works, I guess."

"That's fucking crazy," Peter thought.

"That's why it's illegal. Federally speaking. What goes on at the state level, well, that's a different story. Money changes hands."

"Money between the mafia, you're saying, and state legislatures."

"It doesn't look like that on paper, but, that's some of what we have uncovered."

Peter took this in as the first cold drops of rain dappled the windshield. In addition to the victimized family, he considered the fate of Trooper Ski, a cop who now had a death on his hands. He thought of Althea, dragged across the parking lot, nearly strangled to death by Terry Rafferty. And Rondeau — God knew what was going on with him. It was nothing but lies, violence and death due to some toxic waste, where to put it, and who made the money off it. It felt like it was all for nothing if the family was dead, too.

194

"Why do we believe Spillane? I mean, why take the family to this dump site?"

"The operating theory was that they were taken by men working with Spillane. Put them in the back of a truck, haul it to the dumpsite. I can't sugar-coat it, Deputy: the operating theory is that this family is gone. That unless they managed some way to escape their captors down there, maybe hide out in the tunnels, stay alive — they're dust. It would be a miracle."

Agent Jackson pressed a finger to his earpiece again.

The convoy hurtled down the interstate. After a moment, Jackson released his finger and spoke to Peter. "Any reason to suspect Detective Rondeau would have found out about Bluestone on his own, and kept it to himself? Maybe gone on ahead?"

"No," said Peter.

"Well, in about a half an hour we'll get there and find out," Jackson said.

Peter put his thumb against his lips and gazed into the side mirror, where the lights of the other vehicles blazed behind them. He thought of kissing Althea. He thought of being kept in some kind of underground prison, maybe alive, and what that could do to a person.

CHAPTER THIRTY-FOUR / Escape

Rondeau's strength had gradually returned. He'd been picking at his bindings, acting weaker than he actually was. When the men got along side of him to keep him steady, the woman pointing the needle at him, Rondeau was sure of it — they meant to drug him some more, leave him for the police to find, all part of some story they'd spin.

He drove his legs into the ground and stood up hard and fast, aiming the crown of his head at one of the men. The chair came with him, and the ropes around his chest and stomach cinched tight, burning through his skin. The man's teeth cracked together and he stumbled back, flailing his arms. Rondeau spun the chair so that the legs batted into the woman's shins. She howled, and dropped to the ground, the needle tumbling.

He was still caught by the ropes around his torso though his hands were free. The second man came for him, gun out. Rondeau grabbed it, headbutted the man and wrested the firearm free. He jabbed it in the air. "Back. Get back."

The man instantly raised his arms and took a step away, his eyes blazing.

Everything seemed suspended for a moment. The man on the ground was moaning behind Rondeau. Probably his jaw was broken. The other man continued to stare at Rondeau until his eyes darted to look at the woman on the ground.

Rondeau swung the gun on her. She had her own weapon pointed right back at him. There was no time. He fired twice and fell away. She took two bullets, one in the upper chest, one in the neck. He hit the ground and the chair broke apart. The other man advanced on him, coming lightning quick, and Rondeau shot him in the shoulder.

The ropes had slackened now that the chair was busted. He wriggled free and got to his feet. No sooner than he was upright, the first man grabbed Rondeau from behind in a bear hug. Rondeau flicked his head back, smashing him in the nose. Rondeau spun around and pointed the gun at his head and fired; the man crumpled to the ground in a pink mist.

His father had taught him self-defense; they'd sparred with each other almost every day of his teenage years. Corporal Rondeau had been in Special Forces, and he'd passed on the ruthless training to his son.

The melee had all happened in a matter of seconds. Six, maybe seven seconds and three people were dead. He stood looking at them, scratching at his shoulder, then stepped over one of the dead men. A smooth face, clean-shaven; a guy in his mid-thirties. Could have been anyone, but was most certainly not mafia. An independent agent, someone for hire.

Rondeau looked at the woman. He squatted and stared at her face. Not Connie. Just someone, like the other two, paid to be here. The needle she'd been holding was shattered, the drug spilled out, sucked up by the dry ground.

He stood and walked away. He blinked at the colors still hemming his vision, tried to brush them away with his hand. He smeared something across his face and winced. Blood on his fingers, on his wrist. He wiped it off on the bare flesh of his legs. He was naked except for his underwear. He was cold, but he felt alive.

Rondeau moved toward the bright lights and confirmed the stereo speakers, and electronic gadget on the floor with wires coming from it. There were large wooden crates stacked against the curved walls of the enclosure. Behind him, the large room tunneled into darkness, with smaller tunnels branching off and away. He bet that either in those crates or down one of those tunnels was Kemp's editing equipment. The whole thing felt staged. Was the family packed away into one of those crates, too? He doubted it. They might have been tucked into one of the tunnels, or hidden in an underground room . . .

He couldn't chance it. He moved to the crates and searched for a crowbar, but found nothing. He put the gun down and tried to rip open a crate with his bare hands. His heart was thundering in his chest; he stopped, took several deep breaths. He tried to slow his pulse, and listen. He heard the echoes of dripping water. He felt the vibration of something, like a machine — a generator, perhaps, which had powered those lights and speakers. And this place stunk, it smelled of decay, toxic waste.

He moved among the crates, rapping them with his knuckles, pressing his ear to the wood. They sounded hollow. Each was sealed with thick metal staples. No matter how hard he tried, he couldn't open the lids. The sense of desperation closed in — he felt like he was back in the stone tomb, running out of air. His body was shaking, racked with the cold and damp and adrenaline from the killing. Hallucinatory colors swirled in the air, melting the walls.

He stepped away from the crates, turning towards where the tunnel sloped upwards, potentially rising to the surface. He headed in that direction, but found the tunnel forked not far along. Which way to go? There was a draft coming from the tunnel on the left — maybe indicating an exit. He made his way along, the light waning with each step. He found a hole in the ceiling which revealed a pinhole of the surface — but fifty feet above. In front of him, the tunnel stopped. A dead end. He retraced his steps, hurrying now, shuffling along.

Back at the fork, he paused, listening. He heard movement deeper in the tunnels. Footsteps. He took the other branch of the tunnel, and he ran.

CHAPTER THIRTY-FIVE / The Quarry

The quarry was like a giant stone stadium. Huge slabs of smooth rock formed a circular excavation the width of a football field, several stories deep.

Peter felt dwarfed by the massive pit. Rubble resembling destroyed buildings was piled in the center. The slabs of stone forming the stepped walls were the size of bridges. State troopers and FBI agents moving single file down a winding ledge. An agent named Eldridge led them, Peter just behind.

When they reached the bottom, Eldridge held up a fist and the group came to a halt. In front of them, a tunnel entrance formed a dark mouth in the stone. Eldridge unfurled the schematics he carried, a long sheet that showed the underground tunnel network. The rescuers had already been over it, now Eldridge pointed to it again.

"Main trunk here branches into three smaller tunnels. One of these dead ends, two branch again, and then this one a third time. We're looking for the family, nothing else matters right now. But be on constant alert. You see anything, you stop, you radio me immediately."

The sun broke free of the greasy clouds and bathed them in light. The rock formations threw stark, angled shadows. There was an odor emanating from somewhere, sharp and bilious, riding on currents of air. The wind gusted, kicking up the dust. Eldridge looked them over.

"Be safe, protect yourself, but no wild shots. Get on your radios. If you're worried about giving away your position, transmit signal only."

Eldridge rolled up the map and peered into the dark opening. "Okay. Right there. That takes us down."

Sets of tire tracks fed into the tunnel. Peter imagined the large trucks trundling slowly down the inner edge of the excavation, then disappearing into the shaft. Trucks potentially loaded with toxic chemical waste. Trucks potentially containing human beings.

"We don't know the condition of the vics," Eldridge reminded. "If they're alive, they could be in seriously bad shape. They could even be still in perp custody." He was square-jawed, his dark hair close-cropped. He wore a Kevlar vest beneath a dark winter parka, handgun on his belt. "The perps could be armed."

Peter looked down at his M&P9, gave it a quick check for debris and snapped in the magazine. The others in the group followed the same procedure, gun parts clattering, the sounds reverberating off the stone. They checked flashlight batteries, performed two-way radio checks for the umpteenth time. Peter recognized Maize and Crowley, two troopers. He didn't know all of state police, or any of the dozen agents with their own Kevlar vests displaying the FBI letters in yellow. They were trusting their lives to one another, to strangers.

"We go in by pairs. Person next to you is your buddy. Watch your backs." Eldridge pointed at Peter. "You're with me."

Peter stepped beside the agent and together they moved towards the dark, gaping mouth. He felt like it swallowed them up as they slipped into the earth.

The tunnel was pitch black. Flashlights probed the dusty dark as they made their way down the sloping ground. The smell intensified with each step, rolling toward him in waves. A deer could give off quite an odor when you field-dressed it in the forest, he thought, but this was ten times worse. It reminded him of trips into the medical examiner's building, where within its tiled walls, drifting over its stainless steel gurneys, was the stench of death.

He hoped to God there weren't dead bodies down here.

He listened to the soft footfalls of the group behind him, crunching over the grit. The sounds of breathing, the whisper of clothing. He walked next to Agent Eldridge, the man's words echoing through his mind. *Protect yourself.*

The silence felt oppressive.

A funnel of wind came twisting down into the tunnel. It was warmer down here, the heat palpable, growing by each step. Finally, the slope ended and they walked along the level surface. The tunnel opened wide into a cavernous space. Far up ahead, a row of work lights shone in the gloom.

Peter heard a noise, like a person shouting. Everyone in the group tensed. Peter dropped into a crouch and moved towards the tunnel walls, his heart pounding.

It looked like there was someone there, on the far side of the lights.

Peter felt his muscles tightening, ready: *this could be it.* The kidnappers were in the quarry after all, waiting to ambush the rescuers. The whole thing was a set-up: Spillane had hooked them, and they'd taken it, and now they were down here, underground and easy prey. The group held their breath, watching as the figure in the distance drew nearer, hands in the air. Eldridge's finger slipped through the trigger loop. The agent stepped away from the wall and took a firing stance.

"Stop!" he shouted. The figure was a hundred yards away. Whoever it was, he was speaking, shouting at them, but the words seemed lost in the echoing tunnel, just garbled.

The others in the group were falling in alongside Eldridge, taking aim. Peter hesitated. Something wasn't right. He kept looking from Eldridge, and his gun, to the figure in the distance. It was hard to see — there was light coming from behind the man, silhouetting him — but, was he naked?

Whoever he was, he kept advancing, waving his arms, trying to communicate.

Eldridge took a threatening step forward, then another, the phalanx of agents and troopers following suit, while Peter lagged behind and off to the side. Who the hell was down there? Naked but for underwear, arms in the air, yelling at them. "Hey," Peter said. It was just a whisper. "Whoa," he said, his voice rising. "Whoa whoa whoa — that could be one of the missing family. That could be Hutch Kemp."

"That's not Kemp," Eldridge said. "I don't know who that is but it's not Kemp."

The figure kept approaching. He should've been still as a statue, arms folded over his head. But he kept coming, picking up speed. Eldridge was ready to squeeze off a round. Peter hustled up behind the agent. As they drew nearer the mysterious subject, Peter felt something churning inside. Recognition. The posture, the shambling walk, the shaggy hair . . .

Eldridge was barking commands now, ordering the man to his knees. The phalanx was picking up speed. Eldridge's face was a mask of determination. Regardless of who it was, it seemed, the agent was ready to take deadly action. He tensed, about to fire.

Peter lunged forward and grabbed the agent's wrist, forcing the gun down. "That's one of ours," he shouted. "That's Rondeau."

Eldridge gave Peter a look — something wild was in his eyes, and then it cleared. He seemed to take just a moment, make a decision, and then returned his attention down the large tunnel. "What's he doing here?"

"I don't know," Peter admitted, and let go of Eldridge's hand. The agent was no longer on the verge of shooting, but he was still dubious. If Rondeau was here, what did that mean? Eldridge kept moving forward, gun at the ready, fellow agents beside him. The troopers seemed to fall back a bit — they knew Rondeau.

Rondeau finally slowed his pace. Now that they were closer, Peter could clearly see the detective, even make out his expression. He looked positively manic, his eyes wide, his hair a mess, his body covered in dirt and scratches. "They're down here," he was saying. "The family is down here. They're alive."

"Stop moving," Eldridge ordered. "Stay where you are. Get on your knees. You've seen them?"

Rondeau fell silent. He seemed to be wary of the agents approaching. As if, at first, at a distance, he didn't know who it was that was coming toward him. Now that he knew, he appeared more afraid than relieved. But he did as he was told, lowering to his knees with what looked to Peter like some amount of pain. Rondeau put his hands over his head. Why was Eldridge doing this? Precaution was one thing, and Rondeau's presence was unexplained, but still.

Peter surged forward and went to the detective.

"King!" Eldridge barked, but Peter ignored him. Peter stopped beside Rondeau and crouched down. "You okay?"

The older man looked positively out of his mind. His color was high, his pupils wide and dark as his eyes jerked around in their sockets, taking in the agents surrounding him. He looked ready to fight. "What happened?" asked Peter.

"Step away, Deputy King."

King stood up and squared shoulders with Eldridge. "Let me take him up to the surface."

"No," Eldridge said. One of the other agents circled round behind Rondeau and started to look him over. "Stay still," the agent said.

Peter watched this and found it confusing. Rondeau was nearly nude; no pants, no holster, clearly no weapon — why would they think he was armed? Christ, he smelled like piss, too. The agent brought Rondeau to his feet. "Get him up top," Eldridge said.

"Wait . . ." Peter stepped in front of them, blocking the way out. "What did you see? Did you see the family? Where are they?"

Rondeau only looked at Peter. He had gone completely quiet, his frantic eyes snatching looks at the agents. Eldridge leaned his face toward Rondeau. "Detective? Anything you've got that can help us? Do you know where the family is? Anyone else down here?" Rondeau only stared. Eldridge jerked his thumb in the air. "We'll debrief him out there. Get him medical attention."

The agent led Rondeau away. The detective hobbled along, eyes down, mysteriously silent. Peter watched them walk off, the yellow FBI letters on the agent's vest fading into the darkness.

CHAPTER THIRTY-SIX / Reborn

"Rondeau?" Lights shone in his pupils. Brighter than the sun, dazzling his vision. Rondeau sat on the back bumper of the ambulance, his feet on the ground. A second paramedic took his pulse, checked his vitals. The FBI agent who brought him out stood nearby, asking questions.

"Detective, did you get a visual on the family?"

Rondeau shook his head, cleared his throat. He still had to think the words before he could speak them. But he hoped the worst was over, and that he wasn't going to have any more hallucinations. "I didn't," he said. "See them."

"What happened to you down there? When did you get the information on Bluestone, and why, for God's sake, did you come alone?"

He licked his lips and concentrated. "I didn't come. Call was about Indian Lake. You check with BCI. Dana Gates."

"We know about that. But there's no record of you being there. No GPS, no cell phone pings."

"No towers to ping." He meant the lack of cell phone towers in Hamilton County. "I had my personal . . . vehicle."

"Uh-huh. Okay . . ."

"Tamika Levitt. Talk to her."

The paramedic, a pretty brunette, was taking his blood pressure now. Plastic crackled as another medic opened bandages in the ambulance. He felt warm blood oozing from several places. He knew no matter what he said to the agent, it was useless.

"We've tried," the agent said. "We haven't reached any 'Tamika Levitt.'" He grimaced. "Detective, if you say you were in Indian Lake . . . at what point did you head over here to Bluestone?"

Rondeau swallowed. He had no spit. "Didn't come here of my own volition."

"I don't follow."

"They stuck me," Rondeau said. *But you already know that.* He lifted a hand and pointed at his neck. It was especially difficult to form the next words. "Etorphine hydrochloride knocked me out, but laced with something. I think 25-I."

"I'm familiar with it."

The setting sun had broken through the clouds, darkening the man's features. Rondeau felt a ripple of anger, a bite of fear.

"How long have I been missing?" The words were coming easier. He was asking the paramedic, but the agent answered.

"Missing? Last contact we have logged from you is when you spoke to Detective Gates. That was yesterday morning. It's Tuesday, almost three p.m."

It was hard to hear, but he believed at least that much from the agent. The powerful drug lasted for at least a day. A day spent entombed in hell.

The agent cocked his head and turned to the paramedic. "Can we check that? Etorphine hydrochloride? Or 25-I?" Rondeau felt like the agent was humoring him.

"Not in the field," the paramedic said. "I can draw the blood, but we don't have any way to analyze it." She was putting ointment on his rope burns. *Where do they think the burns came from?* he wondered.

"Draw the blood, hand it over to my team. We'll have it sent to the lab for chemical testing."

Rondeau felt a shiver at the mention of an FBI crime lab. "My brother-in-law can corroborate," he said to the paramedic. "If you can find him. Has anyone found him?"

"Your brother-in-law was *with* you?" The agent crossed his arms. "A civilian? Who is he?"

"Millard."

"Millard? What's his last name?"

Rondeau thought, and came up empty. His mind was still so scrambled he couldn't even recall Millard's last name. The effects of the drug were powerful. He waited for it to come to him. In the meantime, the agent stepped forward, extending the hand down to Rondeau. "I'm Special Agent Marty McDonough, by the way," he said.

Rondeau shook the man's hand. His muscles quivered and he quickly withdrew.

"What *do* you remember?"

Rondeau was silent.

McDonough leaned to the right, looking past the ambulance. "Shit, here they come. Press." He snapped his fingers and shouted, walking away. "Hey, hey! Enforce that line there. No one comes past the barricade. They try it, take their cameras."

Rondeau craned his neck around to see, but the back of the ambulance faced away from the road, towards the low sun, dropping in the west. McDonough stepped back into place. His shadow fell across Rondeau as he blocked the light.

"Can always count on the media to smell the blood in the water," he scoffed. "So you're drugged, you're unconscious, you're brought here. Then what?"

Rondeau liked the way McDonough was looking at him less and less. "I don't know," he lied.

"You don't know?" McDonough spoke to the paramedic. "What's it looking like?"

She stepped back after listening to Rondeau's heart and pulled the stethoscope from her ears. "His pupils are dilated. Blood pressure is ninety over sixty, which is low, but not hypotensive. Heart rate is high, one hundred beats per minute. Because he's not FDP, I'm going to associate the mydriasis with drugs, possible trauma. But it doesn't rule out a drug in his system." She leaned in front of Rondeau, getting between him and McDonough. "Do you remember getting hit with anything?"

He felt the damage he'd inflicted on himself, pounding against the walls of his prison. Launching his body up at the ceiling, trying to budge the stone lid of the tomb. "No," he said.

She looked him over, her kind eyes lingering over his wounds.

"Let me see," he said.

She understood, moved away to get a mirror. McDonough still stood there, staring, the corners of his mouth downturned, expression slack. The paramedic came back and held the mirror in front of Rondeau.

There was blood on the side of his face. His hair was matted to his scalp on that same side. His eyes were black, the pupils consuming all but a thin rind of faded blue. The white of one eye was red with burst capillaries. His split lips were covered in dried mucous, his cheek bruised. And he was covered in dirt and mud.

"Thanks."

He leaned back and lost his balance. The paramedic in the ambulance caught him and lowered him gently to a prone position.

"Detective," McDonough said. "We still need to . . ."

"Find Millard," Rondeau said. *Unless he's been taken, too.* It was a terrible idea, but one he had to consider. Another possibility — a better one — was that he'd run and hidden somewhere. Maybe he'd seen whoever got the jump on Rondeau. It could have been Tamika Levitt herself. She'd been right behind him. She wasn't responding to phone calls? Maybe because she was on their side. Or . . . who knew. Maybe she was somewhere underground, too.

Agent McDonough spoke to the paramedic again. "Is he lucid? Do we think he's still feeling the effects of . . . whatever he says he's on?"

He's feeling it, Rondeau thought about himself. "Where's Eric Stokes?" he asked. "I need to talk to Stokes."

"He's on his way, just relax." To the paramedic, McDonough said: "I'll come back to check on him. Get him stable. Don't let him pass out."

Rondeau felt a strong wind sweep through, rocking the ambulance. A storm was coming.

CHAPTER THIRTY-SEVEN / Saved

Peter King had never felt such elation in his life. There they were, the four of them. Hutchison and Lily Kemp and their children. They were alive. It swept away all the recent strangeness about Rondeau.

Several of the troopers fanned out and formed a protective perimeter. Peter accompanied Eldridge to the family. The search hadn't taken long — after Rondeau had been led up out of the mine, the group had stayed together in the main tunnel, which had gradually wound deeper into the ground. They came to where it forked in the other direction. Half the team split off and headed up the fork, while Peter and Eldridge and the rest had continued on. They'd spotted more lights after a few minutes, and then seen the figures in the chairs.

The parents were tied up, the children on the ground. Maggie was holding onto her father's legs, silent and fearful, watching the rescuers. She was dirty but appeared unharmed. Peter crouched beside her and encircled her with an arm. He thought of Benny, his nephew who was the same age; he suddenly felt very close to her, as if she were his own family. The girl stared up at her father, her eyes shining in the gloom. "It's okay, baby," Hutch told her. "These people are here to help us."

The toddler was wailing, sitting on his diapered butt. Peter slid closer on his knees. The diaper smelled foul. Eldridge and another agent untied the parents. Lily Kemp stood up but her legs were weak. Peter caught her, then helped her to sit and take the baby in her arms. Lily was murmuring, talking too softly for him to understand what she was saying to the baby. She took little William in her arms, cradled and soothed him. Freed next, Hutch tumbled from the chair and gripped Maggie in a fierce hug. Then he slung an arm around Lily and William and drew them towards him. Huddled together, finally able to embrace each other, they cried.

Everything was still for a moment. Peter felt a tear slip down his own cheek. He noticed he wasn't alone: several of the state troopers trying to remain vigilant and protect the scene were misting up. All of the unanswered questions seemed to fade for a moment. This was the best-case scenario. The family was okay.

"Let's give them space," Eldridge said, "and let's lock this place down."

The command brought Peter and the others back to reality: There could still be danger here. The family could have unseen injuries, and their abductors could be lurking. Peter didn't think so, but they were still on high alert and had to check the entire premises.

He stepped away. The Kemps remained bunched together on the ground, amid the foul-smelling air. They cried, and then suddenly laughed, and hugged some more.

"Mr. Kemp," Eldridge said.

Kemp looked up, tear streaks down his dirty face, his smile fading from his lips.

"Do you know where they are?" Eldridge asked.

Kemp shook his head. "No."

"Who kept you here?"

"I don't know their names. I didn't recognize any of them. They used lights, they altered their voices."

"How long ago did they leave?"

Hutchinson Kemp looked up, thinking. Peter watched the man closely. He couldn't imagine what this ordeal had been like. He wondered if the family had been together the whole time. He doubted it. Likely the perps had separated them. Maybe interrogated Kemp. Threatened him.

Kemp was bruised, battered, cut along the ridge of his forehead, swollen knuckles, dried phlegm on his chest, a total mess. But he was coherent. "An hour ago. Maybe two. It's hard to gauge the time . . ."

"I understand."

Everyone was hanging on to Kemp's words. Waiting for Eldridge's signal to continue the search. While they had been tending to the family, the smaller group which had ventured down the fork returned, saying it was a dead end.

"Okay, my agents, stay in your pairs. Let's look at each remaining tunnel. Don't touch *anything*. Just a visual sweep. You find something interesting, you drop your tag. Radios won't reach the surface, but we can keep in touch with one another. Got it? Everyone else, we're headed out."

The agents assented and then got going, splitting off into twos. The troopers seemed dismayed to return to the surface, but kept quiet. A federal forensics team would be ushered in as soon as the family was away from danger. Peter imagined the operation — a place this big, damp, pungent, nothing but rocks and dirt and a few pieces of lighting equipment. Maybe they'd find something down one of the tributary tunnels, maybe not.

Hutchinson Kemp spoke up. "I got the impression something had changed." He looked from Eldridge to Peter. "I saw one of them talking on the phone. Like someone from outside had . . . called it off. The guy talking sounded upset, but then he told us we were free, that people were coming. He dismantled the phone and broke it into pieces. Then they left."

"You think you can ID anybody? Did you see *anything?*"

Hutch looked at his wife, whose face reflected what he was thinking. He shook his head. "They were always in front of those lights." He meant the tripods with area lights off to the side. Peter saw audio speakers, too.

Eldridge started to ask more, but Peter interrupted. "We need to get them out of here."

The agent nodded. The remaining rescuers gathered closer around the family, preparing to leave. Peter helped Lily Kemp to her feet. The baby boy clung to her. Lily was trembling and weak. "You want me to take him for you?" Peter asked.

Lily shook her head. "No," she said in a small voice. "Thank you." The boy buried his face in his mother's neck.

Hutch picked up Maggie. With everyone on their feet and ready, Eldridge got moving ahead.

They emerged into the afternoon, dust swirling in the quarry. Eldridge keyed his radio. "We've got them. We've got the family. Alive. We're coming out now."

Peter's pulse raced; he felt the raised gooseflesh on his skin. The pride of having found the family, the vicarious thrill of their freedom.

They ascended up the edge of the site, along the road, the wind beating harder against them the higher they climbed. Just over the lip of the quarry, the man, Hutch, dropped to his knees. Peter let go of the woman and squatted next to him. The other rescuers crowded around, to see if they could help him back up.

Hutchinson Kemp just knelt there, holding his daughter, rocking, his face turned downward. Peter thought he could hear the man praying beneath the howling wind.

"Oh God," he said. He buried his face in his daughter's hair. "I'm so sorry."

It started to rain.

CHAPTER THIRTY-EIGHT / The Kansas City Shuffle

Something was happening. McDonough was on a two-way radio, looking down towards the giant crater in the distance. He snapped his fingers in the air and a trio of paramedics trotted down the slope towards the quarry. Emergency responders hurried to finish erecting the large tent, loading it with gurneys and medical supplies. A rescue chopper was flying in, ready to take the family to Albany Medical if anyone was in critical condition. There was a buzz in the air. They were coming out.

Stokes stood with Rondeau, but the younger detective started towards the commotion. Rondeau caught him by the arm.

"It's all bullshit," Rondeau said in a low voice. The meds they gave him were working, bringing him back around. The rain spattering against his skin was waking him up.

Stokes stared off toward the quarry.

"Do you hear what I'm saying?" Rondeau tightened the blanket around him. Someone was supposed to be getting him clothes. Where were they? He stunk and he was cold and he wanted to get dressed.

Stokes turned at last, looking concerned. "Okay, I hear you. Talk to me. How's it bullshit? What happened?"

The paramedic pretended not to be listening in; she caught Rondeau's look and walked away. McDonough was preoccupied, but close enough to eavesdrop.

"Not here," Rondeau said.

"Okay — where?"

Rondeau took a moment to think. Good old Stokes. Eager, responsible, a hard worker. He liked Stokes and wanted to be able to trust him. He needed to tell someone — it was burning within him. But he had to be careful.

He called to the group bustling in and out of the tent. "Anyone have a car I can borrow?"

Several of the responders stopped what they were doing and looked uneasy, probably wondering about protocol. Here was a cop who'd mysteriously appeared in the mines, raved about being drugged, and he wanted use of their vehicle? The paramedic reappeared — she hadn't gone far. Even the agent looked around, pulling the phone from his ear. "Rondeau," he shouted over, "we need you to stay . . ."

"Just want a dry place to sit for a few minutes, okay?"

The agent relented. He jabbed a finger toward the parking area. "Get him a car, someone, okay?"

"We could just use mine . . ." Stokes said to Rondeau. "No."

A young man trotted over. He was holding out keys. "Dodge Ram," he said. "Right back there beside those three trees."

Rondeau took the keys. "Thank you." They had maybe ten minutes before the rescuers made the climb all the way out with the family. He stood up, gathering the blanket, and one of his knees buckled. Stokes caught him by an elbow. Rondeau steadied himself. "I'm alright, I'm alright," he grumbled. He hobbled away from the ambulance, throwing a glance over his shoulder at McDonough, whose lips moved soundlessly as he stared back.

The rain whipped up, soaking Rondeau's blanket. But it felt good, walking through the fresh wet air. He found the truck, unlocked the passenger door and tried to hoist himself up. The blanket kept falling. Stokes got behind him and pushed, and his hand slipped beneath the blanket, touching Rondeau's bare thigh.

"Get out of there," Rondeau grumbled.

Stokes laughed. "Sorry, boss."

Once Rondeau was in the cab with the door shut, Stokes jogged around and got in. "Give me the keys." Rondeau handed them over, Stokes fired up the big Hemi engine, and turned the heaters on full blast.

There were food wrappers on the dash, papers and textbooks scattered on the floorboards. Rondeau was checking everything out, sifting through the mess. When he finished, Stokes had his eyebrows raised. "Okay. Find any bugs? Listen, they're coming out, boss, let's—"

"Kemp is a national security threat."

Stokes fell silent. Rondeau let him think about it for a moment. "Alright," Stokes began tentatively. "How?"

"He knows what they don't want anyone else to know. So he's abducted, threatened."

"By whom?"

"I'm not a hundred percent yet. But it's not Spillane."

"So, what — they're throwing blame? Engineering things so that Spillane takes the fall for it — or the mafia?"

Rondeau was frustrated with Stokes' tone. "Don't patronize me. Think about it."

"I am, boss. I am. I'm giving it every thought. But you weren't there yesterday when Nick Spillane was brought in, looking guilty as sin. And you remember John Hayes? Hayes wanted out, and that's why all the distress with Hayes and the Raffertys. Meanwhile the Raffertys, along with Joe Fleming, Nick's nephew Tony, and the rest —

they wouldn't allow themselves to be caught. We've got them red-handed on the manifest violation; it looks like they've been dumping toxic waste. Spillane is in wit sec now, only talking to the feds. The word is he's giving up a bunch of people. We're talking Lucky Luciano types. People exploiting the Adirondacks for professional gain. Making boatloads of money trucking waste at a high price, avoiding all the fees and, dumping. Spillane loves it because he avoids all the citations and regulations. Mafia loves it because they get paid instead of the government. I don't see federal cover-up in this anywhere."

"It's the Kansas City Shuffle. Misdirection."

"The Kansas City . . . Okay. Is that what you're going to take to the DA? I mean, really?" Stokes looked out as an emergency worker ran by, squeezing between the packed vehicles.

"Look," Rondeau urged, "I'm sure Spillane is dirty. And that the dumping is happening. But for Spillane to just lay himself bare, to betray the mob like this . . ."

"They made him an offer he couldn't refuse?"

"When did you get so fucking high and mighty, huh? New guy?"

Stokes played right back. "When Sheriff Oesch told me to keep an eye on you, boss."

Rondeau felt struck. "What?"

Stokes held his angry look for a moment, then feathered his hands over the air vents. A gust of wind battered the truck. The trees out there were being bent sideways. Rondeau watched, and thought the tent was going to blow away if it wasn't really staked down. He didn't like what Stokes was saying. Not one little bit. "You're supposed to *watch* me? What does that mean?"

"Nothing. Never mind."

"Listen to me, Stokes. No, they didn't make him an offer. My guess is Spillane has been an informant for years. He's willing to snitch on multiple organized crime members because he's afraid to get popped for some trucking violations? What was the story they gave you?"

"That he's old. At his age even a short nap and he could die in prison. And he wants to protect his nephew, Tony."

"Uh-huh. So to avoid jail he just happens to know where the family is, waiting to be rescued."

"Rondeau . . . I respect you. But listen to yourself . . ."

"And where is Addison Kemp, huh?"

"What — she's in on it?"

"I don't think so. But she gave me that clip of *Citizen Farmer* for a reason. Remember, Stokes? You were the one who kept bringing that film to my attention. Now — what? You're scared? Okay. Be scared. But do the right thing. This is not what it seems, and I think you know it."

Stokes was silent and looked away.

Rondeau cleared his throat and calmed. "Do we have eyes on her? On Addison?"

"We're looking."

"Don't you think she'd be here?"

"FBI kept this location quiet until the last second. To try and stave off the press parade, bystanders, all that."

"Fuck the FBI. They're manipulators." Rondeau made a fist. He looked at his raw, scraped knuckles. He remembered punching the ceiling of his tomb. He flexed his hand.

Stokes was watching, looking at the grazed flesh.

"You got to give me something, boss. Something solid."

"*I'm* what's solid," Rondeau said, suddenly slapping his bare chest. He felt his lip quiver, felt the emotions rising. "First of all, why am I here? How did I get here? You *know* I went to Indian Lake. They brought me here."

He let the blanket drop around his torso. He watched as Stokes leaned in for a look at the rope burns. The bullet scars. "Believe me," Rondeau said, "I've been through this before . . ." He trailed off, suddenly needing to confess. "I killed them, Eric. I killed three agents down there. Ex-military types. Private security. Hired kidnappers."

Stokes took a long moment before responding. Rondeau felt like he was getting through, in one way, but this last bit might've pushed the younger detective in the other direction. His eyes were still glued to Rondeau's scars, his fresh wounds, like he was working it through.

"They're looking, boss. If anyone else is down there, they'll find them."

"They won't. It'll be cleaned up."

Stokes finally fixed Rondeau with hard look. "See? That, Rondeau. That right there. That's what makes it tough to swallow your story. All of this convenience. There's no evidence for anything, because *they* make it all go away . . ."

Rondeau stared into space. "I had a gun." He held up his hand, open-palm. "I got one of their guns, and I . . . I set it down. I forgot. I . . ."

"Look, I was told . . ." Stokes sounded like he was searching for the right words. "I'm supposed to deal with this in a certain way, you know?"

"Deal with what? What are you talking about? Who's gotten to you?" Rondeau felt a sinking sensation. Like Stokes had been compromised after all. But he needed someone in his corner.

All I've ever had was Millard. It was a crushing realization, a hard truth. His brother-in-law had been a son of a bitch to deal with over the years, a burden. Spouting his favorite operas about the deep state — maybe he'd been his only true confidant all along. Rondeau wanted to see him, to put his arms around him, tell him he was sorry. Sorry for all the times he'd dismissed him, for the times he wished Millard didn't even exist. He needed Stokes to find Millard. That was the priority now. Millard could back up everything up to the point of Rondeau's abduction.

There was commotion outside the vehicle. Stokes sat up straighter, leaning to look out. Another person ran in the direction of the quarry.

"I've got to go," Stokes said. "I think they're here." He opened the door to leave, paused, and turned to Rondeau. "We'll sort this out, boss, okay? We'll sort this out." Stokes lingered for a moment. "I won't let you down." Then he hopped down from the cab of the truck and took off.

Rondeau grabbed the door handle and prepared to exit. He glanced down at the blanket covering his naked body. "Shit," he said.

CHAPTER THIRTY-NINE / Homecoming

Rondeau watched them come up through the sparse saplings, over the wet grass. Cops and paramedics and volunteers circled the family. The air thundered as the med-flight helicopter touched down in a field near the parking area.

Rain pelted them. Most everyone had slipped on ponchos. The press surged against the barricade, camera lenses fixed on the approaching group, reporters barking questions at the troopers who spread their arms and warned them to stay back.

Rondeau found the brunette paramedic in the chaos outside the tent. "I've been looking for you," she said. She gave him a pile of folded clothes.

"Thank you."

Rondeau hurried, limping, to the back of the tent. Cafeteria-style tables loaded with medical supplies filled the space. A defibrillator sat ready for the pads to be attached, an array of field dressings, tourniquets, burn ointments, compression pads. Rondeau shimmied into the pants, wincing as the fabric pulled at the bandages on his legs. The canvas walls fluttered and snapped in the growing storm as he pulled on the sweatshirt, his joints flaring in pain. He slid on the tennis shoes.

You're in shock, Jessy said.

Yeah, maybe. Probably.

You're not thinking straight.

He left and watched as the Kemps arrived at last. The rescuers continued to swarm around the family. Rondeau counted eight cops, all state troopers except for Deputy King. No FBI. He moved towards them and someone stepped in front of him.

"Easy," said Agent McDonough. "We're going to do this by book. We're going to give the family any treatment they need, first, then we'll debrief." He took Rondeau by the arm.

"Please get out of my way," Rondeau said, glancing at McDonough's arm on his. He had questions which couldn't wait. King was with the rescuers, and Rondeau needed to know whether they'd found Millard down there.

"Stand down, Detective."

McDonough was expressionless. Only his eyes seemed alive. The rain drove at an angle, the helicopter blades split the air *whop whop whop whop*. Emergency lights flashed on the roofs of the trooper vehicles forming the media barricade, throwing colors against the dusky landscape.

"Where's my brother-in-law?" Rondeau asked.

McDonough watched the rescue party, just twenty yards away. People began to cheer them, to applaud and whistle. "I don't know who you're talking about."

Rondeau felt despair, then anger. He leaned close to McDonough, his voice a growl. "Anything happens to him, I'll hold you responsible."

McDonough slowly swiveled his head. His eyes were stony. "Exactly how could I be responsible for your mess?"

Rondeau was shaking as he said into McDonough's ear, "I know what this is."

"You're crazy. Do you understand that? I don't know how they put up with you. If it were up to me, you'd be long gone."

Rondeau's anger came to the boil. His hands formed fists. He'd beaten and clawed his way out. He'd gotten free only to find himself in another type of prison — made of lies and deceit. He moved his lips, his voice low, "I know what you are. Hurt my brother-in-law, and I'll kill you."

Some other agents had drawn closer. As McDonough stepped away, he pointed.

Two large federal agents seized Rondeau.

CHAPTER FORTY / Off the Deep End

Peter felt the elation of the rescue deflate, like air from a tire. He watched Rondeau and McDonough's argument with growing trepidation. He could see their angry faces, spit flying, but the words were lost to the thunder of the helicopter.

He stepped in front of the family, an instinctive reaction. The other rescuers did the same, forming a human shield, closing in around them.

Agent Eldridge bolted from the pack and closed the distance. He reached Rondeau, got in front of him and hollered in his face as agents dragged Rondeau backwards. Rondeau was bright red. His hands flailed in the air for a moment, then he slipped their grip.

He was fast for an older guy.

One of the agents jumped him, and Rondeau flipped the agent around in mid-air. Another stepped in, made a tentative grab, and Rondeau put him on the ground, too. Rondeau stepped towards Eldridge, who pulled his gun. Beyond it all, Peter saw members of the press, who'd broken loose, running towards the scene.

The agents surrounded Rondeau and took aim with Eldridge, ordering him to get to the ground. For a moment Rondeau just stood there, feet spread, hands ready, a murderous look in his eyes.

Finally, Rondeau got to his knees and put his hands on his head. Detective Stokes rushed in. He skidded on his heels over the wet ground and fell on his ass. He sprang right back up, looking frantic, pleading with Rondeau.

"Jesus," Hutchinson Kemp said, standing just behind Peter. "What's going on?"

"I don't know." Peter said. He watched the scene with the family. The cameramen flicked on their video lights, the reporters gaped. Everyone else looked mortified.

* * *

They slammed Rondeau into the back of an SUV, hands cuffed behind his back. He threw his head back against the seat. "Fuck!"

He bounced his head off the cushion a few more times. The flames were still there, licking the edges of his vision. His heart was pounding in his chest.

Calm down. You're going to have a heart attack.

The usual presence in his head. His dead sister, her endless commentary.

Still drugs in your system. Confusing you.

Rondeau shook it off. He leaned forward and peered out the windshield. This was ending badly. How had it gotten like this? He'd screwed up, royally. He should have kept his cool. He shouldn't even have gone off with Stokes alone. Stokes could have turned right around and spewed everything to McDonough. *He knows.* Hell, the fix was already in and they were spinning their lies. He'd escaped before they could pump him full of more drugs, or do something even worse.

It didn't matter what you knew, he thought. Didn't matter what you'd seen with your own eyes, or knew in your heart — they could fabricate stories out of whole cloth. Wasn't that how it had gone down in the District? Wasn't that the shit old Ninth Street pulled when they wanted to crucify someone? If they wanted you guilty, you were guilty.

Meanwhile, everyone else saw those "Special Agent" identifications and turned obsequious. They kowtowed to the so-called authority of the feds. By now, Sheriff Oesch would be subverted, along with Captain Bouchard of the state police, the lieutenants and sergeants — everyone would get in line. That was how it went. Whistleblowers walked a lonely, narrow road.

Stop feeling sorry for yourself. Start figuring out how to get yourself out of this.

Good advice. Rondeau consciously slowed his breathing. He watched the slippery silhouettes of men outside the car, heard the murmur of their voices, then tuned it all out. He needed to come up with a plan. If he kept acting crazy, the bonds were only going to cinch tighter.

The thought irritated the skin around his scars. He went to scratch, but the bracelets held tight. Panic stabbed through him. Fear, anger, helplessness.

Stop it. Think. First, start with the truth.

The truth? Who knew anymore? The truth was, there was no truth.

Start with what you know.

He'd done most of his growing up in the District. Even in those days he'd felt like an outsider. When people thought about Washington D.C., they thought of the politicians, the scandals, the architecture. But there was a city surrounding all of that with a high crime rate and plenty of poverty. That was where he'd cut his teeth as a detective, where he'd learned to survive, in the hidden places. He'd learned to see what others didn't. Or wouldn't.

Three days ago, Lily Kemp's hospital had called the police. He'd decided to start a missing person's investigation. He'd gone through all the proper channels. He'd assembled the right team. The search parties were deployed. He'd loaded Stokes with assignments. Short of detectives in his squad, he'd delegated to the deputies. He'd interviewed the next of kin.

All the man's filmmaking materials had been taken. Every scrap of data. Except for one sheaf of papers he'd found in Kemp's basement. Materials on EPA strictures for hazardous waste management. He'd passed the information on to Deputy King. But he'd wondered if it was a plant, something purposefully left behind for investigators to find.

Hutchinson Kemp was a filmmaker who'd set out to make environmental documentaries. But he'd wound up exposing people with a lot to hide. The kidnapping looked like Spillane or his connections' work.

Even the phone call could've been the modern mafia at work.

You have twenty-four hours.

But then there was the tip from Tamika Levitt. She'd seen Kemp's film crew in Indian Lake, where Addie lived part-time. She'd told Rondeau about the Indian Lake Project — a clandestine, black budget project testing experimental drugs on people. The fact that Addison Kemp had bought a seasonal home near the site, and that she had presented Rondeau with footage from Hutchinson Kemp's animal agriculture movie, spoke to her knowledge of something fishy.

It left a lot of questions, and gaps in the narrative of a do-gooder, leftist filmmaker whose family had been kidnapped by the mob for making a movie about waste disposal. The biggest hole in that story — big enough to drive a truck carrying hazardous waste right through — was that Kemp hadn't just got a bullet through the head.

Because Spillane suddenly wanted to turn himself into a federal witness? *Please*, Rondeau thought — Whitey Bulger had been hiding out for years before his capture.

Spillane never would have gone willingly — and he most certainly had friends in the Bureau. Once you were in, you stayed in. Rondeau didn't buy it.

Anyway you sliced it, this was about a major government cover-up. They'd called Rondeau, and him alone, because he'd gotten too close. When that didn't work, they'd kidnapped him, tortured him. Why? What was their next move?

CHAPTER FORTY-ONE / Loyalty

Peter smiled for the cameras but felt deflated after witnessing Detective Rondeau lose it, and with the unnerving encounter in the mine still preying on his mind. He saw Althea in the crowd. She was in the same bright yellow poncho as everyone else, but she was unmistakable to him.

She winked at him, seeming to say, *Yeah, you're a big hero now.*

He returned a sheepish grin. At least he didn't have to address the reporters. Agent Eldridge was doing that, giving them the soundbite summary they craved: "This was a comprehensive investigation involving the cooperation of multiple law enforcement organizations," Eldridge said. "We all owe a debt of gratitude to the Stock County Sheriff's Department and Sheriff Oesch, along with Captain Bouchard and the New York State Police."

Eldridge sounded in control, Peter thought, but seemed preoccupied. The lean, young agent's eyes kept darting to his colleague, Jackson, who Peter had ridden down with. Jackson looked terrible, even sicker than before.

231

The rain whipped Peter's face. He glanced at the Kemp family, lined up beside him. They didn't seem to mind it. It probably felt like bliss to them. Maggie Kemp still clung to her father. Peter saw she was sucking her thumb. The little boy was squawking, the mother rocking him gently. Medics hovered close, eager to check the children's vitals — were they hurt? Dehydrated? But no one dared to pry the family apart to have a better look just yet. Hutchinson Kemp appeared dazed, though the ordeal of the past week was more clearly expressed in his wife's face. Lily Kemp looked anguished. But they all seemed unharmed.

"We ask you now to give the family some room," Eldridge continued. "This is still an ongoing investigation. I understand the public's right to know, but I urge you to show every respect and kindness to this family, and to the process of the law."

Peter scanned the eager faces of the press. One rogue media team had rushed off toward the parking lot, where Rondeau had been taken. Two meaty-looking agents, eyes hidden behind sunglasses, were blocking them.

Peter turned his attention to a cluster of federal agents and glimpsed a familiar figure. The man who hadn't been introduced at the morning briefing was standing near the sickly Agent Jackson. Peter wondered again who he was.

Kemp stepped up beside Agent Eldridge. He whispered into Eldridge's ear. The media was hushed and expectant in the pouring rain. Peter stole another look at Lily. She didn't seem to like where this was going.

"Ladies and gentlemen of the press, Mr. Hutchinson Kemp, after all he and his family have been through, would like to say a few words. As far as the FBI and the rest of the cooperating law enforcement agencies are concerned, there will be a full statement provided tomorrow morning at the Stock County Public Safety Building, 8 a.m. Thank you."

Eldridge turned and smiled at Hutchinson Kemp. They shook hands. Kemp hefted his daughter up higher and stepped towards the shining lights.

"I just want to thank the police and all the volunteers," he said in a soft voice. The media squeezed closer, microphones thrust forward. "All the people who had to leave their own families to search for us. I just wanted to say, thank you, so much, for making our family as important as your own. You saved our lives."

The crowd broke into applause. Peter was surprised, even the reporters tucked their mics under their arms and clapped. Kemp smiled shyly, then rejoined his family. Photographers snapped pictures, cameras clicked and whirred. Kemp would be the next media sensation. Then the troopers moved in, forming a line. The family needed medical attention without further ado, and the investigation had to keep rolling. Reluctantly, the press dispersed and the Kemps were ushered to the tent.

As he passed by Peter King, Hutchinson Kemp reached out his hand. Peter met the man's eyes. "Thank you," Kemp said, and then he was taken away by the medical staff. Eldridge followed him into the tent and closed the canvas flap.

The rain turned to hail.

* * *

The hail hitting the SUV sounded like stones.

The door swung open and McDonough hopped in. He was drenched, his shoulders flecked with white chunks. "Jesus," he said. He glanced back at Rondeau. McDonough's face was flushed from exertion. Or anger.

A female fed Rondeau hadn't seen yet hopped in the passenger side. She spoke to someone before she closed the door.

"It's alright," the agent said. "I appreciate that. I understand. We'll see to it that he's taken care of." She yanked the door shut and ran fingers through her curly hair, shaking out the water.

"Hey, watch it." McDonough held a hand up to shield himself.

The female agent had been talking to the brunette paramedic. She stood there, looking in. Rondeau hated the sorrow he saw in the young woman's eyes, the pity.

"Alright," McDonough said. "You better behave back there, Detective, or I'll drag you out of this car and shoot you myself."

* * *

Althea hurried over to Peter, her arm covering her head. He grabbed her arm as they searched for cover.

"What now?" she asked, running beside him.

"I don't know. I don't know if I'm free, or if I'm waiting on orders, or what. Guess I'll have to see."

Eric Stokes waved at them. He ran over to Peter and Althea, gesturing. "Let's get in my car."

They jumped inside Stokes' jeep. Peter and Althea sat pressed together in the backseat. Althea had apparently ridden down to the quarry with Stokes — her bag was there.

"What a fucking day," Stokes said, igniting the engine. He turned around so he could face them.

"What've you got?" Peter asked. "Anything?"

Stokes nodded. "Yeah. While you were in there, we got a call from the Highway Department in Stock."

"Oh yeah?"

"Yeah. John Hayes. He wanted to talk to you, Pete, but you were in the quarry. So they forwarded it to me. He was reluctant at first, but he sounded desperate."

Peter leaned forward. "What did he say?"

"You know Hayes, right? You guys were in school together. Deep mistrust of government."

Peter remembered the conversation the night he'd picked Hayes up from Moh's. A rant about government tyranny and how small and helpless the people were.

"He says the FBI is all over him," Stokes said. "He's scared. And the boys who put up the fight at Carmelita's Restaurant? He says the feds got them."

"How does he know?"

"Terry Rafferty called him. Less than an hour after the shootout at Carmelita's. Threatened Hayes. Said they were coming for him, that he was a traitor, it was all his fault. Hayes left his place, hid out at the Highway Department garage. He was sure Rafferty knew where he was and was coming for him. But, they never did."

"Maybe they ran, instead."

"Maybe. Anyway, Hayes has wanted out, big time, for a while. Lot of the hazardous waste disposal was happening via these commercial trucking guys, he says. You know, either they're looking the other way, taking payment, or they had a more administrative role. But he was always suspicious, says the feds were lurking, that the feds knew what was happening." Stokes leaned closer, his eyes alight. "What did you see down there?"

Peter shrugged. "Not much. Mining equipment is long gone. Pretty empty. Smelled awful, though." He could still detect the odor lingering on his wet clothes. That stink of death.

"You didn't see any kind of aquifer? Another tunnel leading to some subterranean dump site?"

He shook his head. "But we left the FBI behind. If there's some underground toxic lake, I mean, they're gonna find it. Not something you can keep hidden."

"No . . ." Stokes said, thoughtful. He turned back around, leather seat squawking with his movement. He ran a hand back through his thinning hair. Then he pointed to the mess of parked vehicles ahead of them. "Rondeau's there."

"Which one? Black SUV?"

235

"Yep. No plates. Fed car."

They were silent for a moment. They watched as the SUV left the parking area. A few more seconds passed, and the air in the jeep became heavy.

"Why would the mob just let the family go?" Stokes wondered aloud.

"Spillane called them off," Peter answered, thinking of the briefing with Jackson and the other agents that morning. And how Hutch Kemp explained the way their captors had reacted to a phone call.

"Yeah, well, why were they kept alive in the first place? You got a guy who's going to expose you with his new movie, you just end him. Why all the rigmarole?"

The questions which had subsided in the excitement of finding the family now bubbled back to the surface of Peter's mind. This was ostensibly the mob, protecting their interests, kidnapping a man and his family because of his inquiry into waste shipping methods. But the mafia didn't ordinarily tell people they were going to be okay, then let them go. Instead, mob victims wound up at the bottom of a lake, or dismembered; gone for good, one way or another. Even if Spillane had been arrested and made a call to release the family — Stokes' question had merit — why had they been kept alive in the first place?

Peter watched the SUV as it climbed the hill away from the site. "Let's just follow them," he said suddenly. "See where they go."

"Peter." Althea took him by the arm. "Are you kidding?"

"Yeah," Stokes said. He put the car in drive, hesitated.

"Guys," Althea said. "Listen. This is . . . these are FBI. And Rondeau is . . . well, he's evidently distressed. We know he has problems, yeah? That's clear. So . . ."

Stokes nodded. "I understand. But he's my partner. If you need to go . . ."

Peter turned to Althea. He knew she was the one thinking straight — she always was. But he felt like this

236

was something he had to do. And maybe it was better, given all she'd already been through, for her to stay safe. "It's okay. Go."

She had her hand on the door latch. Then she let go and faced forward with a determined expression. She was staying.

They drove out of the parking lot. The SUV continued up the winding road out of Bluestone, through the sapling trees, and they followed.

CHAPTER FORTY-TWO / A Danger to Yourself and Others

"Where are you taking me?" Rondeau asked.

McDonough caught his gaze in the rear-view mirror. "We're just driving. Let's just drive, okay? Let's just talk."

"You want to talk? Charge me with something and you can talk to my lawyer."

McDonough exchanged a look with the other agent, who rolled her eyes. "A lawyer?" McDonough said. "You need a shrink, not a lawyer."

"Then take me to see one. I'll submit to a full evaluation. If they're not on your payroll, anyway. And first I'd like to see my blood work."

McDonough shook his head, mournfully. "See? Right there. That's what's gotten you into this kind of mess, I bet. Your paranoid delusions."

Rondeau opened his mouth to reply, to argue, but then shut it. This was what they wanted. They were trying to throw him, get him on the defensive. He could begin to see it now — the carefully manufactured expressions, the fake sympathy — they were going to say he wasn't simply mistaken, but that he had mental problems, and discount everything he'd witnessed.

He's a danger to himself and others.

It was the key phrase which allowed indefinite incarceration.

The agents drove in silence for a few moments. Since Rondeau hadn't taken the bait, McDonough kept fishing. "So you don't deny it, then? You're clear, at last? Isn't that what the scientologists call it, Agent Willette? 'Going clear?'"

"That's right." She nodded. "You ascend through these mystical levels, purging yourself of all your uncleanliness. Then you get to this top level — you're 'clear.' And they finally give you the secret documents about the origins of the world."

"Right, right," McDonough went along, amused. "That we come from an alien planet, right?"

"We come from another world. Did you know the whole Scientology thing was started by a writer?"

"You mean like a fiction writer?"

"L. Ron Hubbard. Guy came up with this whole science fiction story about aliens and super beings and all this. Then he turned around and sold it as a religion. And I mean *sold* it. Getting rich off of his stories. The American Dream, right?" She turned and looked at Rondeau. "You getting rich off your fantasies, Rondeau? Got a memoir in the hopper? Going to start a religion? Avoid paying taxes?"

He stayed silent. The car was probably bugged. They were doing this little act to get a confession out of him, to make him slip up and incriminate himself.

He remembered Dominic Whitehall. Whitehall had been a supervisory agent in the FBI crime lab. After he'd tried to blow the whistle on procedural errors and misconduct, he'd wound up alone, unemployed, living in the middle of nowhere. The Connie Leifson lookalike in the quarry had said it: *There are things worse than death.* Like a lifetime of disgrace. And so maybe that was it — Rondeau had already exiled himself, but it wasn't enough. He was causing a stir with the Kemp family disappearance, and now they were going to paint him as crazy.

McDonough kept on the back roads; by now, Rondeau calculated, they could have made the freeway and been on their way back north to Stock County, but they hadn't taken that route. They were going through a small town. The hail had subsided into a steady drizzle. Lacy yellow leaves twirled to the ground. Only the oaks held out, their bronze foliage rustling defiantly in the wind.

"Here," said Agent Willette. "Let me show you something."

She leaned down and rummaged through a bag at her feet. She produced an electronic gadget, a black box the size of a pack of cigarettes. She got two small speakers out of the bag and plugged them into the box. "This is nice," she said of the equipment. "I like these."

McDonough gave the gear a glance. "Oh yeah. Interceptors. Can't live without them."

They were enjoying this. Rondeau checked out the window again. They passed a gas station, a weathered barn converted into a mechanic's shop with a *New York State Inspection* sign hanging over the large doors. He wondered if anyone knew where he was.

Willette held up the device. "We've got three days of your phone calls on here, Detective. I understand you've lost your phone? Good thing you have us. We're like a message service. This one is my favorite." She pressed a button.

Rondeau heard the outgoing message from his cellular phone. *"This is Detective Rondeau. Please tell me who you are and what you need, and I'll get back to you right away."*

A beep emitted from the device, and then a caller's voice. An older man, someone Rondeau didn't recognize. The caller began tentatively: "Hello, ah, yes, Detective Rondeau. My name is Doctor Aaron Lang. I'm a colleague of Connie Leifson's."

Just hearing her name sent a spike through his chest. He tried to stay settled, but was afraid to hear what was coming next.

"First of all," said the tinny voice of Lang, "let met convey that I'm just in shock over Ms. Leifson's tragic accident. But I . . . I just wanted to reach out to you, right away. Please don't think of this as a solicitation . . . Connie and I regularly referred patients to one another. In the event something happens and a therapist is not able to attend to patients, there is a referral list."

Rondeau felt the anger really corkscrewing up through him now, despite his resolve to stay calm. Beneath the anger, though, something was cracking open. Rondeau felt hot around his neck and ears. And itchy. So itchy all over his chest.

"So," the kindly voice continued. "I want to offer my services to you. Connie, she . . . she spoke of you. In all professional discretion, of course. Not in any detail. Just in how she thought you were a good man. Unique. She . . . she strongly urged me, Detective, to get in touch with you if she was ever unable to continue providing you with services."

Rondeau stared at the device. He pulled his gaze away. Willette was stone-faced, watching him.

"Where's my brother-in-law?" Rondeau asked. But his words lacked conviction, or power. *You don't even know his last name.*

"As it appears Ms. Leifson will not be able to return to her practice for some time," Lang said on the message, "I hope you get in touch with me."

Willette continued to glare at Rondeau. The heat seemed to drain from him. Despite the blasting vents in the SUV, he was cold. Empty. The bugs on his skin writhing, driving him crazy.

As Aaron Lang left his phone number, a grim smile spread across Agent Willette's homely face. She clicked off the player when the message ended.

"You don't have a brother-in-law," she said. "He's a figment of your imagination." She pointed at her head with her free hand. "You, Detective Rondeau, are what we call in the Bureau 'pants-shitting crazy.'"

Rondeau let out a long breath. His lips pursed, he then continued to breathe deeply, in and out, through his nose. He thought maybe he was hyperventilating as he started to see stars in the air, dancing around Willette's head.

"So you paid someone," he panted. "To call me and deliver that message."

She frowned. "Nice try."

"Why don't you play the call you placed, telling me to shut down the investigation?"

"Oh? The one we traced to New York City? The one that led us to several of Spillane's conspirators? I got to tell you, Detective, I mean, I really got to hand it to you. So does the Kemp family, really. Don't you think, Agent McDonough?"

"Oh yeah," he said. "For sure."

"They are alive right now because of you. Once we got the call, we opened the book on your checkered past — all that fun you had in the District, blaming the Bureau for whatever you could come up with in your delusional brain. We're tapped into you now."

"Tapped, yeah. You stuck me with hydrochloride," Rondeau said. He felt far away. "You dosed me with 25-I . . ."

The agents looked at each another. Then Willette silently packed away the electronic gear. Rondeau felt a tiny thrill of victory in their silence, just enough to cut through the panic that had been building. They'd actually had him going there for a minute. Almost believing he had some sort of split personality, or an imaginary friend, for God's sake.

"I understand it's hard for you," Willette said, facing forward. "Schizoaffective disorder — I think that's the

242

official title. Sounds like your therapist, Leifson, was not really able to get a handle on it. Didn't it, Agent McDonough?"

"Too much for her," McDonough agreed.

"Sounded like she was considering turning you over to a real shrink, get you medded-up. And then, she did. Maybe not the way she would have hoped, not the best circumstances for her — terrible what happened — but at least you're going to get the care you need, right? And perhaps a more experienced professional will get the diagnosis right. Frankly, I think you're full-blown schizophrenic. Either way, you're a danger to yourself, Rondeau, and you're a danger to others."

CHAPTER FORTY-THREE / Intervention

"Where are they going?" Peter gabbed the back of the passenger seat, peering out.

He caught a glimpse of the fed car as it crested a hill in the gathering twilight. Were they speeding up? He checked the speedometer: sixty-five miles per hour. Not exactly breakneck speed, but along these country backroads, he felt like Stokes was having trouble keeping the pace.

"I don't know." Stokes had a GPS monitor on the dashboard. He used the touch screen to spread out the map, show more of the surrounding area, with a hundred mile radius. The feds were headed west. The interstate was a ways behind, and there were no other major routes out here. *Indian Lake*, Peter thought, then pushed the idea aside.

Stokes phone chimed with an incoming call. He snatched up the phone and answered. "Stokes here." He listened, then said, "Let me put you on speaker."

He tapped the screen a couple times. Althea and Peter listened in.

"Okay," Stokes said, speaking loudly for the microphone. "Detective Gates, you there?"

"Yes."

"I've got Deputies King and Bruin with me, Stock County Sheriff's. Can you repeat to them what you told me earlier today? I relayed it to Deputy King already, but let's refresh."

"Sure. Hi guys."

"Hello," Peter and Althea chorused. Peter sensed Althea tensing beside him.

"I got put on the TC in Essex," Gates said, referring to the vehicle collision. "Vic is Connie Leifson. The kid who was driving, was released, then taken into federal custody."

"Federal? Why?"

"That's just it, I don't know. We did total crash reconstruction. We downloaded the vehicle data. It looks like an accident. But your Detective Rondeau had asked me to keep him in the loop on the case. He seemed to think that there could be some connection between the TC and the missing family."

"And?" Stokes asked. "What did you find?"

"The feds are all over it. I've been bumped."

Peter eyed the black SUV in the distance. It slipped around a bend in the road and went momentarily out of sight. He spoke up. "They took you completely off the case?"

"Yep. Sent me off with my hat in my hand."

"What did you have up until that point?"

"Well I was looking into the victim, see who her clients were. Thinking maybe if this *wasn't* an accident, it could be some sort of payback; someone who hates their therapist, that sort of thing. But that's all protected under confidentiality, even post-mortem."

"And that's why the feds broke into it?" Peter questioned. "Supersede that confidentiality?"

"I don't know. Maybe."

"Okay," Peter said. "What else, Detective?"

"What else? They're all over that hospital. There's something going on there, I don't know what. But it's beyond the accident. Something else that's got everyone in a twist."

The sickly Agent Jackson came to Peter's mind. Everyone was quiet for a moment. Then Gates's voice came through again. "So where's Rondeau now? I've been trying him all morning. That's why I called you, Stokes."

"When was the last time you spoke with Detective Rondeau?" Stokes asked.

"Yesterday at the hospital. We talked about the TC, and I told him about the Indian Lake call."

"You spoke to the caller originally. What was the nature of her tip?"

"Her, ah, *tip*, was that the whole thing — the family disappearance — was related to top secret drug testing."

Stokes and the deputies exchanged looks. Peter had more questions, but Stokes quickly wrapped it up. "Thank you, Detective."

"Okay . . . Not a problem."

Stokes ended the call. The FBI vehicle was getting too far ahead. Stokes pushed the Subaru to seventy.

"I don't know how much more I wanted to discuss over the phone," Stokes said.

Althea frowned, incredulous. "Are you serious?"

"Look," Stokes said. "I've been working with Rondeau for two years. If he followed this call to Indian Lake, he had good reason. For one, Addison Kemp has a house there. But, then there's this other thing . . ."

Peter looked at the GPS monitor. He stretched so he could point close to the screen. "Indian Lake is right there."

Stokes looked ahead at the empty road. The feds had accelerated out of sight. "Maybe that's where they're going. And — I think they've made our tail."

"Okay," Althea said. Peter could sense she was very uncomfortable. She sat back and waved her hands in the air. "This is out of control. We're actually considering that this has something to do with — what?"

Stokes kept up the speed, hurtling past the trees. "I watched *Citizen Farmer*," Stokes said. "Twice. Beyond the claims that the meat industry is responsible for vast amount of pollution and global warming is the idea that we're surrounded by these deadly animal-borne pathogens all the time, and it's this unseen wall of antibiotics keeping it at bay. Only we're running out of antibiotics that are effective."

"I'm not a conspiracy theorist," Althea said.

"Neither am I. But I'll tell you what. Dismissing all conspiracy theories as crazy is just as intellectually lazy as accepting every wild allegation at face value. So, just ask yourself — what if the government is testing a new drug to combat some new illness? A really bad one? If untreatable, we're talking bubonic plague. You noticed how many people are sick lately?"

"Oh my God," Althea said, rolling her eyes. She turned to Peter, incredulous. "Pete . . ."

"I know," he said. "I know . . ."

She looked at the river. She sighed. "So we're — what? Making leaps that the FBI are covering up this impending crisis, and people are being experimented on in some underground *lab*?"

"Maybe not underground at all. Indian Lake might be a base of operations, or it could be a big red herring for conspiracy types while the real testing is happening in the field."

"That's crazy."

"It goes on in Third World countries; it goes on all the time. Clinical trials right out in the open with human guinea pigs."

"That's different! Those people are aware of the risk. They're desperate. They have no choice."

Stokes brought the Subaru to a stop at the T-junction. There were no other cars around. He put an arm up on the back of his seat and faced the deputies. "Could be hospitals, could be flu shots. Hell, the drugs could be distributed using this trucking system, but the feds have seized all of that, closed it down on us so we can't find anything. Look, all I'm saying is we have an obligation here . . ."

"We're cops," Althea said, getting in Stokes' face. Peter pulled at her shoulders, but she shrugged him off. "We're not journalists, and we're not DCI, Eric." She meant the Department of Criminal Investigation, which looked into crimes relating to misconduct in office.

"He's one of ours," Stokes said.

Althea shook her head violently. "Maybe. But this isn't right. I'm getting out."

Peter reached for her and tried to stop her. She batted his hand away and glared at him. "You? What do you think? You think we just risked our lives to take Spillane down when — what? He's a patsy?" She grabbed the door handle. The jeep idled at the stop sign.

They heard the approach of another vehicle. The fed's SUV was coming back, roaring down the crossroad toward them.

The SUV screeched to a halt, blocking the intersection. A single red light was flashing behind the windshield. The front doors opened and two male agents in black suits stepped out.

Peter watched them approach, then held his hands up in full view. Althea remained next to the door, but let go of the handle. The agents separated, coming up on the sides of the Subaru.

One of the agents knocked on the glass by Stokes. He rolled down the window, keeping his other hand up. Peter looked at the SUV, but the windows were tinted. He couldn't see if anyone else was inside. His fingers brushed the grip of his sidearm.

"Hello," Stokes said. "How we doing?"

"You need to turn around," the agent said.

"Turn around?" Stokes nodded toward the SUV. "Who you got in the vehicle?"

Peter could see Stokes was shaking. He turned his attention back to the dark vehicle — the rear doors opened, and two more agents hopped out. With that many agents in the car, he doubted Rondeau was even aboard. This was a decoy vehicle; since the parking lot, they'd been chasing the wrong car.

"Step out of the vehicle," said the agent beside Stokes.

"Let me see your credentials," Stokes said.

"Get *out*," the agent barked, and pulled the door open.

Shit, Peter thought. *Shit shit shit shit*. Stokes did as he was told, and left the Jeep. The other agents reached the car and opened the rear doors, going after Peter and Althea.

They were done.

WEDNESDAY

CHAPTER FORTY-FOUR / A Place to Put the Pain

"Unbelievable," said Sheriff Oesch. He looked like a pissed-off parent. He strode back and forth in front of the three of them in his office at the Public Safety building. "Un-frigging-believable." Oesch was a firm Christian, and didn't curse. Instead he used phrases like *frigging* and *darn it all.* He hardly ever lost his temper. Some people thought he was a pushover and that he lacked the confidence of the former sheriff. But not today. Today, Oesch looked ready to spit fire.

"You three," he said, stabbing a finger at them. "You're done. You've humiliated this department. You've humiliated yourselves."

He directed his ire at Stokes. "Two months suspension, no pay," Oesch said. Then he focused on the deputies and he softened just a little. "Guys, I mean . . ." He dropped his arms, defeated. Finally, Oesch singled out Althea. "What were you thinking?"

It was a rhetorical question. She hadn't slept a wink the night before. Peter knew because his night hadn't been much better. After the feds delivered them home, they'd showered, gotten into bed, and not said a word. She'd slept with her back facing him. By the time the first dawn light painted the sky, the anger retreated, and all that remained was to face the music.

Oesch glowered at Stokes. "Do you even know? Do you even know what you were thinking? Let me summarize for you, because after spending the night talking with the Federal frigging Bureau of Investigation, I have a pretty good idea. You were thinking that little green men were behind this whole thing, am I right? Stokes?"

Stokes looked at the floor, humiliated, shrinking in his seat.

"Because—" Oesch went on.

Peter interrupted. "Alright," he said. He held up his hands.

Oesch snapped a look at him. "King? Got something to say? Your father is a district court *judge* for God's sake. You're hoping to make detective. You ought to know better."

"Just . . . you know. Can you go easy? We're all a part of this."

Oesch shook his head. "I'm not. I'm not part of this."

"You have to admit, it was pretty sensational the way they took Rondeau out of there. They made a huge fuss. What were we supposed to think?"

"What were you supposed to *think*? He assaulted federal agents. They got him out of there, they had security riding tandem; they had every right!"

"Why was he there? Where was his truck?"

"They found his truck, Peter. Half a mile away. They also found his suit jacket in the quarry. And in the pocket, a reference to something called 'Zedekiah's Cave.'"

Peter opened his mouth but Oesch put up a hand to silence him and finished. "He got it from Kemp's basement, didn't log it out; they figure he made the connection to local quarries and that's why he went to

Bluestone — 'Zedekiah's Cave' is what some locals call the mines. I checked – there's a Zedekiah's Cave in Jerusalem. Kemp traveled around there. So who knows what Rondeau was putting together in his brain."

Peter watched him. "Where's Detective Rondeau now?"

The question seemed to change Oesch's mood. He sat down with a sigh. He ran a hand over his face then propped his elbows on the desk. "Detective Rondeau . . ." he began. "You know, when I took this job, I wanted to build up this department. Rondeau had a phenomenal clearance rate. He was seasoned. I knew about the controversy in his past, but I had no idea he was mentally unstable." Oesch singled out Stokes. "I asked you to keep an eye on him, Eric."

Peter was confused. He spoke up. "What? Why?" It seemed Oesch and Stokes had a secret between them; Peter wanted in. He already had his ideas about Rondeau but this seemed like a whole new level. "Mentally unstable?"

"Rondeau was seeing a professional," Oesch said in a small voice.

"How do know? He told you?"

"I have it on good authority."

Peter figured he meant the feds. They'd hijacked the Connie Leifson accident from the state police. They were all over it, Gates had said. Gates had her own curiosity about who Leifson's clients might be, someone with an axe to grind, maybe. But that was privileged information. The feds had pried into it, and then disclosed it to the sheriff.

"Do you know where he is?" Peter asked.

"That's out of my realm, Peter. The FBI has ensured me he's receiving the best care. But the fact is, Rondeau went completely off the rails — he had vital information which he didn't share with us. Because he's paranoid, apparently. Delusional. Maybe worse. They think he's schizophrenic."

"Schizophrenic?"

Oesch looked like he'd swallowed a bug. His mouth worked as he tried to find the words. At last, he came up with something. "Rondeau believes people exist who don't. Like his supposed brother-in-law. Someone he calls 'Millard.' And there is no Millard. That is a fact. Millard is Rondeau's imaginary friend."

As this sank in, Oesch went on, slowly now, as if he'd let something out of his system which had been hurting. "Meanwhile, Spillane is in full witness protection and I understand that the FBI is working with the EPA on it. They're racking up the charges — racketeering, environmental violations — this thing spreads all the way down the coast. All the way to Miami. And we cracked it open. We were on the verge of looking like one of the most efficient, brightest bastions of sheriff's offices in the country. Then the three of you take off, chasing down the FBI." He shook his head again and placed his forehead in his hands.

"You really care about all of that, Sheriff?"

His head jerked up. "*Care* about it? Get out of my sight." He pointed at the door. "All of you."

They gathered their things and left.

* * *

Peter sat thinking in the deputies' shared office. It was a depressing, barren room with four desks, a water cooler, coffee station, and four rusty file cabinets. He got up from the desk and walked out. He headed down the hall, passing by the adjoining locker room. Althea was there. Peter stopped in the doorway.

She sat on one of the benches, bent forward, like a player after the game. Like him, she was in civilian clothes. No uniform today. Neither of them wanted to go home.

Althea stared at the floor.

"Hey," Peter said.

She responded, eyes down. "Hey."

He thought she would forgive him one day. Whatever his culpability — whatever *she* considered his part in this debacle, she would forgive him eventually. She had to. He didn't think he could go on if she didn't.

Just give her time, give her some space. It was a hard thing to do. He felt angry, for one — he wanted to defend himself against what she was thinking. Stick up for himself and for Rondeau, too. But he was confused about it all. Maybe Althea wasn't the only one who needed some space, some time. Peter moved on.

Rondeau's office was down the hall to the left. The door was shut. Peter halted when a vague shape moved on the other side of the opaque glass. He heard movement.

The room was unlocked.

Britney Silas was the head of the Criminal Science Investigation unit. She started, surprised by his entrance. She was going through Rondeau's drawers, wearing plastic gloves.

"Deputy King," she said, standing upright. She used the back of her hand to push strands of hair off her forehead. It was hot — it was always too hot in the damn building. Peter thought Oesch could slash the budget in half if he'd just dial down the heat.

"Hi Brit," he said.

Silas glanced around, as if seeing things through his eyes, understanding how it looked. "They've got me hunting for anything left pertaining to the Kemp case."

He knew who she meant by "they." The office looked completely different. There was only a little paperwork left, a few magazines, and personal effects. The feds had made a major dent. Peter imagined two or three of them in the tight space all last night, picking it all over. Maybe they were afraid they'd missed something, and that's why Silas was finishing the clean-up.

He nodded that he understood. Yet he remained just inside the room, and she seemed reluctant to continue with him standing there. "You looking for just chain of evidence stuff?" he asked.

"Whatever notes Rondeau had, whatever was logged when it was removed from the Kemp house."

"That's it?"

She put her hands on her hips and raised an eyebrow. Peter knew Silas was a good CSI.

"What do you mean, 'that's it?'" she asked.

"I'm just wondering if they told you to collect anything else."

"Such as?"

Peter dropped his shoulders and leaned against the doorway. He didn't like this. It felt like the presence of the FBI had turned everyone against each other. "Listen, we're on the same team here. You know?"

She stayed rigid for a moment, but then seemed to soften a little. She looked down at Rondeau's desk, cleared of its usual clutter.

"I just . . ." Peter began. "Maybe Rondeau needs help."

Silas cocked her eyebrow again. "You mean mental help?"

"I mean *my* help." Peter leaned his head back and peeked into the hallway. They were alone. "Our help," he said.

She spoke in a low voice. "Look, I'll say this. They also asked me to collect anything he'd been keeping related to this controversy in D.C.: the Valentine Killer."

"Tell me." He took a step forward.

Her eyes flashed, but she stayed cool. "I can't. This is my job, Deputy."

"If Rondeau is crazy, why do they care?" Peter let the question hang for a moment. "Unless they're afraid of what he knew."

He came right up to her. His heart was pounding, like he was back in the quarry. *Zedekiah's Cave.* Silas straightened her spine and gazed directly at him.

He saw fear in her eyes. She was afraid of what she'd found. Maybe they hadn't meant for her to, but Silas was good. Sifting through the tiniest details, seeing the patterns, that was her strength.

Peter had never seen her like this. He leaned close, their heads almost touching. "Just tell me one thing, will you? Who is the lead investigator for the FBI on the Kemp case?"

Silas had her jaw clenched and her forehead was beaded with perspiration. She exhaled. "There's McDonough, Jackson, Eldridge, Willette — there's an army of them. But Lee Angstrom has been calling the shots. That's all I'm saying to you."

Peter recalled the man in the charcoal grey suit and sunglasses. Never introduced, never spoke, was there and then gone. He'd seen him one other time, at Bluestone, standing in a group of federal agents. He wondered if it was Angstrom.

If so, the D.C. fed was a long way from home.

Silas put her hand on his. The clock on the wall ticked off the seconds. They locked eyes one last time. "Peter," she said. "I'm going to need you to leave now, okay?"

"Thank you," he said. He left the room.

CHAPTER FORTY-FIVE / Reunion

Peter wanted a beer, but steered clear of the bars. He stopped by the grocery store and picked up a six-pack of cheap domestic. Althea was still gone, running some errands. The two of them were barely speaking, just short practical conversations. They hadn't made love in days. They were both on temporary leave. They'd be showing up to work only to be interviewed by Internal Affairs.

Meanwhile, the media had been making hay. For days it had been round-the-clock coverage of the family's emotional homecoming. Nick Spillane being paraded from the state trooper barracks into a waiting dark SUV played on an endless loop. Mugshots of the Rafferty brothers, Tony Spillane, John Hayes. It was a major coup for the federal government. Hutchinson Kemp was considered something of a hero, if an inadvertent one, leading the authorities to this huge crime syndicate bust.

Nothing about an illness affecting people in record numbers, though Peter had seen more sick people every day. He was washing his hands constantly, steering clear of public spaces.

He sat on the couch in the small house he shared with Althea, reluctant to turn on the television and see more of the same. Something didn't add up.

He gazed around the room. He and Althea had only been living together for a few months, but there were signs of her feminine touch all over the place. From the hanging pictures to the plants, the throw rugs and the cozy couch blankets, Althea had made it their home. He didn't want to lose her. He didn't want to lose what they were building together. But for the past few days, the woman he wanted to spend the rest of his life with had felt like a stranger.

When the key hit the door and Althea came in, he'd still been lost in thought. He stood up from the couch. An apology he'd been rehearsing all the week was on his lips. Althea hurried in, the outdoor air trailing behind her. She hastily set down some bags and started looking for something.

"What's going on?"

"Where's the TV remote?"

He helped search for it. She found it mashed between the couch cushions and flicked on the flatscreen. She seemed excited not upset. "Watch," she said, before he could ask her again what was bothering her.

She turned to one of the cable news channels. Hutchinson Kemp was being interviewed:

"Journalistic responsibility falls on documentary filmmakers. But as a filmmaker, there's a degree of manipulation involved. You want to tell a compelling story. You're trying to sell a product, hope it works in the marketplace, gets people excited. It's hard to completely divorce yourself from that, especially if there is a sensational or controversial issue to capitalize on." Kemp looked remorseful. "I guess with *Citizen Farmer*, we got a little carried away."

Peter was aghast. A week after he's rescued, Hutch Kemp is talking to the media about journalistic responsibility? A commercial came on, and Peter turned to Althea.

"I just found out this was on," she said. She stared at Peter, her face still glazed from the cold. He wanted to kiss her, to make her warm. "It's weird, right?"

He nodded, momentarily speechless. He'd had his apology prepared for her. He knew he'd been fixating about Rondeau, about the whole thing, when he'd been neglecting her, their relationship. But it seemed like she'd been thinking about it, too.

"It's . . ." she began, and then shook her head. He nodded for her to continue. "It's like, I don't know, it's a bit weird that he's recanting that documentary. Related to the farming, and all of that . . ."

The program came back on. The silver-haired interviewer — Peter thought his name was Cooper something — addressed the camera.

"Hutchinson Kemp, along with his family, was captive for six days. His work-in-progress, *Nothing Disappears*, focuses on the treatment of waste disposal in modern society. Investigators believe that during the process of making the film, Kemp stumbled across an element of organized crime. He was then kidnapped, along with his family. In the days since his astonishing rescue by law enforcement, the public outcry has been a bit surprising — many people on social media sites, such as Reddit and Twitter, are saying that Kemp's *previous* film, the documentary *Citizen Farmer* is really what got him into the hot water. Kemp states that the film was 'exaggerated' and that allegations of a conspiracy between the government and the meat industry are unfounded."

The shot switched to Hutchinson Kemp, sitting in an elegant chair in what looked like a den. Peter wondered if it was at the man's home, but he didn't think so. He studied Kemp's face. Was he ashamed or contrite?

It switched back to the interviewer. "So, you have one film that seems to be spot on, where you really did uncover something tucked away. But you're saying that *Citizen Farmer* was not that film."

Back to Kemp. He didn't hesitate or search for the words, they seemed to come easily to him. Rehearsed, like Peter's apology. "That's right. I think I was trying to get there, trying to have that breakthrough film. And *Citizen* was that for me, but I had to push it to get there."

The interviewer nodded. "Typically, though, the public disdains a dolled-up story, or any embellishments to factual reports. I'm thinking of James Frey's memoir *A Million Little Pieces* or, Stephen Glass and his fabrications while working at the *New Republic* . . ."

"That doesn't matter to me. I regret what I've done, but what matters is the lesson I've learned. That we all want the truth — in this day and age, we're so divisive about so many things, and we have this confirmation bias. People agreeing with us, that's one thing. People *disagreeing* with us, we may say anything to prove that we're right. Even lie. But it's not—"

Peter clicked off the TV. He'd taken the remote from Althea. Now he looked at her, still standing there in her Sheriff's Department winter coat.

"I'm sorry," he said.

She took hold of his arms. "Me too." She let go and slipped an arm into her coat. "I found something," she said, still staring at him.

He glanced down at the paper she was holding. "Running errands?"

She smiled back. "Yeah. While I was running errands."

He unfolded the document. It was a printout of a news article from the *Washington Post*. The article was titled "Ricochet Rondeau." He checked the date — from just over two years ago. He read it aloud.

"'Dominic Whitehall is a whistleblower. After twelve years working as a crime lab supervisor for the FBI in Washington, this past week he alleged that the FBI has been falsifying evidence in a number of cases, including the Valentine Killer.'"

He looked up at Althea. "Keep reading," she urged.

"'Whitehall claims the FBI manufactured evidence on the Valentine Killer and targeted a schizophrenic suspect. Detective Jason Millard Rondeau, a District Police liaison, thought something was amiss before they even arrested and charged the suspect. Rondeau, hospitalized from injuries sustained during the Valentine Killer capture, was unwilling to comment.'"

He paused again. "'Millard,'" he said. "'Jason Millard Rondeau.'"

"Yeah." Althea pulled off her coat and pointed to her chest and shoulder. "Get this. I talked to Stokes. Rondeau has two scars. Here, and here. He was shot during the course of investigation."

"By?"

"FBI. One of the grunts. But, Rondeau took it personally. Thought Angstrom ordered the agent to do it on purpose. To kill him."

"No shit."

"No shit. And, one other thing I learned from Stokes . . ."

"Boy, you've been busy." Peter's eyes swept the room, landing on the finished beer bottles. "And I've just been boozing."

"Look at the byline. The reporter who wrote the article."

There was no picture, just a name. *A. Matheson.* It was vaguely familiar. Part of the Kemp investigation, in the paperwork somewhere. "Who's that?" he asked, looking up at Althea.

She'd lost the smile, her face was serious. "What Stokes told me, what we know, is that Addison Kemp's married name was Matheson."

CHAPTER FORTY-SIX / Surveillance

Peter sat with the engine running, watching the Kemp home.

The lights were on. He could see shadows cast on the curtains. There had been no curtains before the kidnapping.

He'd logged six hours so far over the past two days. He would move off for a while and then come back. He imagined the criminals who'd kidnapped the Kemps sitting out here like this when the windows had been clear. Watching. Waiting. He thought of Rondeau, too. Rondeau coming to the empty dark house. He took a sip of his paper cup of coffee, his hand shaking a little.

He wasn't the only one parked outside; there was a news van across the street. Channel 8. They were likely reviewing footage or preparing the next headline. If they knew he was there, they didn't show it. Earlier in the day there would have been more press around. But it was dark and late.

More importantly, Addison Kemp's car was parked in the driveway. After falling off the radar for two weeks, she'd resurfaced. She was wanted by the department for questioning. At least, they wanted an account of her whereabouts during the climactic moments of her brother's release. She wasn't listed with Incident Command, so she hadn't been a searcher, out hunting in the woods for the family. Stokes claimed Rondeau had scheduled a polygraph for Addison. It was more likely she'd been evading that, and doing who knew what else. For now, they were letting her spend time with the family. They were leaving her alone, Peter had learned, but would talk to her tomorrow. Tonight was his last chance.

She finally came out of the house after he'd lingered there for two hours. He watched her scan the driveway and the road, making the van, and probably him, too. He saw how she hesitated, deliberating over whether to return indoors. She got in her car and the taillights lit up, exhaust smoked out of the tailpipe. She backed down the driveway, hit the gas and drove off down the road, and Peter followed. He detected movement in the news van as he passed.

He followed Addison through the sleepy town to the outskirts, where she pulled into the motel. She got out and stood there as he pulled slowly up alongside her and rolled down the window.

"Why are you following me?"

"Good evening, Ms. Kemp. I'm Deputy Peter King, with Stock C—"

"I know who you are. Why are you following me?"

Peter put the car in park and left the motor on. "Just wanted to have a few words with you, ma'am." He set his hands on the steering wheel and added, "This would just be between us."

She seemed to consider this. Something about her was off — he could tell right away. But she agreed. "Okay. Do you want to come inside?"

"You're staying here? Why not with your brother?"

"I'm just being considerate. And I like my own bathroom."

"Why don't you get in?"

She glanced around first. There were only a couple of cars in the motel parking lot. The main office light was on. "You can trust me," he said.

"It's not you I'm worried about."

He followed her gaze to the news van coming slowly down the road. Only now he wasn't so sure it was a news van. Come to think of it, there was no local channel 8 nearby.

Addison hurried around and got in. She was wearing ripped jeans and a fur-lined coat. Her cheeks and nose were red from the cold. She placed her hands over the heating vents.

"Sorry to sneak up on you like that," he said. He continued to eye the van in his mirrors.

"How can I help you, Deputy?"

"Peter."

"Okay, Peter. I went to see Detective Rondeau," she offered. "They told me he's no longer on the case, is that true?" She seemed to be playing a role.

"No, I'm sorry. He's on medical leave."

She looked concerned. "Oh no. Something happen?"

He relaxed and found himself smiling. "Ms. Kemp . . ."

"Addie is fine."

"Can we cut through the bullshit?"

"I don't know what you mean."

He checked for the van again. Still there. She wasn't going to say anything under these conditions. She thought she was being watched. "Alright." he said. He dropped the car into reverse gear and backed up, swung around, and took off.

The van stayed put. Whoever it was, knew they'd been discovered. They'd either given up or they were calling in reinforcements. He had to be fast.

"What do you know about Detective Rondeau? What do you know about what happened to your brother — beyond the story about Nick Spillane and the mafia?"

"You realize, implicit in your question is that my brother is lying about what happened to him."

"I was thinking more along the lines of your brother and his family being abducted by strangers they barely saw, or came to know. That they, along with everyone else, are sticking by the story provided by law enforcement. Namely the FBI."

He could feel her eyes on him while he drove and spared her a quick glance. Maybe he was imagining things, but it looked like in that moment a mask fell away from Addison Kemp.

CHAPTER FORTY-SEVEN / The Truth

They drove out of town until they came to the long driveway that cut away from the main route. Peter's truck bumped over the uneven road, bisecting fields of brown grass long gone to seed. Rondeau's house was in front of them. A rambling, old farmhouse with a pillared porch and a large yard littered with junk.

"He lives like a hermit," Addison said. "Don't you think?"

Peter kept checking behind them. So far, no one was on their tail. He parked and they got out of the vehicle. He glanced at the dark sky. Who knew what could be circling overhead? They climbed the porch and found the front door unlocked.

"We're trespassing," she said.

"Yeah."

The place was barely warmer than the outdoors. Their footfalls echoed in the empty house. Everything needed a coat of paint. Or a wrecking ball, maybe. In the dining room, the large antique table had a few scattered sheets on it. More papers were on the ground. A cabinet behind the table hung open, its contents all over the floor. The house had been ransacked.

"They took everything," Addie said, standing by the dining table.

Peter picked up a piece of paper. It was a menu for a local restaurant. He grabbed up a few others, finding nothing relevant. "Tell me who you are," he asked. He suddenly felt naked in his civilian clothes — jeans, logger boots, wool sweater, and no gun. No authority to be here in a man's home, treading on a federal investigation. The only thing that reassured him was that Althea agreed with him — they needed to get to the bottom of this.

Instead of responding directly to his question, Addie walked out of the room. "Come look at this," she called.

In the hallway, she pointed to a crooked picture on the wall, one of the few things that remained. Peter leaned in for a look. He took his sleeve and wiped away some of the dust.

There was Rondeau, years younger, standing on a bridge. Peter thought the skyline in the distance could be D.C., the river maybe the Potomac. Beside Rondeau was a pretty woman he didn't recognize. They had their arms around each other. They looked happy, like newlyweds.

"I'm a reporter," Addison said beside him.

Staring at the photo, Peter said, "We checked. You own a cleaning business."

"I set up an LLC a few years ago. Sometimes it helps to be undercover." Addison must've known what Peter was thinking. "I've had my eye on Rondeau since the Valentine Killer case, since Dominic Whitehall blew the whistle."

She went back into the kitchen, looking around. She sat down and placed her bag on the table. "Now look at this." She produced a binder filled with newspaper clippings. She leafed through until she stabbed one clipping with her finger. Peter's eyes fell to an image accompanying the article.

Detective Rondeau was shaking hands with another man. Peter recognized who it was without a doubt — the unidentified man from the meeting prior to Bluestone, and then at the quarry itself, conferring with other agents. The caption identified him as Lee Angstrom.

Rondeau's arm was in a sling. The two men stood with the FBI emblem hanging behind them. Angstrom was smiling, Rondeau was not. The caption read: *FBI hands out award of merit to Detective Jason Rondeau.*

Peter scanned the article. *Supplemental police work turned into something instrumental for the Bureau . . . Detective Rondeau suffered from gunshot ricochets during the climactic showdown with the Valentine suspect . . . FBI congratulates Rondeau for his service, above and beyond . . . Rondeau, whose father was killed in the 9/11 Pentagon attack, said 'I'm honored to accept this award.'*

He didn't look honored.

"I saw another one of your articles the other day," Peter said. "*Richochet Rondeau*. You lied to the police. You've obstructed an investigation. That's a major criminal offense."

She looked unconcerned. Her silence seemed to invite more from him.

"So you've been following up on this story," he said. "On FBI corruption. On Whitehall, on Rondeau. So is it all fake? The idea that he has . . . ?"

"Mental illness? I don't think it's fake, but I think 'schizophrenic' is a long shot. Most schizophrenics can't hold down jobs, let alone be a police detective. Schizoaffective is maybe a bit more likely. Better still, delusional personality disorder. Given his upbringing, his father's work — and death — and what happened in D.C. with the crime lab corruption, the Valentine case, I think he had to find a place to put all of that."

Peter circled around in the trashed kitchen. "How? How do we know? Tell me what you've got. Okay?"

She sat serenely at the table while he paced anxiously.

"Rondeau was married to Jessica Rivlin. That's the woman in the photo in the hallway, standing on the bridge. She was pregnant, but the baby didn't make it to term. Rivlin — he called her 'Jessy' — had cancer, and she died shortly after. You can imagine, I guess, what that could do to a person. First, Rondeau's father dies in the September 11 attacks, while investigating major securities fraud. Then he's got this case in D.C. What he saw, and what Whitehall, a forensic scientist, knew about crime lab corruption. But Whitehall got scared and disappeared. Rondeau felt helpless. I think all of these things could've sparked some mental condition. When his wife and child died, it got worse. He invented something to lessen the pain while preserving the memory of her and the baby — it wasn't his *wife* who'd died, but his *sister*. It wasn't his *child*, it was his *nephew*. See? Still tragic, but removed. Enough so he could keep functioning in the world."

"So you know about this person he believes is his brother-in-law: Millard?"

She nodded soberly. "He even told me about him at dinner. To Rondeau, this was all happening to someone else. It was happening to Millard. He took all of his pain, loss and paranoia, and he created a kind of alternate reality, with this other person to bear the weight of it." She searched the room, perhaps remembering their conversation. "Rondeau even has a story about how Millard was an MTA worker in New York. A transit cop. That was actually a story in the *New York Post* from several years ago . . ." She met Peter's eyes. "We all are capable of living double lives, Peter, some people just more than others."

"You really should have come forward. I don't understand . . . you knew this type of thing had happened before. This misdirection . . ."

"I've been watching Rondeau since D.C., like I said. I knew about his therapist, Connie Leifson. I also hired a photographer, Paul Palmirotto. He's Hutch's friend and collaborator. I had him film around the area." She pointed to the sky. "Using the quadcopter to get pictures."

"And you didn't contact the authorities? I still don't . . ." Peter shook his head. He closed his eyes for a moment. It felt like the world was turning upside down. "How did we not know you were a reporter?"

"I have a cleaning business with my ex-husband. All legit. My journalism byline is not Addison Kemp, as you saw . . ."

It was all hitting Peter; thoughts zipped through his mind. He looked at the old stove and the bare cupboards.

"You knew this about Rondeau," he said. "You knew that we had a detective searching for your missing brother, his entire family — we had someone running the investigation and you knew he was mentally unstable . . ."

"I knew? What did I know? I knew the police were doing what they were supposed to. I knew Rondeau's past, but . . ."

Peter was shaking his head. "No. Too many coincidences. Your brother's family goes missing? And the very detective you've been following is on the case? Following . . . doing your piece on, writing your book, whatever you're doing? World's not that small."

"You're right. It isn't." She smoothed her hands over the binder and closed it up.

"Then what? And the Indian Lake house you bought? Rondeau became convinced that your brother was there doing his film on some government conspiracy."

She nodded. "He was."

"He wasn't doing a documentary on waste material?"

"Hutch and I are both investigative journalists. We work in different mediums; I write, he makes films. We've shared ideas for years. Three years ago he tells me about his plans for *Citizen Farmer*. He'd found a UN report that animal agriculture — the meat industry — is more harmful to life on planet earth than fossil fuels. Superheating the atmosphere with methane, for starters. In the meantime, I knew Rondeau had moved north with his wife. His wife and child were gone, his career there was over, so he came up here. Bought this old place where he started really losing it. Interested in my brother's film work, in the middle of a divorce, and curious about Rondeau, it all lined up for me. I found the place in Indian Lake. Yes, there was also the lore about dark drug experiments."

"So why not come clean right away when Rondeau interviewed you?"

"I was afraid. I didn't know who to trust. It wasn't until Rondeau confided in me, over dinner, that I decided to give him the documentary clip. I wanted to point him in the right direction, stay safe."

"You set him up. You wanted to see what would happen."

"No," she shook her head, adamant. "There was the misfortune of Connie Leifson, there was the call from Tamika Levitt. Rondeau was off and running, his own suspicion of the system taking off."

"Levitt told the press he had a psychotic break. She now says she witnessed him losing it in front of her. The official story is that he went to Indian Lake, all part of his delusional fantasies. But there it all finally got to him and he broke down. He drove himself to Bluestone, went into the quarry."

"And what — tied himself up? Stripped himself naked? You were there — what happened?"

Peter remembered the way Eldridge had reacted when he'd seen Rondeau. He'd been hostile. And the way Eldridge had commanded the search. All the troopers had been sent back to the surface after the family had been found. Only FBI had kept going in the mine. Who knew what they had discovered.

"People are getting sick," Addison said. "I kept going because Hutch and I knew there was more. More he missed with *Citizen*. More to the damage caused by factory farming. Like MCR-1, a genetic mutation. Like antibiotic

272

failure — even the last resort antibiotic, called colistin, has lost its effectiveness. The risks livestock pose to human health — it goes all the way back to the first agrarian societies, it's where smallpox comes from, all sorts of animal-borne pathogens. It's why we have vaccines; all issues with livestock."

"Your brother has been turned, Addie. He was just on national television saying—"

"I know what he said. He has to. He has to protect his family. But I have something that is a game changer."

"What? It's all hearsay. It's all circumstantial . . ."

Addison interlaced her fingers. She looked remorseful, the way the dusted light in the room greyed her skin, the way her eyes downcast. "I have a protected source."

"Telling you what? Giving you what?"

"Evidence that the industry is trying to fast-track a new drug. Something even more effective than an antibiotic. Something invulnerable, nothing can resist it. But having too much trouble getting around the FDA."

"Who? Who is the source?" He slammed his hands on the kitchen table.

"Slow down, Peter," Addison said. She patted the air with her hands. "You need to think very carefully. You need to ask yourself if you want to go any further down this road. Give them any more reason to put you in the crosshairs."

He thought about the dark van. He also thought about Rondeau, who lived in a cloud of these same fears. No wonder his mind had split in two.

"Really ask yourself, Peter, if this is what you want. You and your partner." Addie inflected the word *partner* so that he understood her meaning. His life partner. His future wife. And, did he? Did he want to know more?

"What about you?" he asked Addie. "You're still here. You haven't disappeared. You said you were afraid . . ."

"I am. I'm careful."

"Careful? You bought the house in Indian Lake! You're flying drones around . . ."

"Yeah, I'm afraid, okay? They've tarred Rondeau as mentally unstable, unreliable. My brother's life is a wreck. Who knows if he and Lily will make it through — they were already holding on by a thread." She was losing her cool, getting agitated. "This is what they do to people who challenge authority? Not on my watch. If this is what happens behind closed doors, if you question the powers that be, then I don't care about myself. It's worth the risk."

She fell silent. The house creaked and sighed in the wind. He thought he heard mice scratching around inside the walls. Or something else, like microphone static . . .

Peter collected his scattered thoughts, hoping to synthesize all of this new information in a meaningful way. Rondeau and this Whitehall guy were each trying to blame the FBI in D.C. for faulty evidence leading to a wrongful conviction. They were up against lead agent Lee Angstrom and the reputation of the FBI. Then Whitehall had vanished. Rondeau headed north, tried to start over. *He couldn't let it go*, Peter thought. *He was still thinking about it, two, three years later. Driving him nuts.* Peter was afraid it would drive him nuts, too.

"We need to do something," he said. He found her eyes. "We need to make this right." He thought he saw something in her face. "Whitehall resurfaced, didn't he? Maybe you were looking for him, maybe Rondeau still was . . . he's your protected source, right? Whitehall?"

She dragged a finger across the dirty table, making a streak. "This is the line, Peter. There's no going back over it. You may have ambitions beyond Patrol Division, but I don't know if this is it."

"You've got something. Tell me."

"It's been all around us, Peter. All the time."

He held her gaze, then stepped back and looked around the kitchen. The house was almost empty now, like Rondeau's office. But for two years the office had been piled with files and boxes. Maybe Rondeau was running his own investigation. Probably his messiness meant no one would make heads or tails of it. A person could've spent a week in his office, in his home, not necessarily drawn conclusions. But Addie, like Brit Silas, was detail-oriented. They looked for the little things.

"Rondeau never let the Valentine Killer case go," Addie said. "He moved away, yeah. But he kept working. He just compartmentalized it. As Millard. Millard and his crazy ideas." She sat back, let it sink in. "And Millard talked to me. We had some lengthy conversations when I first came up here a week ago. I'm privy to two years of his research. Nearly half of all wrongful convictions involve fraud or junk science, and more than a third involve suppression of evidence by law enforcement. In D.C., on the Valentine Killer case, they framed a guy who fit the profile. In the case of my brother's abduction, they took something legit — the improper handling of hazardous waste — and diverted all the attention from the illegal drug testing going on, the meat industry cover-up."

"So how do we do it? How do we fight back?"

"You're a good man, Peter, I don't want you to—"

"Tell me." He stared at her, knowing he was speaking for Althea, too.

"Okay. I'm talking with the Justice Department. Department of Criminal Investigation. Whitehall is not my source, but you're right — Rondeau found out where he was. I think we can coax him out of hiding and put everything together we know on this case — what you know, what I know . . ."

"Yeah, but what's different this time?"

"I have proof of the crime lab tampering in the Valentine Killer case. We start there, and the whole house of cards will fall."

"How?"

She gazed at him levelly, her eyes shining, the wind blowing outside, "Because I have found the real Valentine Killer," she said. *"That's* my protected source."

FIVE WEEKS LATER

CHAPTER FORTY-EIGHT / The Light

Rondeau stepped out into the bright morning. The air was crisp and fresh. He drew a deep breath, arched his back and lifted his face to the winter sun.

Today was the day he needed to go into town. Oesch wanted to see him. Rondeau really had no interest in going. Stokes had brought him food, over a months' supply, but now he was running low. Didn't want the new guy turning into the errand boy. It just wasn't right. So, Oesch first, then shopping. Oesch said there were a few things left to collect from Rondeau's old office. It would be Stokes' office now, soon as the poor kid was back on active duty.

Rondeau walked to his truck, rehearsing the things he planned to say to Oesch on Stokes' behalf — Stokes had gotten into a lot of trouble because of him. Before he got in, he surveyed the property. Dr. Lang had said it would do Rondeau some good to take the time and maybe tidy things up a little. He'd been right. Neglecting the property the way he'd been doing since Jessy died hadn't liberated him.

Even with the ground half-frozen he'd taken the riding mower to it. All told, it had taken a week to knock down that high grass. He'd left some — the conservationists said that letting a lawn go, to some extent, was good for the wildlife.

He gazed into the large yard. He'd moved the refrigerator with the dolly, and he was scrapping the junkers one piece at a time. He'd soon have a load to take to the landfill.

The thought of the landfill reminded him of the Kemp case. Lang said that when thoughts of the investigation arose, not to try and suppress them. Just to let them be. Rondeau missed Connie Leifson, missed talking to her, missed her face (her legs, too; he wasn't going to lie), but Lang was okay. A bit of a stuffed shirt, the kind of guy you'd expect to have a bust of Freud in his parlor (he had neither a bust nor a parlor, but, still) but Rondeau felt like in just one month, through eight sessions, they were making progress.

"Well, alright," called a voice. Rondeau saw Millard sitting on an old freezer beside the rusted fridge. Millard raised his hand in a wave, and Rondeau turned away, lowered his head, kept walking to the truck.

One thing was better, anyway, Rondeau thought, mounting the cab and shimmying behind the wheel, sometimes when Millard showed up, he was in a transit cop uniform. It helped to remind Rondeau that he wasn't really there; Lang had pointed out the story in the *New York Post* from years ago. Rondeau looked out the windshield. Today wasn't one of those days, though. Millard was wearing his old flannel shirt and a pair of Carhartt work pants. Rainbow suspenders, even. He swung his legs and hopped down from the freezer. He came towards him and Rondeau keyed the engine.

"Hey," Millard called over the roar of the Chevy. "Hey — you going into town?"

Rondeau backed out, made a turn in the short grass, and pointed the nose of the truck down the driveway. Now Millard was on the driver's side, approaching Rondeau. Rondeau hand-cranked the window down. He propped his elbow on the door and opened his mouth to reply to Millard.

He's not there. Don't talk to him. Jessy's voice. At least he never saw Jessy. He didn't think he could handle that. But she still spoke to him. Just a soft voice, in the dark there with him. *Leave him be*, she said.

Rondeau turned away, hit the gas, and trundled down the long drive.

Ten minutes later, he was pulling into the Stock County Public Safety Building. A sense of nostalgia washed over him. For two years — six, sometimes seven days a week — he had arrived at this same spot. He sometimes caught Mindy (or was it Cindy?) on her way in. He'd see King and Bruin sneaking a morning kiss in King's truck before they went inside, thinking no one saw them. Well, they could do it out in the open now, if they wanted — Stokes said they had plans to get hitched. Good for them.

He shut off the truck and the memories turned to anxiety. Was this crazy or what? The whole of Stock County knew he was batshit (a term he'd borrowed from the FBI, though Dr. Lang didn't approve of it). He'd been the head of a missing person's investigation, while he'd been seeing an imaginary person. Not just one imaginary person — but multiple. Such as secret agents he thought he'd killed deep in the tunnels. Had he been tied up? Kept in a box? No. He'd suffered a mental breakdown. Tasked with finding a missing family, he ended up hip-deep in conspiracy theory and paranoia. He'd even thought Connie's accident had something to do with it all. He'd been completely off the rails. It was only by some miracle it had worked out in the end.

The FBI had grilled him enough, miracle or not. Five days straight they'd interrogated him. And it wasn't just about the Kemps. It was about the District, about what happened when Lee Angstrom had chased down a mass murderer plaguing the city. The whole thing had made him itch. Made his bullet wounds feel like bacterial infections, spreading through his body.

They wanted to know if he'd been in contact with Addison Kemp. Of course I have, he'd replied — she was kin to the missing family. Did you know she was an investigative reporter?

No, he hadn't.

He opened the door and stepped down from the truck. He drew another breath, felt the sun again. Then he went inside.

Within the jail was business as usual. Deputy Kenzie smiled at him, said hello, and led him through the entry process. It felt strange to be a civilian now. It felt okay. He collected his items from the tub on the other side of the metal detector and Kenzie keyed the lock to the main doors. Rondeau was led to Sheriff Oesch's office. He knocked, was invited to enter, and then stopped short when he found Addison Kemp seated across the desk from Sheriff Oesch.

Addie rose as Rondeau entered the room.

Oesch bellowed in a friendly way, standing as well. "The prodigal son returns," he said. Oesch was never that funny.

Addie extended a hand, and Rondeau took the grip. "Detective, I just want to thank you. You did everything for my brother and his family. You and your team."

Rondeau found it hard to look at her. Found it hard, really, to take in any of it. He started thinking of excuses to leave. He let go of her hand, and took a step back, his mouth working, his blood rising. Then his eyes fell to the folded up newspaper in her other hand.

Before he could ask her what it was she was holding, he heard a commotion in the hallway. Oesch got a look on his face like a kid about to launch a surprise birthday party. Addie looked pleased too — Rondeau searched her face for some sign of what was happening — her lips were pursed, her eyes bright.

He turned toward the door to the room. He walked towards it, as if in a dream, and stepped into the hallway. At first his eyes only registered Peter King and Althea Bruin. They were walking side by side down the corridor, and Peter was pushing someone in a wheelchair. Someone very familiar to the detective.

Connie looked frail, but she was smiling. She had some scarring, and her hair was tucked under a wool cap, probably because they'd shaved some of it to operate on her. But she was beautiful. And as she neared she said, "Hi, Rondeau."

"Hi, Connie."

Peter stopped pushing her and came around the wheel chair. He stuck out his hand, and Rondeau shook it, still in shock. Peter threw his arms around Rondeau and hugged him. "Come on," he whispered in Rondeau's ear.

No TV, no newspapers — that was Lang's strict media diet. At least, he'd said, for a few months. Investigators' brains never stopped looking for patterns, trying to solve the world around them. And the work Rondeau needed to do was in here, the doc had said, pointing to his chest, not out there. Corny, but Rondeau had gotten the gist, and he'd stuck to it. He hadn't seen anything in the news for weeks. He knew what the FBI had told him, he knew what Lang had told him. So when they paraded him back into the sheriff's office, Addie laid the newspaper out on the desk. The headline read: REAL VALENTINE KILLER CONFESSES.

That was the first thing he absorbed, and it took a moment, his eyes lingering over the words. There was a subheading, too, though: JUSTICE DEPARTMENT

OPENS UP CASE ON FBI CRIME LAB FRAUD IN
WASHINGTON D.C.

It was hard to take in. Extremely hard. His body was
shaking as his mind tried to make sense of the words. He
could only get bits and pieces. The feds were accused of
framing an innocent man for the multiple murders. The
real culprit had come forward, turned himself in. He'd
made a phone call to a reporter — Addie Matheson. The
innocent man had been freed — there was a picture of the
man Rondeau remembered from the shipyard, and he was
smiling.

And there was an interview with Dominic Whitehall.
Whitehall had come out of hiding and was going to be a
star witness for the Justice Department.

Rondeau saw his own name mentioned next, and his
heart did a somersault in his chest.

The article named him as the "cop who wouldn't
quit," and explained how he had tried to shine a light on
the corruption only to be shut down — but that he
remained in active duty in the North Country of upstate,
New York, where another major case had the DCI
investigating further FBI malfeasance.

The Kemp family, who had gone missing after
Hutchinson Kemp, a filmmaker, had produced a
documentary about the meat industry. The article revealed
that Kemp was still pursuing answers even after the film
was out, concerned about a major public health issue, and
a government scheme to keep the public in the dark about
top secret drug testing in order for the industry's profits to
keep coming in.

Someone took Rondeau's hand as he read. He glanced
over at Addison Kemp. When Rondeau spoke, his voice
was hoarse.

"You write this?"

She nodded.

"Matheson . . ." he said. He remembered the way that
name had rang familiar when Stokes had checked Addie's

background, her husband. A fairly common name, though, easy to overlook given all that had been going on . . . and where the hell was Stokes?

Rondeau searched the faces in the room until he found his old partner standing near the back. "You knew about this?"

Stokes shrugged, then he smiled. "How you doing — you alright?"

Rondeau loved it when Stokes asked him how he was doing. He felt a smile break over his features. But then the smile faded.

Was this real? During his breakdown, he'd imagined himself captive, trying to break free, turning on his captors, killing them. But that imagined captivity had represented his own mind falling apart. No bodies were ever found. The FBI was convincing, Lang was convincing, and it seemed to line up. And the medications were working.

Rondeau let go of Addie's hand and took a step back. He felt light-headed for a moment. He saw looks of concern on people's faces.

Then he heard a voice and looked down at Connie, on the other side of him. "It's alright," she said. "We'll take it one step at a time."

One step at a time, one day at a time. At least that much was familiar.

Oesch walked past and was leaning into the hallway. Rondeau's unease abated as he watched the sheriff, wondering what he was doing. Oesch slapped the doorjamb with a smile. He strode back to his desk, keeping his eyes on Rondeau. "Here we go," he said.

Before Rondeau could ask what, more people showed up at the door. Deputy Kenzie and Sergeant Fransen crowded in. Even Dana Gates, from the state police, was there. Last to appear was Trooper Ski.

"Couldn't get everyone," said Oesch, "lot of people out sick. But I rounded up who I could." Oesch, presiding behind his desk, gave everyone in the room a once-over, then his gaze landed on Rondeau. Rondeau could have sworn Oesch had tears in his eyes. Oesch's chin wobbled. "Rondeau, we all want to thank you. You led this team, and you led us to the safe return of the Kemp family."

Rondeau tried to take it all in, to register each of their faces, smiling at him . . . not like they felt sorry for him, but that they genuinely respected him.

"And," Addison Kemp said beside him, "for persevering in the face of incredible odds. If it wasn't for you, I wouldn't have written that first article. The real Valentine Killer would have never known to reach out to me. I wouldn't have been able to convince Whitehall to come out of hiding. None of this — this new investigation — would've been possible without you, Jason."

He still found it hard to speak. "Thank you," he managed.

They seemed to want more. Some kind of a speech. He wasn't the speech-type. He wasn't funny either. He was an ordinary guy, just doing his job.

"Now everybody get back to work," he said sternly.

They laughed, and then they broke into applause.

THE END

TJB
Etown
9/23/15-
2/23/16

Thank you for reading this book. If you enjoyed it please leave feedback on Amazon, and if there is anything we missed or you have a question about then please get in touch. The author and publishing team appreciate your feedback and time reading this book.

Our email is jasper@joffebooks.com

www.joffebooks.com

ALSO BY T.J. BREARTON

HABIT
SURVIVORS
DAYBREAK

DARK KILLS
DARK WEB
GONE

HIGHWATER